Lynette Rees is a RONE award-nominated author and former writing therapist, tutor and mentor.

She has written in many genres and has seen huge success with her self-published books. *The Workhouse Waif* hit the Amazon Kindle bestseller list and was No. 1 in 'Victorian Historical Romance'. She now publishes orphan sagas with Quercus Books in the UK.

Also by Lynette Rees:

The Workhouse Waif

A Daughter's Promise

The Cobbler's Wife

The Matchgirl

Lynette Rees

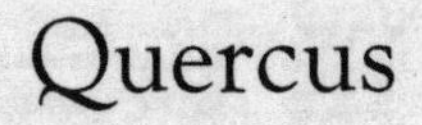

Quercus

First self-published in 2017 by Lynette Rees

This edition first published in 2019 by

Quercus Editions Ltd
Carmelite House
50 Victoria Embankment
London EC4Y 0DZ

An Hachette UK company

A CIP catalogue record for this book is available from the British Library

PAPERBACK ISBN 978 1 52940 073 1
EBOOK ISBN 978 1 78747 289 1

www.quercusbooks.co.uk

Typeset by Jouve (UK), Milton Keynes

Printed and bound in Great Britain by Clays Ltd, Elcograf S.p.A.

'Better remain silent, better not even think,
if you are not prepared to act'

—Annie Besant

This book is dedicated to Annie Besant and the matchgirls for all they achieved to improve working conditions in Great Britain. Without them, we might not have the conditions in this country we know of today. They sparked off something with their campaign that spread like wildfire throughout the land.

Author's Note

The majority of the characters in this book are fictitious and have no existence outside the author's imagination. They have no relation to anyone bearing the same name or names and are pure invention. However, certain characters such as Annie Besant, Mary Driscoll and Theodore Bryant (of *Bryant and May*) did actually exist. This is a work of fiction that is inspired by real life events at the Bryant and May factory in Bow, but some scenes have been dramatised. The strike took place in 1888 as many workers had succumbed to a condition known as 'phossy jaw' from working with the white phosphorus at the factory, which the government of the day refused to ban at the time.

Chapter One

June 4th, 1888

East London

The sounds of shouts and clatters in the street caught the attention of sixteen-year-old Lottie Perkins. She raced over to the living-room window to raise the old lace curtain to take a peek at what was going on outside. She'd risen early to begin a day's work at the Bryant and May Match Factory at Bow. And now she stood watching the Higgins family from across the road outside their house in a state of distress. Mr Higgins was trying to round up all the kids as his wife attempted to settle the baby. All their worldly goods were piled on top of an old wooden hand cart. Why were they leaving? It was a mystery to her. Had they found somewhere better to live instead of this grimy old place? But Mrs Higgins' face told a different story; etched on it was the look of despair as she carried the baby, patting his back to quieten his pitiful cries. A couple of neighbours had arrived to see them off, with lots of hugs and kisses. Oh, how they were going to be missed around here.

She sighed as she dropped the curtain. She had thought it would be a day like any other today; the days were so repetitive at the factory.

She could've been destined for better things in life, Lottie was well aware. The conditions they endured in the factory were sometimes insufferable and she often thought about what her life would be like if her father hadn't passed away and her mother not fallen out with Lottie's rich aunt, Dorothea. Lottie ought to have soft hands like a lady but instead hers were chapped and sore. They never looked clean somehow and no matter how hard she scrubbed them after working at that place, they still looked slightly soiled. Lottie's eyes scanned her humble home, the threadbare carpets and peeling wallpaper making it appear somewhat shabby. Nowadays, they had to make do and mend: with four younger siblings, there were six mouths to feed in the household and money was tight.

Lottie let out a little sigh as she returned to the scullery to sip her hot sweet cup of tea. She became aware of a presence beside her. 'Enough there for another cuppa, is there, love?' her mother asked, gazing at Lottie.

Lottie studied her mother's weary face. She'd worn the same black bombazine dress for months to mourn her dear Albert's death. In truth, Lottie had been extremely worried about her need to remain indoors and how she'd retreated inside her shell when she'd been such a feisty woman when Pa was alive. But today, there were signs she was about to emerge from that very same shell: she wore a grey Linley wool dress just like she had before Pa's death. Was her long period of mourning really over?

Lottie smiled and let out a little sigh of relief. 'Oh Ma, of course there is. It's unusual to see you up and about.'

Ma took in a long breath and let it out again. 'I've decided I need to get a job. I'm coming with you to the factory this morning to ask,' she stated firmly. 'Will your boss, Mr Steed, be in today, do you think?'

Lottie nodded. 'He should be. He's the man you need to speak to, Ma.'

Lottie studied her mother's face. Her sunken eyes and hollow cheeks were testament to her recent grief. Her skin looked pale and sallow. Lottie had recently had a long chat over the garden wall to their next-door neighbour about her concerns for Ma, remembering Doris's words about giving her mother something to live for. She decided not to put her mother off. It was the first time she'd seen her show any interest in anything at all.

Lottie chewed on her bottom lip. 'Are you sure? You know what it's like at the factory, Ma. They are dreadful taskmasters. They don't give us very good breaks and the pay is poor. We work long hours and get treated no better than pack horses.'

Ma nodded and then stuck out her chin, defiantly. 'I realise all of that,' she said quietly, 'but if I don't do something I fear I will live like this for the rest of my life and I can't fall apart. You all need me, particularly the young 'uns.'

For a moment, Lottie wondered what had prompted her mother to change her mind but before her mother could answer, she cleared her throat and said, 'Doris from next door called to see me when you were at work yesterday. Gave me a good talking to, she did.'

Lottie smiled through blurry eyes. At least her mother was trying to get back in the land of the living rather than burying herself in a grave alongside Pa.

'You make the tea and I'll toast the bread,' Lottie said, lifting the toasting fork from a nail that hung on the wall beside the stove.

Her mother nodded and wiped away a tear with the back of her hand. It wasn't going to be easy for any of them. In fact, the past year had been extremely difficult.

'What about the kids when you're at work though, Ma?'

'I've thought of that. They'll be at school most of the day and if I ask for opposite shifts to you, we can work something out.' She rolled up her sleeves as if that was somehow a gesture of confidence in what she had planned for her family. 'Also, Doris has said she can pop back and forth to check on them when they come home from school. Besides, the girls are old enough now: Bessie is twelve and Daisy eleven, both old enough to take care of themselves and their little brothers.'

Lottie's young brothers, Freddy and Davy, were twins and the youngest of the family at just five years old. Identical in almost every way, except that Davy, the younger of the two, had slightly more freckles and that's how most people told them apart. But Lottie could tell the difference between the two in a blackout cellar. To her there were differences that others might not notice if they didn't know them so well. Davy spoke slower than Freddy, and Freddy often answered for his younger twin, which made people think Freddy was the more forward for his age, when in fact, the opposite was true. It was Davy who was the most intelligent and who spent his time reading, while Freddy preferred to be outside in the street playing pitch and toss or marbles.

How she loved her brothers and sisters and wished she could do more for them. It was heartbreaking they'd all had to lose their father at such a tender age.

She supposed her mother was right. It wasn't unusual to see latch key kids around the East End of London. It was quite normal for children to fend for themselves while their parents worked or indeed to even work themselves. Some as young as six years old were expected to work long hours for a pittance; due to their small stature and being light on their feet they could do things adults couldn't do, like going up soot-filled chimneys. Some of the work given wasn't suited to their ages and they suffered as a result. Even worse were those poor children who got thrown into the workhouse as either their parents died young, couldn't cope with them, or entire families were left homeless due to poverty. Lottie didn't want to see their family being split up – what would happen if money became short? Up until now, they'd coped, but money was running out. With six mouths to feed and no longer a male head of the house to provide them with a regular wage, Ma getting a job at the factory would really help keep their heads above water, at least for time being.

Remembering the commotion opposite, Lottie turned to Ma. 'Why are the Higgins family leaving their house, Ma?' She took a bite from the crusty toast which had very little dripping spread on it. Economy was needed right now if they were all to survive, they could no longer afford to be lavish with anything.

Ma frowned. 'Is it today they're off?' She stood and walked over to the window, lifting the curtain to watch them say their goodbyes outside. Then shaking her head she turned back to her daughter. 'Doris told me they couldn't afford the rent. They've been turfed out on to the streets by the rent man. I don't much fancy their chances of keeping out of the workhouse now . . .'

Lottie guessed the family had very little option now than to enter that place. She chewed her bottom lip. 'Ma,' she began.

'What, Lottie?' Her mother's eyes looked full of concern.

'Could that happen to us? Could we get thrown out of our home, too?'

Ma slowly nodded her head. 'It could. It was when Doris told me about the Higgins family that it brought me to my senses. I've been in a daze since your father died. I need to pull meself up by me boot straps. Poor Arnold Higgins got himself in money difficulties when they wouldn't give him no more work at the docks. The poor chap had to line up with all the other men when they were chosen for a day's work and he failed to pass muster. They want strong fit men there, there's no sentiment in business, you'll learn that someday, my gal!'

Lottie thought she'd learned that already the way the bosses were acting at the factory, putting profit before the workers' welfare, but she didn't want to tell her mother that today. She didn't want to put her off. She hadn't seen her mother so fired up in a long while.

Following breakfast, Lottie and Ma donned their jackets and hats and made their way towards the Bryant and May Match Factory in Fairfield Road, Bow, which was only a couple of streets from their home. In the distance, they could clearly see its tall stack standing loud and proud as it beckoned its workers to draw nearer. Three years previously, Bryant and May had merged with the firm Bell and Black which had factories in Stratford, Manchester, York and Glasgow, that's how big the firm had become, yet still they treated their mainly female workforce badly, despite an increase in finances.

Lottie's mother stopped to rap on the door knocker next door to theirs, and then Mrs Munroe appeared bleary eyed on the doorstep.

''S 'oright. I'm up and about, Freda.' She reassured her. 'I'll let meself in through the back way and get breakfast ready for the kids. You feeling 'oright, today?'

'Yes, never better, Doris. Thanks for all of this. I'll make it up to you. Maybe I can take in washing for you or something?'

'Don't worry, I'll think of something,' Doris replied gruffly, rubbing her coal-blackened face. She'd obviously been up early lighting the fire. She wasn't one for glamour, Doris Munroe. Her children were all grown up, apart from one son, Ted, who had never married and stayed at home with her and his father. Lottie was convinced that Doris was lining her up to marry him. She didn't much care for Ted. He was a few years older and she found him tedious to talk to. They had nothing whatsoever in common and she avoided him if she could. But she was unlucky today – as Ma and Doris chatted on the doorstep, she felt someone come up behind her and squeeze her waist with two strong hands. She turned and felt her cheeks flush red with embarrassment. 'I wish you wouldn't do that, Ted!' she snapped, her mother and his oblivious to their altercation as they spoke about the Higgins family's departure.

'Couldn't resist!' He winked. It was then she noticed the newspaper tucked under his arm.

'Just finished a night shift at the docks, have you?'

'Aye. Trouble is the bosses are making most of the workers work day to day now, not like when your father was alive. Things were better then. Our jobs were safer. There's a lot of unrest.' He unfolded the newspaper to show her a headline. 'I reckon there's trouble afoot there.' He whistled through his teeth, a habit she found most annoying.

Lottie nodded and turning to her mother said, 'Come on, Ma, or we'll be late.'

'I'm coming!' She said her goodbyes to Mrs Munroe and Ted, then followed after Lottie, falling in step with her.

As they made their way along the long grimy street with its identical doors and windows and reddish-brown brick walls, Lottie turned to her mother, who marched with extreme purpose. 'Ma, I hope Mrs Munroe isn't helping us out because she plans on demanding a favour in return.'

Her mother stopped in her tracks. 'What the devil do you mean?'

Lottie stopped too. 'Well, I . . . I . . . just get the feeling she would like to see me married to her Ted.'

Her mother chuckled. 'No, don't be so daft, gal. Ted's not the marrying kind. He's bound to his mother's apron strings. No girl will ever be good enough for her son, in Doris's eyes, even you, Lottie Perkins. Come on, we better get a shift on or you'll be late.'

Breathing a sigh of relief, Lottie followed her mother

along the shady street. The gas lighter was in the process of extinguishing the lamps as they spilled out pools of light, casting a golden glow on to the pavements below. Dawn would break soon. It was like going to work at night time. Lottie often thought for the little daylight she saw, especially in winter, that it could be so depressing. The smells of horse manure in the gutter mingling in with the clouds of sulphurous smoke belching from the match factory made Lottie's stomach turn. They were smells she never quite got used to and were stronger in summer than winter.

In front of them were groups of other girls and women marching towards the factory in wooden clogs or hobnail boots. Most were chattering away. They seemed to march to a rhythm that was almost like a drum beat in quality. Lottie had often noticed that, but no one else ever mentioned it. Maybe she daydreamed far too often. Her father used to say she had a romantic soul. Along the way, groups of girls acknowledged others. Every girl with a tale of her own to tell – some happier than others.

When they approached the factory gates, her mother went off to seek out one of the foremen to enquire about speaking to Mr Steed about a job. Lottie worried if her mother had the stamina to stand up and work for ten hours a day with very few breaks in between. It was not for the faint hearted and Ma had been a little delicate of late.

As Lottie entered the factory floor, the din of machinery

and chatter was deafening. Her best friend, Cassie Bowen, was in the process of dipping matches into a chalk-white powdery chemical called phosphorus.

'How are you doing, Cass?' Lottie called out to her.

The girl grimaced. She hadn't seemed her usual self of late and Lottie was becoming quite concerned. 'Fed up to the back teeth of it all, tell you the truth, Lottie. This stuff is starting to sting me face and I keep getting headaches an' all!' she shouted over the din, then she brushed back a lock of hair that had fallen from her mob cap onto her face and began to cough. 'It's even affecting me lungs now as well.' She wiped the back of her powdered hand under her nose. 'My nose is always dripping too.'

Lottie laid a hand on the girl's shoulder. 'I think you need to be careful with that powder on your hands, Cassie. You need to wash them when you can.'

'I know but the foreman plays hell if I leave me work station. Sometimes I even eat me food here and still have powder on them.'

Lottie frowned. 'This isn't right at all. I've seen how you've gone downhill since working here. We need to ask Mr Steed if he can move you elsewhere, maybe the packing department. He might move you if you explain things to him.'

The girl working beside Cassie laughed. 'Stop acting like a lady, Lottie. Yes, Lady Lottie is what I'm going to call you from now on with your big ideas!'

'I was only trying to help.' Lottie was fed up that some of the girls poked fun at how she spoke. Aunt Dorothea had taught her to speak properly and given her piano lessons too and said how her father had been from good stock, but the girls here wouldn't understand any of that so she never told them about her family's past. 'I still think it wouldn't hurt to ask.'

Cassie glared at the girl. 'Look Polly, Lottie was only making a suggestion, weren't you?'

'I was and all,' Lottie said feeling most affronted. 'I just think if you don't ask you don't get!'

Polly shook her head. 'Ha, you're jokin' aint you, gal! I been asking to be moved meself for months, but it's fallin' on deaf ears. Mr Steed keeps refusing. He ain't interested in how we feel as long as he gets the work out o' us.'

Lottie sighed. They shouldn't have to put up with this kind of thing. But what could they do about it? 'I'll speak to you later, Cass,' she said. 'I can see the foreman watching me. I need to get to my work.' She couldn't risk a ticking off or a cuff around the earhole today of all days as it could scupper her mother's chances of landing herself a job.

Cass nodded and smiled. 'All right, Lottie. It's only you that keeps me going in here. Will I see you later?'

'You can count on it. We can walk home together and think what can be done about this.'

Flossie, Lottie's workmate, cornered her before she even

had time to remove her shawl and hang it on a peg. ''Ere, have you heard the latest news?' Her eyes shone excitedly.

Lottie shook her head. 'Sal's had the baby?' Sal was a young unmarried woman who'd got pregnant out of the blue. Rumour had it that the father was one of the foremen, but Floss and Lottie had no idea which one and Sal hadn't told them either. Floss frowned. 'No, not that. There's a woman who's been asking women questions about the working conditions here.'

Lottie blinked several times. 'That's the first I've heard of anything like that. Who has she spoken to?'

Flossie drew a quick breath as if she wanted her words to tumble out as quickly as possible before she was overheard by anyone. 'I spoke to her last night. She clocked me on me way 'ome and she asked questions of a few others outside the factory gates.'

Lottie quickly scanned the factory floor to ensure they weren't being watched. If they were caught gossiping it could mean a back hander from one of the foremen, and it would have been even worse if they realised the subject matter. 'Do you think that was wise? You could lose your job, Floss! It's not worth it.'

Floss lowered her voice to barely a whisper. 'Look, Lottie, yer know as well as I do 'ow bad things have got here. 'Alf the time we're not even allowed to go to the lavvy for a pee. Poor Ginny Malone had her courses last week and needed to go to the lav and wasn't allowed out, and as a result, bled all over the factory floor. It was like a slaughterhouse in here!'

Lottie sighed. She guessed Floss was exaggerating the situation, though she felt for the poor girl. 'That's dreadful.' Lottie sympathised.

Floss nodded and carried on. 'Yeah, it is. It were the boss's fault. She was made to clean up all that blood and they wouldn't even allow her to rest up afterwards neither, even though she had a bad belly.'

Lottie nodded. 'I know it is wrong. I'm not saying it's not, but what I mean is we could lose the jobs we already have if we speak out against what goes on here. There's no woman going to change anything for the likes of us. I reckon we ought to talk to Mr Steed ourselves first.'

Floss's eyes glittered. 'This woman is different though, Lottie. She's a real lady. She talks proper, dresses posh 'an all. Educated, like. She knows what she's on about. She told me she's going to help us all by getting the word out. Ain't that grand? She wants to tell everyone how badly we get treated 'ere!'

Lottie gulped. 'I hope she doesn't go naming names and dropping any of us in it. My poor mother can't manage as it is – that's why she's come to ask for a job here today. If I should lose my job it could be the workhouse for us all. I couldn't bear to be split up from the kids. I really don't want to get into trouble over some posh woman and what she says.'

'I know, and we do have to be careful, but there's other

stuff that's not right 'ere. Poor Martha keeps getting headaches and her jaw is swollen. Me Ma thinks she's got that phossy jaw thing from that white stuff we're using to make the matches.'

Lottie knew her friend was right. One woman had been sent home with something similar and never returned again. There'd been a rumour that she needed an operation to have part of her jaw removed but she didn't have the money to pay for it. Didn't Cassie just say she'd been suffering from headaches too?

One thing was certain, never mind the poor pay and working conditions at Bryant and May, there was a danger to the health of those working there. The British government, so far, hadn't banned the dangerous substance, unlike America and Sweden.

The common work-day was ten hours long and for most of that time, Lottie and Floss were on their feet cutting in half the long strips of wood, both ends of which had been dipped into a compound of chemicals to create the matchheads. The cut matches were then packed into boxes by a team of young women. It was a dangerous job and Lottie was aware of the need to keep her concentration.

Flossie had told Lottie that Bryant and May had actually lowered wages earned over the years, so they weren't even earning as well as workers were twelve years ago. Though she didn't know that for certain, she guessed it was rumour mongering amongst the women who had older relatives working there.

There was also a tale Lottie had heard of how a statue of William Gladstone had been erected at Bow Road outside the church, in honour of a planned visit from the prime minister. Surely it couldn't be true what she'd been told that the women had to pay towards the statue themselves from their very meagre wages?

Floss had told her that her mother had said each girl had a shilling deducted from her wages. When the women discovered this, they were outraged. Why should they have to spend their hard-earned money on something like that without even being asked? Many of them went to the unveiling of the statue armed with stones and bricks to fire at it and then they cut their arms allowing their blood to spill on the marble plinth. It all reminded Lottie of a sacrificial altar of sorts. Maybe that's what the women had been trying to convey – how much they'd sacrificed working at the factory, even their life blood.

The smell of the white phosphorus from the match-dipping machines lingered in the air, causing the women to cough and wheeze. Lottie noticed that some of them had a strange yellow tinge on their skin. They really looked unhealthy. She was glad that she worked on the cutting machines with Floss and not like poor Cass and some of the others dipping the match heads. A woman called, Aggie, who was around Ma's age, had worked at the factory for years and now her skin was as yellow as custard. Lottie hoped that wouldn't happen to Cassie.

She wondered what Mr Steed was saying to her mother in his office. More than likely Ma was giving him the sharp edge of her tongue. She didn't suffer fools gladly and was a hard woman to say no to. But in her heart she hoped Mr Steed would refuse her work as she didn't want her mother to end up like poor old Aggie. And even if she was spared that, the long hours standing all day were too much for a woman of her age.

Every so often, she glanced towards Mr Steed's room. She'd been in there a long time and still hadn't come out. Deciding she'd better concentrate more carefully on her work she returned to it, setting up the matches for cutting, but she was disturbed as she saw Mr Baker, one of the foremen, escorting Sal away from the factory floor. He was pushing her in front of him as if he wanted her out of the building and the way her shoulders were shaking, it appeared as though she were crying. The other girls and women knew better than to stare in case he turned on them.

'What's going on there, Floss?' Lottie looked at her friend. 'Sal looks pretty upset to me. I don't like the way Mr Baker is pushing her like that in her condition.'

'Baker's probably getting shot of her as she's been running 'er mouth off about who the father of 'er child is, I expect.' Floss turned back to her work.

Lottie did know indeed about the circulating rumours

from time to time at the factory and they often involved something to do with one of the girls and either a foreman or manager. Whether these tales were true or not, they never knew for sure. Lottie wondered what would become of the girl now. She sighed heavily and returned to her work before she was caught gawping at her. Finally, she heard Mr Steed's office door open and the sound of footsteps approaching.

By the frown on her face, Ma didn't look best pleased. She drew alongside Lottie.

'Better stop what you're doing a moment there, love,' she warned. 'Don't want you being distracted in case you have an accident and lose a finger or something.'

Lottie glanced around worried in case one of the foremen should happen to see her, but luckily, there was no one around. Otherwise, she might be punished for stopping her work.

'What's the matter, Ma?'

'He can't give me a job here, only working from home making the matchboxes he told me.' She sniffed loudly. 'Although that Mr Steed is very polite an' all, I reckon it's down to my age – he thinks I'm too old. He favours young girls like yerself.'

Lottie sighed heavily. 'At least it's a job,' she said hopefully, though secretly, she was relieved.

'Aye, it's a job all right. Everyone knows how badly out-workers are paid, though. The sweaters take most of the money and run the women and children ragged.'

Lottie nodded. Her mother was right of course. Mrs McKeague from Dublin who lived down the road took in work and her children helped her. They worked all hours. Trying to think of something positive to say, Lottie cleared her throat. 'Well, one good thing, Ma, at least you won't be getting phossy jaw. And another thing, you'll have no more worries about having to get someone to look after the kids if you work from home.'

Her mother nodded, but her lips were firmly set in a grimace. 'I've said I'll do the job as I have no other option. One of the sweaters will drop the stuff around later, but I have to pay for my own glue and other things.' She shook her head. 'But I won't give up trying to get a job here. It's what I really want. I'll keep asking!' Her mother was a persistent sort if nothing else.

'At least the kids can help out, Ma,' Lottie said cheerfully.

Her mother forced a smile. 'I suppose so. Now I won't keep you any longer. It's stew for tea tonight. I made that bit of scrag end of lamb stretch a bit. Won't be much in it but at least there'll be 'tatas, carrots and onion.'

Lottie's stomach growled. Who knew when she'd get to have her break? It was nice to see a little spark back in her mother's eyes though, but deep down Lottie knew that packing at home didn't pay as well as working at the factory, and even here, they were underpaid at just four shillings a week.

Lottie sometimes watched the girls in the packing department, daydreaming about being one of them. They stood in rows each shift packing the boxes, much better than being on dipping or cutting machines. The girls seemed happier too and if the foremen weren't around they chatted happily with one another, cracking jokes and winding each other up. Some would even sing while they worked. That's where she'd rather be.

'Penny for 'em, Lottie?' Floss said. 'Yer were far away there?'

'Yes, I was thinking how much better it would be for us to work in the packing department rather than risking our fingers here.'

Floss nodded. 'Yer ain't far wrong there, gal. I'd give my right arm to be one of that lot!' Then realising what she'd just said, she burst out laughing, causing Lottie to giggle too.

Floss coughed as the floor manager drew near.

'I hope you pair weren't making fun of anyone then?' Mr Steed's watchful eyes scanned Lottie's face.

'Er no, Mr Steed.' She carried on cutting the matches into length.

'As it happens,' he said with both hands behind his back, 'we've thought of introducing a new method which will halve work time. I'll tell you about it later.' He smiled broadly, then drew up closer to Lottie. 'Sorry I can't find any work at present for your Ma inside the factory but I have arranged for her to work from home, but maybe sometime in the future, Lottie.'

'She did tell me, Mr Steed, and thank you.'

'No problem. If she's anything like her daughter, then she'll be an asset to the company.'

Did she imagine it or was Mr Steed flirting with her? Lately he had taken to saying lots of nice things to her and chatting more to her than the other girls. It was beginning to make her feel a little uncomfortable. She didn't want some of the girls thinking she had ideas above her station.

Lottie looked away, hoping he'd leave and find something else to do.

'Yes, I'll have a little chat with you in my office soon to explain the new cutting procedure.'

Some of the girls were watching with avid interest, but then he was suddenly called away and he made his excuses and departed.

Floss winked at Lottie, causing her face to burn with embarrassment.

When the manager had left them to walk off to another line of girls who were being spoken to by a foreman, Floss said, 'See, I told you the other day he fancies you. Wants you in his office for you to offer yer 'onour!' She laughed a deep throaty chuckle.

'Not on your bleeding Nellie!' Lottie said loudly. Smarting with indignation, she turned back to her task in hand.

'Sssh. I was only joshing with you.'

'Well, I don't find it at all funny, Flossie Gittings!' Floss often embarrassed her, and she didn't much like it. She feared Mr Steed might hear the girl laughing behind his back.

Flossie turned away from Lottie and returned to her work. She spent the rest of the morning biting her tongue and ignoring Floss. Conditions were hard enough at the factory without having the girl constantly wind her up, but at least she was better off than some, she thought, sneaking a peek across at the women stirring the phosphorus in a large silver vat.

Floss caught her eye and nodded sadly, as if to say, 'There by the grace of God go you and I.'

Suddenly there was a loud ear-piercing scream. 'What on earth is that?' Lottie ran from her workstation to see a young girl kneeling on the floor, frantically trying to pick up some matches she'd spilled, but it was too late. Mr Baker, the foreman, stood towering over her as the girl looked up at him. She was only about twelve years old and, by the way she trembled, it was obvious she was petrified of the man. Hauling her up by her collar until she was on her feet, he bellowed, 'You shall be punished for that, you young upstart.'

'Please sir, I'll pick them all up, 'onest I will . . .'

'You clumsy little cow!' He cuffed her around the head with the back of his hand so that she stumbled backwards on to one of the work benches behind her. 'For your cack-handedness, a half day's pay will have to be docked. No question about it.' Then he turned on his heel and marched off back to his office, leaving the young girl stood there crying, and then Lottie heard a splashing noise and realised the child had just wet herself.

She shook her head and put her arms around the girl. 'Sssh, it will be all right. What's your name?'

'Geraldine Morgan. I only started 'ere today. I couldn't 'elp it.'

'I know you couldn't, love. I'll pick up the matches. You run along to the lavvy and clean yourself up. Your undergarments will be soaked through. Swill them in the sink and leave them to dry somewhere, hopefully they'll be dry by the time you are ready to go home.'

The girl smiled at such kindness, but it was obvious to Lottie how humiliated she must have felt in front of everyone. Under her breath she cursed Mr Baker for his hard-hearted approach to his workers, particularly the very young girls on the factory floor.

Chapter Two

On the walk home from work with Cassie, Lottie took a look at her friend. 'I really think we need to do something about all of this – about the conditions we work under at that place,' she said firmly.

'But what?' Cassie asked.

'I'm not quite sure. Maybe a few of us should speak to Mr Steed.'

Cassie paused a moment. 'There was a woman hanging around outside the factory the other day trying to speak to some of the girls.'

'I heard about that. Floss mentioned it too. Did you get to speak to her?'

Cassie shook her head. 'I wasn't feeling too good at the time, didn't have the energy for it, but Polly reckons she wants some of us to protest about the conditions here. I didn't want to say anything earlier on the factory floor in case one of the bosses caught wind of it.'

'Really? But where she does want us to protest?'

'You know that statue of the prime minister outside Bow Church?'

'I do indeed. You mean there?'

Cassie nodded. 'But I don't think we can do that, we'll lose our jobs I reckon.'

'I was told the hands of the statue were painted red and the women protested as they'd had their wages docked to pay for it!'

'Never!' Cassie said as shuddering coughs wracked her body.

'Do you want to go on coughing all your life?' Lottie placed a hand of comfort on her friend's back.

'No, of course not.'

'Well then, something needs to be done. But I don't know if that lady is the one to do it. None of us knows her or who she really is, do we?'

'Suppose you're right. Perhaps your idea of speaking to Mr Steed might be better.'

'There's no suppose about it.' Lottie reckoned she had some sway with Mr Steed as he seemed to favour her over the other girls. Perhaps he had picked up on her family's background? He did always say she seemed more educated. But Flossie's words came back at her full force like a warning: 'See, I told you the other day he fancies you. Wants you in his office for you to offer yer 'onour!'

*

Lottie stood inside Mr Steed's office, trembling. She never felt safe in his presence. It was as if he always had his beady eyes on her, almost as though he was mentally undressing her, but nothing could be proved. She suspected he was a letch and the factory gossip confirmed that as such, but there was no real proof, no evidence that she was aware of. Besides, he was married, wasn't he? In any case, girls were afraid to speak out for fear of being fired from the factory, so, if there were any shenanigans, maybe she wouldn't find out anyhow.

He was a very good-looking man and this morning he wore a brown tweed suit with a matching bow tie. His dark moustache was well trimmed. When he smiled he didn't look half so scary. Looking directly at her, he said, 'I've brought you in here, Miss Perkins, to tell you about a new way we have of packing boxes. It's far more efficient and will stop the matches firing off.'

Packing boxes? She was confused. Hadn't he said he wanted to see her regarding a new cutting procedure. What was he up to?

Lottie twisted her hands behind her back, it was the only way she could cope with her nervousness without revealing it to her employer. She would have liked to have a word with him about Cassie and the others, but daren't right now as it was obvious he was intent on telling her something.

'Don't look so frightened, girl. This is for all our benefit. It will make your job more efficient. I plan to move you to the packing department. You're a good worker here, an asset to this firm, not like some I could mention.' He sniffed loudly. 'You're not like the others, Lottie. You're special and much more ladylike. I never hear you cursing like a navvy like some of those do. You deserve to do well so I'm granting you this little favour. The other girls will envy you.'

But I won't get a pay rise though, Lottie thought to herself. They were all trying to get more out of them for as little as possible. And Lottie definitely didn't want to be treated as something special. Some of the girls thought she put on airs and graces as it was, and she didn't want to give them any more ammunition to poke fun at her. She felt trapped in the middle of it all – not a boss, yet not one of the girls either. It was so unfair and now if she was moved the girls will probably hate her all the more for it, particularly Floss. And even if she was moved, she'd still get pushed around by those above her. *I just can't win*, Lottie thought sadly.

Now there was something new to be learned. What if she couldn't do it?

Mr Steed explained the entire process to her. It didn't make a lot of sense to Lottie but apparently, there would be less waste this way even if it would make her job more difficult. As he spoke. he drew nearer to her so she could feel his warm breath on her face. He circled her as if inspecting his quarry. 'Miss Perkins, you have grown into a very fine young woman.

You could go far here if you play your cards right and do as I tell you.'

A hot flush spread from Lottie's neck and, to her absolute horror, to her face. What did he mean? She could go far? Her whole body stiffened in response to his suggestion. Could he hear how fast her heart pounded? She sincerely prayed not.

He lowered his voice which gave it even more husky overtones. 'Yes, a pretty young girl like you should use her assets. In fact, if you're compliant with what I have in mind, I'll ensure that your mother gets the next available job here. Just imagine, you'll be so much better off. It will be to our mutual benefit, as it were. I'm quite sure you understand what I mean. One good turn deserves another . . .' He smiled wolfishly, which made her tremble.

Staring absently at the small wooden clock on the wall, Lottie noticed that its tick seemed to get louder by the second and how it reflected her own thudding heartbeat. She cleared her throat. 'I think I have the right idea now, Mr Steed. I mean about the packing.' Finding the courage to speak up about the girls, she cleared her throat. 'Mr Steed, I wonder if some of us could come to speak to you about a problem here at the factory?'

He drew closer, looking into her eyes. She mustn't give up. She needed to stand up for everyone, so she stuck out her chin defiantly.

'Go on, Lottie. I'm listening.'

'Well it's like this you see, Mr Steed. Some of the girls are becoming sick. My best friend, Cassie Bowen, is coughing her lungs up after working with the phosphorus from dipping the match heads. I'm really worried about her. She's getting head and jaw aches as well.'

He rubbed his chin. 'Is that so? Of course, we don't definitely know it's down to that, do we? Her house might be damp and therefore giving her respiratory problems.'

'Then how do you explain Aggie's skin turning yellow like that? She was involved in match dipping as well.' He seemed to have no answer to that and a long, uncomfortable silence fell between them.

Then he drew even closer as her heart pounded.

After circling her, he stepped forward and stroked her face. She tried to school her features into a mask that protected against any discomfort she might be experiencing at his implications. Her whole body was guarded as the hairs on the back of her neck prickled, dangerously. 'Yes, you have the complexion of a real English rose,' he continued.

She knew Mr Steed had daughters around her age. His wife was always smart and well-dressed when she visited him at the factory, wearing clothing that was the height of fashion. Despite her portly frame, she was still a smart woman. What was the matter with him? He drew up behind her and blew on her neck. 'This isn't the right place, of course. We wouldn't want to be seen, but if you'd like to meet me on

Sunday afternoon, I'll make it worth your while. We can speak about your fears for your friends then. I might be able to help you.' He placed both hands on her shoulders and she felt him bring his body close to hers.

Momentarily, she froze, both internally and externally, feeling like one of those Greek marble statues she'd once seen at the museum. Then a wave of revulsion coursed through her body. What was he saying to her? She thought she knew, and of course she wanted to keep herself for the man she would eventually love. She had no desire for a quick fumble that could get her in the family way, even if it would improve the family finances. She just wasn't that type of girl. There were many of those sorts about, she saw them almost every day loitering around the pubs in their gaudy, gay dresses, waiting to be bought a glass of gin and slipped a few coins to provide their services, often to married men. Well, she wasn't like one of them, not on her Nellie, she wasn't one. And it sickened her that he wanted her to be available to him just so he'd listen to her fears. Was that what he meant? Surely not?

As if not wanting to totally scare her away, he added, 'Aye, I could maybe take you out for tea. Just imagine it, a nice plate of sandwiches with the crusts cut off and some fancy cakes.'

The mere thought of it made Lottie's mouth moisten with hunger. She could have a slap-up meal and secure her mother's employment at the factory. But at what cost? There had already been a couple of pregnancies at the factory and both pregnant girls were supposedly knocked up by one of the managers, rumoured to be the same one, though his name wasn't Steed. Yet, this man was respectable. He wouldn't be taking her to some seedy East End pub to partake of his jollies. He was just offering her an afternoon in a tea room. Totally respectable. She could really do with feeding up. Her mouth salivated at the thought of all the delicious concoctions at the tea room – iced custard tarts, jam doughnuts, French fancies . . .

She feigned a smile, doing anything that would get her out of the claustrophobic office. It was a warm day and she'd had nothing to eat since breakfast time. Her stomach rumbled.

'I'd better let you run along so you can have your lunch now,' Mr Steed said. He had a funny accent. It wasn't Cockney nor Irish. There were plenty of Irish workers in the factory. Floss reckoned Mr Steed came from outside of London, but Lottie had no idea where that was, she'd never been further than the West End herself. His accent was quite refined for the East End, but then again, so was hers, so she had been told by the other girls. They found it quite amusing that she didn't speak like they did, but she didn't let it get her down. There was a good reason why she spoke so well and it was all down to her father's upbringing, for all she knew about it.

*

When she arrived home, there was no odour of stew cooking as she opened the back door of the scullery. Often the first smell that greeted her would be some sort of hearty meal or at least the beef dripping being warmed for the kids for them to soak their hunks of bread in. She sauntered into the living room where her mother, brothers and sisters were huddled around the table. Layers of cardboard, paste and hemp string were scattered between them, where they sat with their heads down and their fingers working away.

Bessie seemed to be enjoying herself and Daisy was deep in concentration, but Freddy and Davy didn't look too happy. Freddy was scowling and Davy looked close to tears. No doubt, Freddy would be happier playing in the back alley and Davy would prefer to have his head in one of his picture books.

Her mother looked up from the matchbox-making process. 'Sorry, Lottie. I haven't had time to even start the supper. Can you do it, please?' Ma smoothed back her hair and carried on pasting the boxes.

Lottie could see there was still a lot to be done. She nodded, noticing the jars of glue and mountains of little cardboard boxes that seemed to cover just about every surface.

Lottie removed her jacket and bonnet and hung them on the coat stand in the corner. The fire in the hearth had almost dwindled away to nothing, so she knelt down and added a couple of lumps of coal and stoked it up with the poker. 'Yes, of course, I'll help, Ma, but what happened?'

'Well, I didn't have enough money to buy the scrag end of lamb after paying the sweater for this paste and string. He'll be calling around first thing in the morning for the matchboxes. It's taking me longer than I thought. Fiddly bloomin' things they are an' all!'

Lottie drew close to the table and patted her mother's shoulder. 'Never mind, Ma. You'll soon get the hang of it. What can I make us to eat instead, then?'

'There's some meat dripping left in the roasting tin in the scullery and some bread. Warm that up and give it to the kids. Don't worry about me.'

'Don't be daft, Ma. If you're working you have to eat something or else you'll faint. Any cheese left?'

'There's a bit left in the pantry but you might need to cut the mould off it. And check no rodents have got at it. Last thing we want is to all go down sick after mice droppings in the food!'

'Shall do. I'll roast some tatas in their jackets in the fire for me and you and we can have some with melted cheese,' she said soothingly.

'That sounds good, our Lottie. Go see to the kids first though. They must be starving. They've been helping me since they got in from school. The boys 'ave been complaining as I wouldn't allow them out to play in the alley, I feel bad keeping them 'ere in the house, but if this order ain't ready on time, I won't get paid.'

Bessie and Daisy looked up and smiled.

'Yes, we are hungry, Lottie. This is hard work,' Bessie said, blowing away a strand of hair that had got in her face.

Daisy grimaced. She obviously wasn't enjoying the task at all. Lottie guessed she'd rather be out in the back alley talking to Patrick Donovan a few doors up the street. They were both sweet on one another – she could tell by the way she blushed whenever his name was mentioned.

Freddy and Davy almost jumped out of their seats at the mention of food. 'Stay where you are, both of you,' Lottie scolded, good-humouredly. 'I'll just heat up the dripping but you must wash your hands before you eat, all right?'

The boys nodded and said, 'Yes, Lottie,' in unison.

'Carry on helping Ma, then. I'll call you when it's ready.'

She smiled to herself as she went off to the scullery to warm up the dripping. It wasn't really adequate for their tea. Tomorrow she would tip up some more housekeeping money until her mother got paid for her work. What she was going to do about Mr Steed's proposition was another thing, though.

Ma sighed. 'I stayed up most of the night to finish these off.' She looked at the large box of matchboxes she'd filled. 'I sent the kids to bed their normal time. They were dog tired. I couldn't expect them to miss out on their sleep as well. It was ever so hard. I'm sure the sweater won't pass them, Lottie.'

Lottie lifted one and inspected it and then another. 'Well most of them look fine to me, Ma. I'm sure it'll get easier the more you do it and you'll speed up,' she said cheerfully.

'I hope so.' Ma sounded as if she didn't quite believe that herself.

'You'll see, this time next week you'll fly through the lot.'

The sweater, Mr O'Hara, when he arrived, appeared to be out of breath and perspiring profusely. *No wonder they call them sweaters*, Lottie thought to herself. But the real reason, of course, was because they were employed by the match factory to use home-workers to make the boxes for the matches. They were akin to a go-between, sandwiched between the out-workers and the factory. Mr O'Hara mopped his brow with a dirty-looking handkerchief.

Ma had worked her guts out for a pittance and now what if the work didn't qualify as it was substandard? Lottie held her breath as he lifted a matchbox and inspected it with his beady eyes.

'Hmmm not too bad,' he said. 'You're going to have to learn to work quickly though if you want to earn decent money.' He sniffed.

'Oh I will, I'm getting the hang of it already.' Her mother winked at her.

He hefted the large box packed with all the matchboxes and handed her a few coins. Her mother beamed and dropped them into her pinafore pocket. It was nice to see a little spark of light switch on in her mother's eyes once more.

As soon as he'd departed, her mother chuckled. 'Good job he didn't see those few I made a right pig's ear of. I threw them on to the fire. Hopefully, he won't know there's a few missing.'

Lottie nodded. 'Hopefully not. You made hundreds of them there. I doubt he'll sit down and count every last one.'

Ma smiled. 'I hope you're right, gal. Now, eat your porridge. You need something substantial before you get to work, my girl. I've got enough money now, and more, to get us that scrag end of lamb and vegetables for tonight's supper.'

'I'm glad of that, but allow me to make the breakfast next time if you're going to be up half the night working!' Lottie patted her mother on the shoulder.

Ma smiled. 'Aye, I'll get used to it, I suppose. An' I'll work a lot quicker once I get the 'ang of it.'

Chapter Three

Lottie avoided Mr Steed as much as possible at work. She thought he'd forgotten all about Sunday as he seemed busy, so she tried to put it to the back of her mind as she and Floss prepared to leave at the end of the day.

'Hey, Floss,' she said, taking her shawl from a peg on the wall. 'Is it right what I heard – that the lady who was here the other day wants to organise a protest at the prime minister's statue outside the church?'

'Sssh,' Floss warned. 'Walls have ears.'

Lottie lowered her voice. 'Well, is it?'

'Yes, it's true. She's going to stir this place up, that's for sure! A lot are interested in attending. Why don't you come along?'

Lottie didn't know if she liked the sound of that. 'Be careful,' she warned. 'We don't even know her. She could cause all sorts of trouble. I'm hoping to have a quiet word with Mr Steed about it all.'

Floss's eyes flashed. 'Aw Lottie, yer not going to dob us all in, are you?'

'No, of course not.' Lottie realised Floss had misunderstood her. 'I meant to discuss our health here, particularly Cassie's on the match-dipping machine.'

'Ah, I see. Well, ask all yer like but I don't reckon you'll get very far.'

Lottie longed to tell Floss that she had already planted a seed and hoped to speak to Mr Steed as soon as possible, but daren't. Mr Steed might not appreciate that.

He finally cornered her as the other girls were donning their shawls. Floss glanced across at her and rolled her eyes, but then turned and walked down the stairs, her hobnail boots clomping away. 'Thought any more about our little assignation on the Sabbath?' Mr Steed spoke quietly. 'Come on, we'll speak about this in my office.'

She followed him inside.

He really made her skin crawl; the mere thought of being in his presence creeped her out as she feared his motives. 'I . . . don't think my boyfriend would like it,' she lied, as if it would somehow afford her protection.

For a moment, his mouth opened and closed. 'Boyfriend?' he said, narrowing his eyes to barely slits. 'I bet your father, if he were still alive, would have something to say about that, young lady. In fact, he told me to keep an eye on you.' So that's what it was. Mr Steed knew her father. 'We worked together at the docks at one time. I was a clerk in the offices and your father was in the shipyard.'

'That's very thoughtful of you, Mr Steed. But it's not necessary. We are managing fine at home.' Lottie hoped he'd drop the subject and made to turn away, but he caught her by the elbow and steered her back towards him so she was forced to face him once more. She looked up at the clock as it ticked away. Normally she would have left by now and the last rhythmic movements of the girls' retreating steps were fast fading away. She swallowed a lump in her throat at the thought of being left alone in the factory with him.

'Tell you what,' he said, his eyes now widening, 'How about I bring both my daughters along? They're just about your age; they'd be pleasant company for you. It will be a nice treat for you, a reward for all your hard work here, Lottie. Out of all the girls on the factory floor, I know I can trust you the most.'

Relief flooded through her. Had she got his intentions all wrong? Maybe he was just trying to be helpful as he'd known her father? 'Th . . . thank you, Mr Steed,' was all she managed to mumble as her pulse slowed back to its normal beat.

'There you go then,' he said softly. 'We'll meet you somewhere suitable on Sunday at about one o'clock. I'll send a note to confirm.'

She nodded and left his office in a complete daze. Should she tell her mother about this? She had enough on her plate at the moment and if she realised that by keeping in with her boss it would eventually secure her a job at the factory, maybe she wouldn't like it.

When she left the building, Floss was waiting for her outside. The girl looked her up and down. 'Boss's pet, eh?' she teased.

'No, not really.' She shook her head vehemently.

'What did he want you for, then?' Floss stood with her hands placed firmly on her hips. She wasn't giving up without a fight.

'If you must know, he called me to say that my father had told him to keep an eye on me before he died. He wants to take me out Sunday afternoon with his daughters and he has a job lined up for me in the packing department.'

Flossie's mouth gaped open, then snapped shut again. She was at a loss for words. Inside, Lottie felt she had one up on the girl. She was envious, that much was for sure. Maybe she'd wanted that packing job herself.

Lottie tried changing the subject, but Floss hardly spoke to her on the way home.

The following day, Lottie caught up with Cass at work. 'How are you feeling?' She draped an arm around her friend's shoulder.

'Not a lot better to be honest with you. Me jaw was aching something chronic last night.' Lottie could tell by the dark rings beneath her eyes that her friend had had little sleep.

'Don't worry,' she reassured her. 'I intend on speaking to Mr Steed this Sunday about getting you moved.'

'But how are you meeting him on a Sunday, Lottie?'

'Never you mind, Cass. An opportunity has presented itself, which I'm going to grab with both hands.'

Cassie smiled, but then Lottie noticed Floss whispering to a couple of the other girls behind the closed palm of her hand. Then she thought she heard the words 'Who does she think she is?' and 'la de da!' Had she imagined that? Was she being too sensitive? Well, she didn't care, she was going to have a nice afternoon out on Sunday and make some new friends in Mr Steed's daughters. Cassie was the only friend she trusted at the factory.

She gave her friend a peck on the cheek and walked over to her work station to notice some of the girls had gathered at the window and were looking outside the factory as some of the workforce were still arriving.

'What's going on?'

One of the girls turned. 'It's that woman who's been hanging around asking questions. She's stopping some of the girls at the gate.'

Lottie pushed her way through the gaggle of girls to see what was going on. A well-dressed lady stood there, her arms moving around in an animated fashion as she spoke. A small crowd had gathered around her. They appeared to be listening with avid interest, while others, who probably feared getting caught, avoided her as they marched in, their eyes forward as if wearing blinkers. To those workers the woman simply didn't exist. Who was this woman who didn't seem to fear anyone, not even the bosses?

Lottie had a sense of foreboding. This was a woman who wasn't going to let things lie – she was a woman on a mission by the looks of it.

Floss didn't speak to her for the rest of the day and much of the next and, with all this relative quiet, Lottie found herself daydreaming about the lady. Maybe she was someone who knew Aunt Dorothea? She imagined the life she must live, in a big fancy house with servants and beautiful dresses hanging up in her wardrobe. Oh, what it must be like to own fine things, not to have just one dress for work, another for every day and a best one for Sunday. Lottie was quite sure that woman would have one for every day of the year.

The following evening, Lottie was one of the last workers to leave the factory and as she was about to head off home, a dark-haired woman, who looked a little older than Ma, blocked her path. Was this the lady who had consumed all of her thoughts? The woman wore a dark blue dress that had a white collar and cuffs and a matching jacket with a straw bonnet. She was definitely no factory worker.

'I wonder if I might have a word with you, miss?' the lady asked.

For a moment, Lottie thought maybe she would ask for directions to some place. 'Yes?'

The woman cleared her throat before saying, 'My name is Annie Besant. I'm a journalist. I've been speaking to some young women from the Bryant and May factory and discovering you're all working in appalling conditions in there.' She studied Lottie carefully for any reaction.

Immediately, the hairs on the back of Lottie's neck bristled with fear. She could not afford to lose her job by discussing these matters with a complete stranger. She glanced around warily to ensure no one was watching her. What if Mr Steed saw her? Or worse still, Mr Bryant himself?

'I'm sorry, I don't know which girls you are referring to, Madam. But there are no girls unhappy at their job that I'm aware of.'

Annie Besant looked at her in such a way that radiated kindness, almost as though she could see into her very soul and knew she was telling an untruth but preferred not to embarrass her. 'It's all right, dear, you will not get into trouble for speaking to me, I shall see to that. But there have been cases where young women have been dismissed for not doing anything bad that I can see of. One pregnant woman was sacked because she refused to work with the phosphorus as it might harm her unborn baby. Now, you have to admit that's not right, is it?' She paused as she waited for Lottie to reply.

Lottie's mouth became dry. She swallowed hard. 'Sorry, I

know of no such case.' Wasn't she right, though? That a young pregnant woman had been forced to leave the factory? She remembered asking Floss about it at the time. But the rumour had been that one of the bosses had got her pregnant and that she had to leave. Lottie hadn't seen the girl since, so it was probably true.

'Then, there's the case of you working long hours here, shorter hours in winter, but in the summer your working day is tremendously long, with very few breaks.'

Lottie had to admit that Mrs Besant did have a point there. She nodded.

'And some of the girls have to eat at the workplace where phosphoruus gets on to their food. You've heard of phossy jaw, no doubt?'

She nodded. 'Yes, one lady has left due to it. Her face was badly swollen and looked a bit green and there was an awful smell whenever she came near.' Lottie shuddered as the memory seared through her.

Mrs Besant's eyes looked full of compassion. 'There are lots of other issues too, and I'd like to make them known to the public, that's all. Otherwise you poor girls will be bearing the brunt of the bosses' brutality. You already are in a manner of speaking.' This lady seemed so self-assured and honest, it was hard for Lottie to dislike her. 'Could you tell me anything you're not happy with? Sorry, what's your name?' Annie touched Lottie's shoulder.

Lottie glanced around her to see if anyone was watching them, but the last of the stragglers had already left. 'Lottie. Lottie Perkins, miss. Now I must get home as I have to help my Ma with the tea for the little ones.' She turned to walk away, not wanting to risk being seen with the woman.

'Lottie, I think it in your best interest to speak to me.' Mrs Besant's tone was insistent. *What right does she have to persuade me to speak? What good will it do me when I could lose the only livelihood I have?* Lottie did not want to end up like the Higgins family across the street out on their backsides, all thanks to some rich woman wanting to fight her cause.

Lottie turned towards Mrs Besant, her chin held high as she met the woman's strong, penetrative gaze. 'I really do have to leave, now if you'll forgive me . . .'

'Very well. I will not prevent you from leaving, Lottie, but if you'd like to meet with me on Sunday afternoon, we could chat then?'

'Sorry, miss. I'm otherwise engaged. Some other time, maybe.' She turned and headed off home before Mrs Besant had the chance to say anything else. Her footsteps echoed on the pavement beneath her and she kept her eyes focused ahead. If she was caught talking to Mrs Besant there would be hell to pay.

This time, when she arrived home at the old familiar street, the only home she'd ever known, with its reddish-brown brick walls, there was the smell of lamb stew cooking in a pan on the fire. It was such a comforting odour and it reminded Lottie of when Pa was still alive.

'How are you late, Lottie?' Ma asked with a tone of suspicion in her voice. She looked up from the table she was in the middle of laying. 'Your cheeks are flushed, my girl!'

'Oh, just rushing that's all.' She fibbed. 'You managed to finish the matchboxes, then?'

'Yes, I've got into the swing of it. One of your sisters helped me towards the end.'

'Which one?' As if Lottie needed to ask.

'Bessie. She said she likes doing it and wouldn't mind working at the factory herself. She has quick, nimble fingers that one. Not like a string of sausages like my own.' She chuckled. That wasn't true at all, her mother had lovely, shapely hands, except they were roughened with all the hard work she did at home such as washing clothes, cleaning the house, making coal fires and now assembling matchboxes. The list of the things she did for the family was endless and it was a thankless task, Lottie reminded herself. She valued her mother and she wasn't getting any younger so Lottie liked to do as much as she could to help out. 'Bessie has a knack of assembling those matchboxes. She'd do so well at the factory.'

Lottie let out a heavy sigh. 'Oh, Ma, I should hate it if any of the girls follow me into that place.' She removed her bonnet and jacket and hung them up on a peg behind the back door.

'No, it's not what I want for any of us either, but needs must and all that,' Ma said stoically.

Lottie chewed her lip as a pang of guilt overtook her. 'I should have told you the truth, Ma. I just didn't want to draw you into it all. I felt a bit flustered earlier as I was stopped by a lady coming out of the factory gates. She wanted to talk to me. She was most insistent that I speak with her as she thinks she can help us all with our cause.'

Her mother put down the loaf she had just started slicing. 'And what happened? What did she want from you?'

Lottie let out a long breath. 'I thought at first maybe she wanted directions to somewhere as she seemed out of place around here, very ladylike looking she was, but then she started asking questions about working conditions at the factory which put me on my guard.'

Her mother raised a quizzical brow. 'Who is she?'

'A lady called Annie Besant. She says she's a journalist who wants to improve the conditions at Bryant and May.' Lottie shook her head. It was useless: she wasn't free to speak out to anyone.

'If I were you, I wouldn't speak to 'er – the bosses might see and send you packing.'

Lottie nodded in agreement, but at the back of her mind, there was something that fascinated her about Mrs Besant. It was a dilemma whether to speak to the woman or not as it could mean the end of employment at the factory if she got caught out.

Lottie's eyes were drawn to a dirty cup on the counter in the scullery. It was a cup she hadn't seen in a long while, a china blue one her father used to use that Ma had stowed away since his death. Narrowing her eyes she asked, 'Who's cup is this, Ma?'

Appearing flustered, her mother's cheeks reddened. 'I couldn't find no other one when Mr O'Hara called with the work for me today. I felt I had to offer him a cup of tea as he's been so helpful to me.'

So, they'd been spending a bit of time together, discussing things over a cup of tea in the morning when he dropped the work off for her while the kids were in school. That surprised Lottie. She didn't know what to think about it all. Ma was just lonely, she guessed.

The following morning, Floss was waiting for Lottie at the factory gates talking to two handsome lads. By their appearance, Lottie guessed they were dockers off to work. She'd seen them hanging around the gates trying to chat up girls before now. It annoyed Lottie that Floss would talk to just anyone, particularly of the opposite sex. Although she knew she was a good girl really, she thought it could create the wrong impression to be seen with those young men alone, particularly at her work place.

The taller lad appeared to be teasing Floss. He tugged her blue ribbon from her hair and ran off with it, while the other stood there laughing.

'Give Floss her ribbon back!' Lottie said angrily.

'Hark, what have we here – Miss Prim and Proper Drawers!' he sneered as he waved the ribbon around.

'I don't care. That's not your property, now return it at once before I—'

'Before you what, love?' he challenged.

'Never mind what, just give it back to her!' Lottie gritted her teeth. If she wasn't such a lady, she'd love to smack him in the face.

'Aw, give it back to her.' The other lad mocked her as he pranced around as if he was Lottie himself. Lottie's cheeks burned with embarrassment.

The lad who had taken the ribbon swaggered over to Floss dangling it in front of her face. 'Gis a kiss or you can't have it!' he teased, holding it above her head, so she had to stretch on tiptoes to try to snatch it from his grasp, but it was too high up. Floss glanced at Lottie, who shook her head.

Then he lowered it again. 'C'mon, let's have a smacker on the lips, darlin'!'

Quick as a flash, Floss snatched her ribbon from the lad's hand and walked to stand beside Lottie.

'So long, beautiful!' the lad shouted at Floss blowing her a kiss, who blushed as she watched the lads turn their backs on them and walk down the street together, laughing and nudging one another as they went. When they were out of sight, she turned to Lottie and said, 'What did yer want to do that for? I liked him an' all!'

'Well it's not proper behaviour for a young lady, is it? Being on your own with two lads like that. Do you want to get talked about? And if the foreman saw you flirting with that one who stole your ribbon, he might have cuffed you or even docked your pay as it's just outside the factory gates.' Lottie folded her arms and stuck her chin in the air.

'You're really hoity toity sometimes, Lottie. The boys were doing no harm. They were just teasing me, 'aving a bit of fun that was all. You really should try it some time!'

Lottie was still wary of Floss. She felt the girl had been gossiping about her the previous day. She didn't want to rile her up any further so she changed the subject. At least Floss was still speaking to her after days of giving her the cold shoulder.

'Well, I meant no harm. Were you waiting for me, then?'

Floss nodded. 'Yes, to ask you if you saw Mrs Besant on your way home last night? Don't worry I won't say anything if you did. I've spoken to 'er meself. I give her all the gen on 'ow we're not allowed a toilet break when we wants 'em. I nearly wet meself the other day. I also told her how little Geraldine Morgan got her pay docked on her first day for dropping a box o' matches on the floor and was so scared she wet her bloomers!'

'Sssh, keep your voice down,' Lottie said, turning to glance around her. There was no sign of any foremen around, only the voices of the girls and women as they marched past to head into work.

Floss drew nearer and lowered her voice. 'Well, what did you say to her?'

'Nothing, I went home instead.' Lottie hoped the girl would forget the topic and speak about something else instead. 'I gave her a short shrift as I didn't want to get into trouble with the bosses.'

'You numbskull!' Flossie shook her head. 'What a chance to tell her our story and you could put it over better than I can. I've told her some stuff but you'd make it clear, with your big words an' all. Bet if you met her she'd give you some money for your time or take you to a fancy tea room some place!'

'Well, I'm not after any money and I can't afford to lose my position here now Pa is no longer alive.'

'In any case, why are you so shirty with me this morning? Is it because of those lads?'

Lottie drew in a breath and let it out again. 'If you must know it's not just that, it's because of how you acted the other day!'

Floss frowned. ''Ow come?'

'I saw you gossiping about me to a couple of the girls after Mr Steed spoke to me.'

Floss's face reddened. 'Yes, I did talk to 'em about you, but not in the way you fink. I was just worried about you, 'onestly. I asked the girls if the rumours were true about 'im and they said they didn't know. But now you've explained he's just looking out for you and taking you out with his daughters on Sunday, I've changed my mind. You lucky thing. I wish I was going with yer, Lottie.'

At this very moment in time, so did Lottie. The very fact Mr Steed had asked her to go alone had rang alarm bells, but when she thought of him and how good looking and charming he was, she found him hard to resist. It made her feel sophisticated and grown up that he would ask to meet her at the park and not any of the other factory girls.

Chapter Four

Lottie was sitting at the table with the family as they ate their supper. It was only bread and dripping again – she was fed up of eating the same things. Oh to eat a lovely slice of beef and not just the dripping. They were all sick to the stomach of not being able to eat as well as when Pa was alive.

'I don't want this,' Freddy said, looking at his twin for support.

Davy shook his thick mop of hair. 'I don't want it either.' He pushed his plate away.

'You'll eat it and be glad of it,' Ma snapped. 'The way things are going, who knows what we'll eat tomorrow! That's why I've had to make the matchboxes.'

Freddy's face reddened and Davy looked as if he was about to cry.

'Just eat your food, boy,' Lottie said tactfully.

There was a short sharp rap at the front door which caused

Ma to rise to her feet. 'Now who on earth can that be this time of the night?' she grumbled.

She disappeared in the passageway and Lottie strained to hear. It was a male voice and he didn't sound too pleased. She put her index finger to her lips to warn the kids to keep quiet and she went to the scullery door and listened.

'I want that money by tomorrow at the latest, Mrs Perkins!' the voice said. She recognised the voice as belonging to Mr Fripps, the rent man.

'Can't you just give me another few days until I'm on my feet?' Ma was asking.

'If I do that for you, I'll have to do it for everyone,' he said. 'I'll call again this time tomorrow night and I better have that money waiting for me, or else.'

There was the sound of the front door closing. Lottie rushed back to her seat.

Ma entered, her face looking downcast as she took her seat. 'What's up, Ma?' Lottie asked.

'Nothing for you to worry about, sweetheart. Now finish your meal, then you can make us a cup of tea.'

Ma wasn't letting on about the rent money and that worried Lottie a whole lot more.

Lottie managed to avoid the watchful eyes of Mr Steed most of the following morning, but when it was lunchtime he handed her a letter. It stated: 'For your eyes only, Miss Perkins.' For a moment, she feared she was going to be sacked because Mrs Besant had stopped her the previous evening. Maybe he'd been watching from his office window? But, after slitting open the envelope with her thumb and unfolding the paper, she saw written, in his best penmanship, 'Victoria Park, one o'clock sharp, this Sunday.'

Her heart pounded in her chest. Despite the fact she'd been partly dreading the meeting, part of her was excited by the fact someone like Oliver Steed would invite her out. For her eyes only – it made her feel special that he'd singled her out from the other girls. What was so special about her for him though? Did he think she seemed more grown up than the others? What did he see in her that she couldn't see in herself? It was then she noticed there was a silver sixpence in the envelope, she assumed for her to take a cab or the omnibus.

She chewed her bottom lip. She wasn't allowed much time for her lunch – none of them were – so she replaced the letter back in its envelope and hid it in her skirt pocket. She could never tell her mother about the meeting. She knew her mother would insist she take one of her brothers or sisters to get them out the house. It was hard sometimes for Ma, having to cope with so many of them. The kids were always under her feet.

She didn't entirely trust Floss – there was a danger she might tell the other girls, and her biggest fear was if any of the girls knew of her association with Oliver, she would be ostracised. As it was, some of them thought she was a bit la de da because of her accent. The truth was her father's family had been reasonably well off but her father had fallen on hard times when he'd married her mother against their wishes. 'A woman beneath his station,' everyone had said. And they'd run off to the East End of London together which caused a big scandal at the time. His parents had never got over it. The only one who'd kept in touch was Aunt Dorothea, his sister, until Ma had put paid to that.

When they were back at their cutting machines, Lottie turned to Floss. 'I did speak to that Mrs Besant on the way home yesterday evening,' she said quietly, so none of the others could hear.

'Did you now?' Floss said, blinking with interest. She drew near. 'So whatcha think of 'er? Did you tell 'er how bad it is working for the bosses?'

Lottie tensed up, quite affronted by Floss's questions. 'No, I did not! I haven't told her a thing. Yes, she did seem a nice lady, but she's a journalist. She's only after selling papers which will be yesterday's news tomorrow.'

Floss sniffed and ran the back of her hand across her nose, a habit that irritated Lottie as she felt the girl should use a clean handkerchief. 'Well I never, I fought there was something about the woman. I mean I know she's a lady an' all, but I never realised she worked as a journalist. She must be well educated.' She paused as she drew a breath in and let it out again. 'I'm telling you now, Lottie Perkins, whether you have a gander and a gossip with the lady or not, somefink's going to happen – lots of the girls and the women 'ere are fed up to the back teeth of how we're getting treated. It just ain't fair!'

Lottie softened her tone and touched Floss's shoulder. 'It's not that I don't agree with you all, Floss. But why bite the hand that feeds us? We could end up with no jobs at all, and then, where would we be?' It really worried Lottie that she could end up out of a job, especially after what she'd heard the rent man tell her mother.

Flossie gave her a hard stare and turned back to her work. If Lottie wasn't careful she was going to make an enemy of the girl and that was the last thing she wanted to happen.

When Lottie left for home that evening, she glanced over her shoulder to see if there was any sign of Mrs Besant, but there was none. She breathed a sigh of relief and went on her way. But as soon as she approached the back lane of the house, she could sense something was amiss. The hairs on the back of her neck began to bristle.

'Get out of here now this minute!' she heard her mother shouting. She hadn't heard Ma shout like that since well before her Pa had died. What was going on?

Quickly, she unlatched the back wooden gate to see the

sweater, Mr O'Hara, marching down the path and her mother behind him, waving a sweeping brush after him.

His face looked red with embarrassment and he snorted loudly as he passed Lottie. 'Tell your mother to calm down, will you, lass? 'Tis the last thing I need to be chased out of here by a mad woman.' He lifted his black bowler hat and replaced it back on his head as a sign of respect. 'It's only my intention to help your ma. She's been kind to me, making me cups of tea and baking for me but now she's gone all strange and angry!'

Lottie looked at him in amazement. She had to admit that Ma had seemed a lot happier with him around, so why the change today? Was it something work related? Maybe he'd piled too much work on her and she couldn't take any more of it. After all, she had been working hard lately. Lottie thought she was beginning to get the hang of things by now and seemed to be coping well. But Mr O'Hara seemed to be fleeing from Ma like a rat deserting a sinking ship. Ma could be quite scary when angered. What had he done that was so bad? She watched as he left through the back gate.

Lottie opened her mouth to speak, then closed it again. She was at a loss for words for once. Then, looking at her mother, who appeared a right comical sight as she still waved about the brush, she turned to her and asked, 'What's the matter, Ma? What has Mr O' Hara done to you?'

Her mother dropped the brush to her side and looked at

her daughter. 'Nothing, except flamin' well asking me to marry him! The cheek of it. I'm still in mourning for your father.'

Lottie tried to stifle a giggle at the thought of Mr O'Hara being sweet on her mother. She took a breath. 'Well, you could do worse I suppose.'

'So, you suppose now, do you? The brass neck of the man, coming here and giving it all the niceties saying how I'm a rare English rose. I bet he says that to all the ladies he drops the work off to.'

'Now, come on, Ma.' Lottie draped her arm around her mother's shoulder. 'He seems decent enough to me and you are a rare English rose.' Although her mother had been through a hard time of it of late, she was still a good-looking woman.

'Well, thank you, Lottie. I can take that from me own daughter, but not from a man like him. He's like Don Juan the second!'

Lottie chuckled. She hadn't taken Mr O' Hara for some sort of Lothario, he just looked like a respectable middle-aged man to her. 'Come inside, Ma. I'll make you a nice cup of tea.' She was still bemused that Mr O'Hara had designs on her mother. She realised she didn't know his first name. 'What is his Christian name, Ma?'

'Shamus. And he'll shame the bleedin' devil that one an' all!' She began to chuckle herself.

It seemed to Lottie that if her mother knew the sweater's first name then maybe they had been sharing more than niceties. It must have been lonely for her when they were all out of the house. 'Well, you know what I think?'

Ma's eyes widened. 'No, but I guess you're going to tell me anyhow.'

'You both like one another's company and what could be so wrong in that?'

Her mother nodded and then, quite unexpectedly, shed a couple of tears, which she wiped away with the edge of her pinafore. 'Maybe you're right, our Lottie. You usually are.'

Somehow Lottie felt her mother was crying for her own loneliness.

She followed her inside the scullery. The kids were due home from school soon and there would be the supper to get on with before they settled down to helping with the match-boxes again. It was all go.

She noticed her father's twill jacket hanging on the back of a chair. Ma must have been looking through his things again. No doubt, Shamus had probably chosen the wrong time to approach her about such matters when her heart was still yearning for her Albert. Pa was never far away from any of their thoughts. It was then Lottie noticed a jar of coins on the counter. Where had that come from? It looked enough to pay the rent. Surely it had to be something to do with Mr O' Hara – had he given Ma the money to pay the rent or loaned it to her?

Oh dear, Ma? What are you getting yourself into?

Chapter Five

Lottie dressed with care that morning. She planned to slip away following the church service with the excuse of popping over to Floss's house. If her mother's suspicions were aroused, then she wasn't saying so. Lottie smiled. She was lucky indeed to be asked out by Mr Steed, but if she wasn't that wary, why hadn't she told Ma?

Although she wore her Sunday best – a striped linen dress, nipped in at the waist and matching jacket – she feared she would not be as well dressed as Mr Steed's two daughters. Her best dress was well over two years old and quite worn at the cuffs. The hem had been let down as she'd grown an inch or so over the past year. She imagined that Charlotte and Amelia Steed would be swathed in satin dresses edged with fine white lace, the type that rustled when they walked and shimmered in the sunlight. They'd carry parasols and their bonnets would match their dresses. In her mind, they were a pair of refined young ladies. She'd caught sight of them once when Mrs Steed had called to the factory to visit and both girls had accompanied her. They were breathtakingly beautiful, stunning in fact. Both girls had smiled at her and she'd longed to speak to them but they'd been ushered away from the machinery by Mrs Steed, who no doubt intended they keep their gowns in pristine condition. How she'd love to wear one of those dresses, befitting of a young lady, and not a dress she'd outgrown and had to let the hem down on. It was make do and mend at home, a far cry from the lives of the Steed family.

Lottie had noted that day at the factory that Steed's wife was a pleasantly plump woman whose features appeared to be set in stone. Lottie had immediately taken a dislike to the woman, but the girls, she recalled, were very pretty. They both wore their hair in tightly coiled ringlets, though Charlotte's hair was as blond as Amelia's was dark. They bore a striking contrast to one another, like chalk and cheese.

The church service seemed to go on and on and Lottie found herself glancing at the clock behind the vicar's head. It felt like a thousand butterflies had taken flight in her tummy at the thought of seeing Mr Steed later and she hoped that Ma wouldn't notice how jittery she was. She needn't have worried though; her mother seemed totally absorbed in the service. The vicar was speaking about a lost little lamb and how Jesus, the good shepherd, would search for just one missing lamb to bring it back to the fold but that was about all she heard as her mind kept wandering to later that afternoon in Victoria Park.

Freddy was trying his best to stifle a yawn while Bessie had to nudge Davy to stop him kicking the pew in front of him. Daisy, though, looked as absorbed as Ma was in the service.

Finally, there were signs that the minister was bringing it all to a close as he uttered a final prayer and everyone bowed their heads. Then the organ struck up a few chords of a hymn in preparation for people to leave. Usually they either stayed and chatted for a few minutes to their friends in nearby pews or else they rushed to the door to shake hands with the minister and his wife before rushing off home for their Sunday dinners.

It would take some time to walk to Victoria Park as the church wasn't that close to their home but, at her Aunt Dorothea's suggestion, it was the one her family had preferred to attend over the years. Her aunt was a member here too, but Ma acted as if she was blind to the woman. The other kids might have forgotten their aunt, but Lottie, being the eldest, certainly hadn't. She took a quick glance over at her auntie's pew, the one all Lottie's family used until the family breach.

As if sensing she was being watched, Aunt Dorothea turned and smiled at her niece. Lottie smiled back and gave a little wave without her ma noticing. She didn't want to incur her mother's wrath but neither did she feel like ignoring the woman who had been so kind to her in earlier years. So whenever she had the opportunity, she smiled at her aunt. Once last year when Pa had taken ill, Lottie had tried to tell her aunt, but Ma had pulled her away at the final moment.

The family had stayed away from church during his illness, but now, Ma had decided to return. Heaven knew why now, but Lottie was glad to be back and by the look on Aunt Dorothea's face, so was she, even if they couldn't speak to one another.

Lottie planned on keeping the silver sixpence Mr Steed had given her to spend on a few sugar glazed ha'penny buns for the kids. They needed feeding up especially now they were helping Ma assemble those match boxes. But her mother would ask her where the money had come from. How would she reply?

The hymn ended with a boom, boom, boom of the organ, and then there was total silence as the vicar walked the length of the aisle to the main door to shake hands with people as they departed. Lottie was already on her feet, brushing down the skirts of her dress, her heart hammering madly.

Why was she like this? Was she afraid of Mr Steed? After all, he had told her he'd promised her father he'd watch out for her.

'I'll see you all later!' she called to her family over her shoulder as she jostled out of the wooden pew. Heads turned in her direction and, before anyone had a chance to reply or object, she marched off up the aisle. If Ma asked she was going to say she'd called over to Floss's house; she'd pretend she needed to see her about a work matter. Ma had stopped making their usual Sunday roast as money was tight, so she wouldn't be missed around the table anyhow. Now they dined Sunday evenings instead and it was usually a stew made from a cheap cut of meat. The days of the roast dinner were well and truly over.

Off she strode, down the squalid streets outside. It had been a very wet June so far and it had rained most days, but today, for once, it was dry and the sun was trying to peer out from behind the grey gloomy clouds overhead.

She walked at a brisk rate and it took her a good twenty minutes to reach the park. It was a splendid place. Ma had told her it was the 'People's Park'. The very first park assigned to the people of London. It had been Queen Victoria's idea to appoint a park for the ordinary, everyday folk in the area as there was so much abject poverty and disease.

It was somewhere for them to go in their leisure time to sail a small wooden boat on the lake, sit on a bench and reflect, stroll around admiring the greenery and pretty flowers or attend the refreshment rooms for a nice cup of tea and a fancy cake. Many people counted themselves fortunate if they owned a backyard but some lived in rooms owned by other people with no lawned gardens or blooms to admire, just dark brick walled houses on grim, grimy streets, which often stank to high heaven of drains and horse manure – and that wasn't even with the fumes coming from the local factories. Many lived in rooms huddled together, sometimes several families under one roof. But Victoria Park was heaven on earth, as Ma liked to say. Lottie had to agree, it was indeed.

As she approached the park she looked around for any sign of Mr Steed and his daughters, shielding her eyes as the sun was now beaming down strongly. All she could see were a few couples walking arm-in-arm, a nursemaid pushing a baby in a stroller, no doubt from the posh end of the place, and an old man feeding the ducks with what looked like stale bread. The cherry blossom trees in amongst the oaks, chestnut and hawthorn trees, gave the place a bright feeling almost as though it were God's way of decorating the place. She took a little walk around and thought to herself if they didn't show within a quarter of an hour she'd return home. Then she turned suddenly to see a shadow cast behind her.

Mr Steed stood before her in what was obviously his Sunday best. He wore a dark long jacket with a striped waistcoat beneath and matching trousers. His crisp white shirt looked well starched and he wore a grey cravat which was affixed in place by a small silver pin. She took a sharp breath as her heart raced; out of the work environment, he did look astonishingly handsome.

'Lottie.' He smiled broadly.

'W . . . Where are Charlotte and Amelia? Couldn't they come?' She raised her hand to shield her eyes from the sun which was just behind him in the sky, giving his body a strange ethereal glow.

'They shall be along presently. They went to church with their mother. Meanwhile, how do you fancy a stroll around the lake?'

She nodded, satisfied with his answer, though she did feel strange as he linked arms with her as though they were like every other courting couple in the park. He directed her the opposite way, and now the sun was out of her eyes and she could see clearly. She tried to reassure herself he was just looking after her best interests. After all, he had promised her father as much.

The sun glistening through the trees and the shrieks of children's laughter made a welcome change from working in that dark, dismal old factory.

'A penny for them, my dear?' he asked, as he stopped and patted her hand.

'Oh, I was just thinking how lovely it is here. I could stay here all day.'

'And all the night too, I'll be bound. I agree it is rather spectacular, and being here makes my heart glad to be away from all my troubles.'

She paused to look at him quizzically. 'Your troubles, Mr Steed?' Then she wished she had remained silent. 'Sorry, I shouldn't have asked. That was so rude of me.'

He smiled. 'No problem. And please call me Oliver while we're together.'

Lottie felt strange that he was asking her to call him by his Christian name, and then, as if realising her discomfort he added, 'Well, only when we're alone together like this. At work it is best to keep calling me, Mr Steed.' He chuckled and she smiled too.

'I hope your troubles, whatever they are, will be over with soon, Oliver,' she said.

'I don't think they will be, dear sweet Lottie.' He shook his head and for a moment she thought she heard a catch to his voice. 'It's my wife . . .'

'Your wife?' She felt strange that he should talk about such a personal issue.

'Yes. I fear she no longer loves me. It's since the birth of our baby son, Arthur, last year. She is very cold towards me.'

Lottie shook her head, absently. 'I'm sorry, I had no idea.'

'To be honest with you, I wouldn't be much surprised if she doesn't send Charlotte and Amelia here this afternoon, as a sort of punishment. She's like that.' He paused to gaze into her eyes. 'But you'll stop with me and keep me company, won't you?'

She nodded, now feeling so sorry for him. How could she refuse his plea? 'Y . . . Yes, of course I will.'

'In fact, if they don't show up soon, then I guess she won't have sent them here in our carriage, and if that's the case, would you care for a trip on one of the boats?'

Her heart hammered beneath her bodice, and mouth dry, she replied, 'Yes, please.'

In all her wildest imaginations, she'd pictured herself being in one of those boats, reclining back and trailing one hand in the water. It was a luxury her family could ill afford, especially now since her father had died. When he was alive he had promised one day he'd save up and take all his children on one of the boats. After his death, she had found the jar of coppers he'd been saving on a shelf in a cupboard in the scullery, the very same jar that she had witnessed on the side the other day. She had meant to tell her mother she believed it was for the family boat trip but they were so strapped for money, it would have seemed churlish to remind her mother of that fact, particularly when young bellies were growling with hunger.

'What's the matter, Lottie?' Oliver asked.

'Oh, I was just thinking that my pa always wanted to take us children out on a boat ride.'

'I see, and that never happened, I take it?'

She shook her head as tears began to form in her eyes. 'No, it didn't . . .' She feared she'd break down and cry in front him, and next thing she felt him pressing a gentleman's handkerchief into her hand. She unfolded it to see the initials O.S. embroidered into one of the corners. It was such an intimate act of kindness that she couldn't help the tears from flowing.

'Please don't cry. I couldn't bear to see a beautiful face such as yours crease up. All shall be well. We shall take that boat trip in memory of your father, Lottie.'

'I'd like that very much,' she said.

Oliver drew closer towards her. 'Oh Lottie, you're not like the other girls.' He cupped her face in his hands and looked deep into her eyes. 'How is that? You speak differently, too.'

Lottie swallowed as he let her go and took a step back. 'My Aunt Dorothea, my father's sister, taught me good manners. You see, my father came from a well-to-do family, but he was ostracised when he married my mother, who was an East End flower seller of Irish heritage – her parents came over here from the Emerald Isle before she was born. Yet, he said, he fell in love with her at first sight. There was no class barrier to him. We used to visit my aunt regularly at her lovely home and she taught me to play the piano. She used to visit us in the East End now and again, but Ma felt ashamed of our humble home. Eventually, there was some sort of disagreement in the family and they fell out. She doesn't even know her own brother has died. Ma hasn't told her. I feel so bad about that.'

'I see,' he said. 'Then we both have something in common as my accent is different too.'

'I did wonder about that. Where were you from originally?'

'The north of England, an industrial town with lots of factories, nowhere you'd have been to. I came here to seek my fortune –' he chuckled, which made her feel all warm inside '– and found you.'

She smiled, despite her tears, and he took her hand to lead

her to the boating lake. People were already queuing up on the wooden jetty. Lottie enjoyed being so close to Mr Steed – Oliver – as he was the last link with her father. She felt it natural as he wrapped one arm around her as they walked towards the waiting rowing boats.

She took this as her cue to ask him a favour. 'Oliver . . .'

'Yes, m'dear.'

'I was wondering if it's possible for you to have a word with Mr Bryant about the working conditions at the factory. I have a good friend, Cassie Bowen, and I'm worried about her as she works dipping the match heads in phosphorus.'

'Oh, not now, Lottie. I promise we'll speak about it some other time when it's more appropriate to do so. I like to forget about that place when I'm away from it.'

She nodded. 'Sorry to have bothered you then.' She felt guilty for asking but hurt at the same time that he had dismissed her comment.

As if realising this to be the case, he whispered, 'I promise we shall speak of such things back at the factory. I shan't forget. Oh, look, we're next.'

The boatman dragged the rowing boat nearer to them with a long wooden pole which had a hook on one end.

Oliver helped her on board, lifting her at the waist and gently setting her down inside the boat. She had never felt so cared for since her father had died and, in a way, she now felt a pang of guilt that she was glad Oliver's daughters hadn't turned up. The poor man must have endured a dog's life with that wife of his. But now his daughters weren't here, this made it more of a proper date than a family-style outing.

Once he'd paid the attendant, he clambered on to the boat himself and seated himself opposite her. He removed his jacket, folded it up and placed it in front of him, then rolled up his shirt sleeves and took the oars.

It felt so tranquil on the lake and she laid back, closing her eyes, and she let her hand trail through the water as she'd always longed to do, feeling the cool water glide over her skin. Moments later, she opened her eyes to see Oliver gazing down at her. His earlier expression had changed and his blue grey eyes had taken on an intense look.

'Is there anything wrong?' she asked, sitting up.

He shook his head. 'No, dear Lottie, there's nothing wrong at all, quite the opposite in fact. I was thinking how beautiful you are and if only . . .'

'If only, what?' she sat forward in the wooden seat.

He hesitated as if carefully choosing his words. It felt as though her heart had stopped and time stood still. 'If only, you were my wife.'

Her stomach somersaulted over and a flitter of excitement coursed through her veins as she felt her heart beat once more. As if not believing her ears, she asked, 'What did you just say?'

'I said, if only you were my wife, I know we'd be happy together.'

She had to agree. She thought she would be very happy as Oliver's wife. She'd feel so protected, but she said nothing, just smiled. But at the back of her mind was the thought that he wasn't really hers to have. He was a married man and divorce wasn't simple, it was a scandal. And after all, she was still only young herself. Maybe it would be something to think about for the future. After all, if Mr Steed was so unhappy in his marriage, there was a good chance his wife was too. Maybe she'd be the one to divorce him and set him free.

They sat in silence for a while until Oliver brought the boat to rest near a heavily shrubbed area where weeping willow tree branches cascaded over their heads, casting a shaded area over and around them. The rest of the boats were far off in the distance and the only sound Lottie could hear was the thud of her own heartbeat pulsing a rhythm of its own. What was happening brought to mind a Christina Rossetti poem she had recently learned by heart, called, 'In the Willow Shade'.

It was mesmerising being on the lake.

'What thoughts are you having?' Oliver brought her back to reality.

'Seeing that willow tree reminded me of a poem I know by Christina Rossetti. I think it's about a love that can never be. It's such a beautiful poem.'

He gazed at her for the longest time before saying softly, 'I wish I could kiss you right now, Lottie. But I suppose that would be wrong. It's just my wife is so cold towards me, she always rebuffs any advances I make towards her.'

What would be the harm in a kiss?

'Have you ever been kissed before?' he asked gently.

She startled for a moment and sat up straight. 'No, not really, not unless you count a peck on the cheek from my next-door neighbour once. I didn't much like it either!'

He laughed. 'Well, this wouldn't be that sort of kiss. Lottie, if I could just kiss you one time I would be forever happy, and no one need know about it at all. Here we are in another world.'

No, there would be no harm in it at all and no one need see. But she'd know, wouldn't she? For a moment she imagined all her family watching them as they hid behind a large bush, Ma pursing her lips in annoyance as she shook her head. *Nice girls don't do things like that, Lottie. Unchaperoned with a married man.* But her need to be kissed by Oliver was so overpowering it outweighed the risk she was willing to take, so she found herself nodding.

Slowly, he stood and came over towards her. 'Look, I can tether the boat to that iron post there and we can get out and sit on the bank. It's quite private.'

He threw the looped rope that was attached to the boat over the post and guided the boat towards the bank. He leapt off on to the grass and stood with his arm extended to allow her to disembark. Trembling, she took his hand as he helped her on to dry land.

He laid his jacket down on the grassy verge for her to sit and he followed suit. Then, all at once, she was in his arms, his warm breaths covering her as he pushed her gently down on the grass. His lips brushed against hers and she opened her mouth to respond. She had never been kissed this way before. It took her breath away as his kisses became more passionate and intense and she yielded to them. He stroked her face, all the while telling her how beautiful she was; all the while as the poem kept flitting through her mind.

She had never felt so much passion in her life. Was this love? Was this what it was all about? Was this what the painters, poets and writers depicted so well? Stolen kisses and breathless embraces? The poem continued to recite itself in her head and without prompting, she found herself adding her own words:

'*And on that shimmering summer day*
The willow covered her as she lay
In such strong arms, embraced, entwined,
His kisses tasted just like wine . . .

Then all at once, she was brought back to reality as she felt his hand roam up the skirts of her dress and she froze. She pulled away. This wasn't supposed to happen. 'P . . . please, Oliver. I am a virgin. I'm s . . . saving myself for marriage.' Her mouth felt dry with fear and her limbs trembled. A moment ago she had been dreamy and wistful and now she felt threatened. It was like Oliver had thrown a bucket of cold water over her.

As if keeping himself in check, softly he replied, 'I'm sorry, I should have known better. You're a good girl, not like some at the factory who flirt with the foremen. I can wait until the time is right and I can make you my wife. You do things to me, Lottie, that drive me wild with desire.'

How could she, Lottie Perkins, an ordinary young woman of sixteen, have such an effect on him? Though she liked that he respected her, and would not force her to do anything she did not want to. 'I am glad you are prepared to wait. But what about your wife, Oliver?'

'I think she'll leave soon and take the children with her. She has already spoken of divorce. Meanwhile, I don't think it will harm if we have a little dalliance together without going "the whole hog" as it were, if you catch my drift?'

She thought she caught his drift very well indeed. Floss had told her that she had got up to that with her boyfriend, Charlie, once. She'd allowed him to take liberties, but they hadn't actually done the deed, but nevertheless, she'd enjoyed it.

'I think,' Lottie said firmly, 'as I have never even been kissed before, that kissing is enough for the time being.'

He nodded. 'I quite understand.' Tenderly, he carried on kissing her and as he lay on top of her, she felt his hardness against her leg and it made her feel a little cheap. If only her mother knew what she was getting up to right now, she'd feel disgusted.

On the boat ride back, Oliver lightened the mood by joking with her, and she reassured herself that they were good for one another. Just inside the park gates was a vendor selling Italian ice cream from a little white cart that bore the name 'Bellini's' in red and yellow lettering. Oliver dipped his hand in his jacket pocket and extracted his leather wallet to purchase an ice cream each. 'I know I promised we'd visit the refreshment rooms for tea and cake but as it's such a lovely day I want to treat you to one of these.'

'I don't mind one bit,' she said, meaning it.

She hadn't had an ice cream since her father was alive and it made her feel good to recall the memory. In the distance, a group of children were playing with a kite as their father looked on as they ran around whooping with pleasure. That scenario reminded her of afternoons with her father many years ago.

'Have you enjoyed yourself this afternoon, Lottie?' Oliver asked, a gleam in his eyes.

'Oh, I have. Truly. Thank you, Oliver.'

'There will be plenty more like this, my love. And as soon as my wife files for divorce we shall be engaged to be married, I promise you that.'

Warm sensations engulfed her body, emotions that belied how she should feel. It would be easy to get carried away and want a time of passion with Oliver. His wife was a foolish woman to want to throw it all away. No one seemed to get divorced that Lottie knew of where she lived. The type of people she knew of who got divorced were wealthy people who were gossiped about in newspaper columns. In her world, women were expected to lie in their beds once they'd made them, no matter how messed up those particular beds were.

Oliver took her hand as they walked, eating the ice cream that was sandwiched between two wafers. They went to admire the gardens and Lottie imagined what their garden would look like once she was Oliver's wife. The thought made her heart gladden inside. It was such a conflicting feeling – she felt her heart beat furiously for him but at the same time a little voice in her head was warning her. What was it telling her? That falling for a married man would only cause her grief, that's what. She fought to ignore it.

The voice was telling her one thing, but Oliver was telling her another – he wanted her in his life and he intended marrying her at any cost.

Chapter Six

'What's going on over there?' Lottie asked as her eyes were drawn to a large crowd beginning to gather around a man stood on a soap box. It looked as if he were speaking passionately to the people in front of him.

'That's William Morris. He's probably talking about workers' rights. Far too boring for you to listen to.' Oliver chuckled. 'Believe me, it won't be your cup of tea, my dear.'

But Lottie was interested, particularly because of the unrest at the Bryant and May factory. 'How do you know it wouldn't concern me, Oliver?' she asked, with her head held high in the air.

Oliver stiffened as if realising for the first time a woman would be interested in that sort of thing. 'Come on now, Lottie, let's go and view the gardens as we'd planned to do.'

Reluctantly, she followed after him. Those people watching William Morris seemed to be mesmerised by his oratory. He spoke with obvious passion and there was plenty of applause.

She remembered well how her father had described him as a socialist and how he had spoken at Hyde Park from a cart that bore a red flag. He'd been giving out leaflets to everyone that day and her father had brought one home with him. There had been some unrest at the dockyard at the time, particularly amongst the Irish.

But Lottie's thoughts were jarred back to the present as Oliver led her through the gardens to admire the pretty flowers. Surely, Oliver should be interested as he'd once worked at the docks? It amazed her that he didn't really seem to care one jot.

Intruding into her thoughts, he said, 'Someday, I'll buy you the biggest bunch of flowers you've ever seen. But for the time being you shall have to make do with something else.' He led her past the colourful flower display to where a young girl stood offering red roses from a wicker basket. Although it was a warm day, she wore an almost threadbare woollen shawl around her shoulders and peeping out beneath her grey linen skirt was a pair of dirty, bare feet. Oliver slipped some coppers into the girl's grimy hand and she handed him the well-trimmed rose which had a pretty white ribbon attached to it.

'Thank you kindly, sir!' she said. It was obvious that Oliver had paid more than he needed, and the girl skipped off bearing a huge smile on her face. The poor thing looked even younger than Bessie and Daisy. But there was someone she reminded her of – now, who was it? She thought for a moment. Geraldine

Morgan, the young girl who had dropped the matches her first day at the factory.

'Oliver,' she began. 'That little girl looks so much like another who works at the factory, I wanted to talk to you about . . .'

'Not now, Lottie, remember what I said?'

She nodded wanting to bite her own tongue. Maybe she was making him feel stressed by mentioning these things right now on his day off from work. She vowed to speak no more about it but would choose her time more carefully on the next occasion.

'A rose for a rose,' Oliver said, skilfully changing the subject, handing the rose to her. Her cheeks flamed with pleasure. No one had ever bought her flowers before, let alone presented her with a red rose. Didn't that spell love?

'Thank you, Oliver,' she said, wrapping her arms around his neck and kissing his cheek.

Gently he pushed her away. 'Not here, someone I know might see us and it will get back to Mrs Steed,' he said sharply. Then seeing the expression on her face, he softened his voice. 'We do have to be careful in case she makes trouble for us.'

In an instant, the little bubble that had ballooned inside her, burst, and she was back to reality. Here she was, walking out with a married man in the park in broad daylight, without his wife's knowledge. The thought made her feel so sad. Somehow, that afternoon she had forgotten all about Mrs Steed and the children. A deluge of guilt washed over her.

As if realising her disappointment, Oliver said, 'Seeing as how you were interested in speaker's corner, why don't we head off over there and see what's going on?'

Brightening up, she nodded, swallowing down her disappointment, and they walked together, not arm-in-arm this time as there were so many people around. They found a spot and stood at a comfortable distance as William Morris finished his speech and people applauded loudly.

'And now, without further ado, I shall leave you with my very good comrade, Mrs Annie Besant!' he announced, before leaving the podium.

A shiver coursed Lottie's spine. She was just about to tell Oliver this was the woman she had met outside the factory, then realised that he was the last person she should tell.

Annie Besant stood firm on the wooden podium, the red ribbon in her hair – her trademark – fluttering in the summer breeze. 'The people have been silenced. I will be the advocate of this silence. I will speak for those who aren't able to speak. I will be the Word of the People.'

There was a tremendous ripple of applause and, for the first time, Lottie noted there were a lot of women in the crowd, even one or two she recognised from the factory.

'Go on, give it to them, Annie!' a man shouted from the back of the crowd.

'There is one factory in this area where the young girls and women are battered into silence. They aren't allowed a voice, but I am, so I will be their voice. This is the same factory where they work long hours for little pay. They work with a chemical called phosphorus which is so dangerous it can eat away at your bone and, believe me, there have been deaths! Our government is refusing to ban this substance so they are as bad as the bosses at that factory!'

There was a huge collective gasp from the crowd. Lottie turned to look at Oliver who was staring intently ahead, his eyes fixated on Annie Besant, but his glare was hard and unflinching. It was obvious he was no fan of the woman or her politics.

'That's terrible!' a woman shouted.

'These poor girls, if they even drop a box of matches on the floor they're forced to pay for it from their own money!' Annie Besant continued. 'Those young girls and women can't speak for themselves, so I propose that there is safety in numbers and that soon there will be a walk-out at the Bryant and May factory!' she shouted and people cheered. Some threw their hats in the air.

Oliver remained stone-faced. 'I think it's time we left before unrest breaks out,' he said firmly, and although Lottie yearned to stay, she guessed there might be truth to his words. In any case, her mother would be worried about her. He took her by the arm and guided her through the jostling crowd, which was listening with avid interest.

How she longed to stay behind and hear more of what Mrs Besant had to say on the matter!

'That woman is a trouble maker,' he said, once they were

well away from the throng. 'She was involved in that demonstration at Trafalgar Square last November when all that unrest broke out. Two thousand police and four hundred troops were brought in to halt the demonstration.'

'I remember hearing about it,' Lottie said, not having any idea that Annie Besant had been involved. How powerful she must be if she could have that sort of effect. Lottie stopped again to hear what Annie had to say, mesmerised by the woman's words. She didn't want to leave the spot but Oliver was determined she listen to him instead. He raised his voice.

'Lots of the demonstrators were injured as the police laid into them with truncheons and trampled them with their horses. There were both infantry and cavalry present at the time. That William Morris and George Bernard Shaw were involved in it as well. Marxists the lot of them! They called it Bloody Sunday. That's the sort they are – revolutionaries under the red flag!'

Lottie could tell Oliver was angry. There was no way she could mention that Annie Besant had approached her outside the factory. He grabbed hold of her arm and tried to pull her away, but she resisted.

'Don't make this more difficult than it needs to be, Lottie. We can't hang around here. Arrests could be made at any moment. This woman isn't only opposing the factory, she speaks out about our government! It could be an offence she might be arrested for!'

'Well I can't see any police, can you?' Of course she realised it would be such an embarrassment if, as one of the bosses at the factory, he were caught listening to the likes of such a political activist as Annie Besant.

Lottie noticed a lad who had been listening to the speech staring at her. He was quite handsome and lifted the brim of his cap to peer more closely at her. 'Are you all right, miss?' he asked.

'The lady,' Oliver emphasised the words, 'is with me and she should know better than to listen to the likes of that Marxist. She talks a load of rot!'

'Let the lady speak for herself,' the lad continued. Lottie watched in total disbelief that a lad who didn't look much older than herself would dare to intervene and cut in on Oliver. 'I should be interested to hear what she has to say. Unlike yourself, I think what women have to say is as important as what a man has to say. Mrs Besant is a fine example of that. And for your information, she doesn't speak rot, she speaks the truth and also backs the dockers!'

Lottie could have hugged the lad. Who the heck was he? She cleared her throat and realising she needed to keep Steed sweet, said, 'I'm fine. Thank you for your concern. We were just about to leave any way.'

'Well, that's all right, then.' He cocked a smile. 'You better run along with your daddy.' He winked to show he knew Oliver wasn't really her father but that it would wind him up anyhow.

Lottie had to stifle a giggle. Oliver's face was beetroot red with anger as he led her away.

When he calmed down and they'd reached the park gates, she turned to him and asked, 'Do you think it's true what Mrs Besant is saying about the workers at the factory being badly treated and underpaid?' Of course, she knew this to be the case but wanted to see how he reacted.

In a hushed tone, he replied, 'Look, I'm caught betwixt and between. I'm not one of you lot and neither am I one of the bosses up the top.' She noted the guarded look in his eyes. 'Honestly, I do realise there are a lot of practices going on at the factory that aren't in the girls' best interests, but I have to be careful not to step on anyone's toes else I might lose my own job otherwise.'

Sticking out her chin, she said, 'But you are my boss, aren't you? You'd be privy to all that goes on and what the higher ups are saying about all of this.'

He let out a long breath and ran his hand through his tousled jet-black hair before replacing his bowler hat on his head. 'Yes, and I could get the sack for my thoughts on all this. I really can't afford to do that as I have to provide for my wife and family.' He softened for a moment, then added, 'And if I lost my job, how would I look after you?'

'Well, I won't tell anyone. It's just between you and me,' she said, glad he had calmed down. 'You do trust me, don't you?'

He nodded, and his eyes cleared again. 'Of course I do. I

agree, the girls aren't treated fairly at all and should be paid more for the graft they put in, but it's out of my hands. I've heard a tale from the factory floor that Mrs Besant has been accosting some of the workforce trying to get them to say things about the working conditions . . .'

Lottie's face grew hot and she hoped he wouldn't notice. 'Yes, I've heard the same thing.'

He narrowed his gaze. 'You haven't spoken to her, have you, Lottie?'

A pulse pounded in her head, then she swallowed. 'N . . . No of course not.'

A look of relief swept over Oliver's face as he let out a long breath. 'That's good. I want it kept that way – no good will come of it. You girls will end up losing your jobs and there's plenty that would snatch them right out of your hands.' He stopped and placed both palms of his hands on her shoulders, gazing into her eyes. 'Promise me, Lottie, you'll never speak to that woman. Please give me your word on that.'

She gulped. What could she do? She hadn't intended answering her questions anyhow, until she heard her speak today – she had a fire in her belly that Lottie had never witnessed in a woman before and it impressed her greatly. Crossing her fingers of both hands behind her back, she nodded. 'No, I won't go looking for Mrs Besant to speak to her.'

Oliver let out a long sigh of relief. 'Good. I want it kept that way. I'm glad we understand one another.'

She had promised that she wouldn't go looking for her, though if Annie Besant came to her instead, that was a very different matter indeed. She was beginning to experience a newfound respect for the woman. She knew of no other who could cause so much unrest and division. The ordinary people like that lad at the park seemed to love her and all she stood for. But why would a young lad think so highly of the woman? As far as she knew she hadn't seen him working at the factory.

One thing was certain, if Oliver caught her talking to the woman he wouldn't be happy about it and that would scupper her chances of getting Cassie moved to a new department at the factory before it was too late.

Lottie entered the house via the back door and she quickly rushed to her bedroom to hide the red rose in a drawer. She intended to put it in water later so she could press it between the pages of her poetry book, so she could keep it forever.

'Where have you been, my girl?' Ma stood on the landing with her hands behind her back, her chin thrust forward in a manner she hadn't seen in a long while. She was annoyed that much was certain.

'I . . . I told you, Ma, I went to see Floss.'

Ma looked her up and down. 'Your cheeks look a little too flushed to me. Have you been spooning with a lad?'

Lottie shook her head. 'Sorry I'm late getting back, Ma. I

know I promised to help you in the house, but the time flew by.' She felt bad for lying to Ma, but if she found out what she'd been up to she'd surely forbid her to leave the house again.

''Orright, your sisters helped instead and now I know they can do it, they can do it again.' Both girls giggled and popped out from behind her. 'I've kept you some dinner, it's on the hob.'

'Thanks, Ma.'

She hated keeping secrets from her, but what could she do? They were from two different generations and she knew she wouldn't understand, both the fact she had spent the time in the company of a married man today, and that she wanted to hear more from Mrs Besant.

The following morning, Lottie looked out for Oliver at work, but he was nowhere to be seen. Floss glanced over at her. ''Ere, Lottie, what's the matter with you today? Yer not your usual self.'

Lottie cleared her throat. 'Just got a cold coming on, that's all. Where's Mr Steed today?'

'How would I know? He ain't been on the factory floor all morning. I ain't seen Cassie Bowen either, maybe they're together!' She chuckled.

'What's happened to Cass?' Lottie felt suddenly alarmed. There was something wrong, she just knew it.

'Polly might know,' she said flippantly, then changed the subject. 'So, what did you get up to yesterday? I called over to your house in the afternoon, but your Ma said you weren't in.'

It felt as though every drop of blood had drained from Lottie's body as her heart quickened a beat. So, her Ma must have realised she was lying yesterday when she'd said she'd gone to visit Floss. No wonder she was so angry with her when she arrived home.

'I, er, stayed on after church to help tidy up the hymn books and then the vicar said I could practice on the piano as we don't have one at home.'

Floss glared at her. So, she didn't believe her either, but then she said, 'Humph, it's 'orright for some, ain't it? No one offers me to play the piano.'

Lottie let out a long breath of relief. 'Well, are you able to play?'

She shook her head beneath her white mob cap that was keeping her wild, unruly mane in place. 'No, 'fraid I can't. Who taught you, anyhow?'

'My Aunt Dorothea plays, she has a piano at home, but we don't get to see her all that much.' Relieved, Floss had fallen for her untruth, she turned back to her work. Maybe she'd see Oliver later. She couldn't wait to be with him once again. He had promised to move her to the packing department soon, so she was disappointed that hadn't happened as yet.

After work, Lottie walked home alone. She missed Cassie's

company and went to the girl's house to enquire how she was. A very pale Mrs Bowen opened the door.

'Hello, Mrs Bowen. I've come to see how Cass is.'

'You'd better come in, sweetheart,' she offered as Lottie followed her inside. 'It ain't good. We paid to have the doctor out and he reckons it's that phossy jaw she's got.'

'But is there anything they can do for it, any medicine they can give her?'

'Only for the pain.' She shook her head, her eyes misting with tears and then her hand went to her mouth as if she was just realising what it all meant. Lottie put her arm around her. 'Come on, Mrs Bowen, I'll make you a cup of tea,' she said. The woman nodded gratefully.

After they'd drank their tea and had a good chat, Mrs Bowen led Lottie to her daughter's bedroom where she lay fast asleep. She looked so peaceful it was hard to believe she was really so poorly. 'I'm glad she's asleep now,' Mrs Bowen said. 'She was awake all night long coughing and spluttering and her jaw hurt something rotten. Me and her father took turns to stay up with her. The doctor gave me some medicine for the pain to give her.'

Lottie nodded sympathetically. No doubt it was laudanum or something similar, she guessed. She so wished Cassie could see she was here to visit her and that she hadn't forgotten all about her.

As if reading her thoughts, Mrs Bowen, after they'd stepped

away from the bedroom door said, 'Don't worry, Lottie. I'll tell her you were here and you were kind enough to make me a cup of tea and have a little chat.'

'Thank you,' she said with tears in her eyes as she stooped to kiss Mrs Bowen's cheek. 'If there's anything I can do, let me know.'

The woman nodded, but Lottie just knew there was no more any of them could do for poor Cassie any more.

Oliver did not show up at work the following day, nor the next. Rumours circulated the factory floor. One girl, Minnie, said he'd got a young lady 'up the spout' as she put it. Lottie shuddered at the thought, though she realised it was all talk. None of them knew him like she did. They didn't know the promises he'd made or that she could speak to him about the health of the girls at the factory. What a kind man he was. Someone else reckoned he'd taken his family away on holiday. Lottie believed neither could be true. If he had been going away he'd have told her, she was sure of that. It was pure speculation. If only they knew the real Mr Steed.

That lunchtime she decided to tell the girls what she'd discovered about Cassie. Most were shocked, particularly Polly, who now worried about her own health, but there were those like Floss who had seen it coming.

'It's 'ardly surpising, is it? Look at Aggie, she's now gone off sick too. The woman was walking around with yellow skin like a bleedin' canary, she was, and the bosses let her carry on working!'

'Girls, we can stand for this no longer!' Lottie said, to murmurs of agreement.

When she left work that evening, there was a small crowd gathered near the factory gates and in amongst them, Lottie noticed Mrs Besant, her dark head nodding beneath the frills of her bonnet as she appeared to be asking the girls questions. As Lottie approached, Mrs Besant turned her head and stopped speaking. She gazed at her with a look of familiarity. And for a moment, Lottie feared Mrs Besant only recognised her from speaker's corner that Sunday in the park.

She needn't have worried as she asked softly, 'Have you come to join us?'

Lottie found herself nodding, even though she was going against everything Oliver had warned her about. Cassie was at the forefront of her mind and she knew she had to be involved in this somehow. With the girls, Mrs Besant made arrangements to meet at a later date, away from the factory, away from loose lips, where she could question them about their employment.

'Do not fear, girls, for I am on your side!' She finished her speech boldly, raising a finger.

As the girls walked away in dribs and drabs, talking amongst themselves, the sway of opinion was moving fast.

'Just a moment. Lottie, isn't it?' Annie Besant stood, blinking in the early evening sun.

Lottie nodded. This time in no rush to leave. 'Yes, ma'am. I know I told you I wouldn't speak about conditions at that place, but I have changed my mind.'

Annie Besant's eyes twinkled with kindness. 'What or whom, made you change it, pray tell?'

'It was hearing you speak at Victoria Park on Sunday. The passion in your voice, you really know what you're talking about. I was so impressed.'

Mrs Besant smiled broadly revealing a set of even white teeth. 'Ah, but I am not out to impress anyone. I am out for justice.'

'For the underdog?' Lottie asked.

'If you'd like to put it that way, then, yes, for the men, women and children who have no voices of their own.'

'But there's also another reason I came here today. My friend, Cassie Bowen, has just been diagnosed with that phossy jaw. She's in a terrible state and her mother doesn't think she'll pull through. It's made me realise we need to do something now before it's too late.'

Annie's eyes were full of compassion. 'I think we'll have to see what we can do about raising money for Cassie and her family. Just leave it with me.'

'Thank you, Mrs Besant,' Lottie said feeling relieved. She was just about to walk away, when Annie continued speaking.

'I was just about to pack up here for the day anyhow. How would you like to come for some tea with me?'

She looked around as the crowd began to dwindle away, then smiled. 'I'd like that very much, ma'am.'

'Very well. My carriage awaits.' She gestured with her gloved hand to where, Lottie noticed for the first time, a man in a top hat was waiting at the end of the road. She guessed he was the carriage driver.

Once inside the carriage, Mrs Besant said, 'So tell me a little about yourself, Lottie.'

'Oh, I don't know there's much to tell.'

'Everyone has a story, my dear. Even the poor who sleep on the streets of Whitechapel. Do you know one day I almost stumbled over what I thought was a bag of rags and it turned out to be a young woman who had been forced on the streets after becoming pregnant? Her father drove her away.'

'What happened to her?'

'I managed to get her to the Salvation Army women's shelter at Hanbury Street. Now that young woman is married and has a family of her own and is a valuable member of society.'

'What happened to her baby?'

'That was a sad tale: the poor mite couldn't survive the harsh winter after the mother had been living out in the cold. She had just perished to death the night I found her mother.'

Lottie watched Annie turn her head to look out of the window, blinking back tears.

'That's very sad. I'm lucky I live with my mother and brothers and sisters. Our father died last year.'

'That must have been hard for you all, Lottie.'

'It was and, to tell you the truth, it still is sometimes.'

'So, that's why you work at the factory?'

'Yes, ma'am. But I don't like it there. It's true, every word you say about that place.'

Annie smiled. 'The truth always outs in the end. So, how would you like life to be for you?'

Lottie laughed. 'I'd like to be a lady like yourself. You see my father came from a wealthy family but was cut off when he met my mother as she was from a poor family.'

'So, you've glimpsed what it's like to be wealthy, you mean?'

'Yes. We used to visit my father's sister, Aunt Dorothea, quite regularly. She taught me how to have nice manners and play the piano, but there was a falling out between her and my mother.'

'I see,' Annie said. 'But believe me, being wealthy isn't always the best thing in life. I mean, it is better than being poor and sleeping rough, but even rich people aren't always happy.' She looked out of the window again, and Lottie wondered what she was thinking. Maybe about her marriage and her child and how things hadn't worked out for her?

'Mrs Besant, what do you think the best thing in life is, then?'

She turned back to face Lottie. 'To be kind, Lottie. Kindness costs nothing at all. Whether you're a pauper or a king, you should be kind, always.'

Annie's words ran through her mind as they continued their journey to the tea room. Mrs Besant was kindness itself and Lottie smiled, realising that despite whatever background Annie came from, she would have been kind.

Lottie enjoyed herself in the tea room and she hung on Annie's every word as they drank their tea and ate some fancies.

It made her feel so grown up to be seated with such a powerful woman. She noticed people staring at them and some even came over to speak with Annie and shake her hand. Lottie felt that she was a star. And later, when she dropped Lottie back home as the carriage drew up outside her house, she felt quite proud as the neighbours stared. What on earth would Ma say about all of this? And more importantly what would the factory girls think? But it was all in a good cause.

Before she said her goodbyes, Mrs Besant said, 'Don't worry Lottie, Cassie and her parents shall be taken care of, you can be sure of that.'

Chapter Seven

From her work station, Lottie noticed Mr O'Hara picking up boxes of matches to load into his wooden handcart to take to the outworkers. She really didn't know what to make of him and his intentions towards her mother; she hoped they were honourable.

She looked at Floss. 'What do you think of him?'

'Who?' Floss looked vacant.

'Mr O'Hara, the sweater. He's been bringing work to my mother. I think he might be sweet on her.'

Floss grinned. 'I think he's a decent man. Someone told me 'is wife died in childbirth. He's lonely I expect. And so's your Ma.'

Lottie guessed Floss was right. Maybe he just liked her mother's company. In any case, she was pleased for them.

Lottie was dying to tell Floss about having tea with Mrs Besant the previous evening, but decided against it. She would only get jealous and wouldn't understand how someone like

Lottie could feel at ease being in a tea room with such an elegant woman. Though the factory girls respected her they would never expect to have the right etiquette to be in her company in a place like that.

Soon after their meeting, Annie Besant published a searing account in *The Link*, her own publication, entitled 'White Slavery in London.'

'Look, here!' Floss exclaimed to a group of workers. The crowd of girls huddled around as someone kept watch to ensure that no bosses were about. 'You read it, Lottie,' she urged, thrusting the article beneath Lottie's nose. Floss could read but wasn't as literate as Lottie was.

'*Born in slums*,' Lottie read, '*driven to work while still children, undersized because under-fed, oppressed because helpless, flung aside as soon as worked out. Who cares if they die or go on to the streets, provided that Bryant and May shareholders get their 23 per cent and Mr Theodore Bryant can erect statues and buy parks?*'

There was a murmur of agreement from the group.

'*Girls are used to carrying boxes on their heads until the hair is rubbed off*,' Lottie carried on, '*and some young heads are bald at fifteen years of age. Country clergymen with shares in Bryant and May, draw down on your knee your fifteen-year-old daughter; pass your hand tenderly over the silky clustering curls. Rejoice in the dainty beauty of the thick, shiny tresses.*'

Lottie swallowed hard as she and the other girls digested the article. Annie Besant had used bold facts and weaved compelling imagery into the article to drive home the extreme working conditions. It wasn't that the workers just lost their hair, but often over time, their skin turned yellow, then green, and finally black as they succumbed to a deadly form of 'phossy jaw'.

The article outlined the fact the girls at Bryant and May earned less than five shillings a week, and along the way this pay was further docked for taking lavatory breaks or arriving late for work.

'Well, it's all true anyhow!' Floss said, taking the paper from Lottie, folding it up and slipping it into her pinafore pocket.

'It might be true,' one of the girls, Mary Driscoll, said, 'but we don't want to be caught discussing newspaper articles or else we'll be out on our ears!' There was a swell of agreement, and Lottie knew in her heart that the girl spoke sense even if the facts in the article were true. 'Girls, you must cross your hearts and hope to die that you never breathe a word of what we're telling Mrs Besant to the bosses,' she said. All the girls muttered their agreement as they nodded their heads.

'We're all in this together,' Lottie added. 'Careless words could cost jobs.'

The day after the article was published, Oliver finally showed up at work, though he appeared to be avoiding Lottie. Did he know she had spoken to Annie Besant. Surely not? If so, who could have told him?

She was eventually summoned to his office, where she found him grim-faced. Was he about to reprimand her? Had she gone down in his estimation after her defiance in the park? Or did he suddenly have mixed feelings as he felt guilty about his wife and daughters?

'Please sit down, Miss Perkins.'

So, it's Miss Perkins now, is it? What happened to 'dear sweet Lottie'? Tears filled her eyes.

He let out a short huff of breath, on seeing her expression. 'I'm sorry, but while we are at work, I have to address you in a manner befitting your position. I called you here to fill you in on something.'

She nodded and took a seat. She felt the palms of her hands perspiring as she fretted over what he had to tell her.

Oliver sat opposite her. 'I'm sorry, Lottie, there was no way for me to pass a message on to you. I have been away from work as my wife has been very sick.'

Lottie felt the hairs on the back of her neck bristle. 'I'm sorry to hear that. What happened?'

He shook his head, gravely. 'No one knows for sure. It doesn't appear to be contagious, but she's been very unwell and doesn't seem to be getting any better. I have been greatly concerned about her.'

Lottie bit her bottom lip. 'I'm so sorry, Oliver, I mean Mr

Steed. Perhaps we shouldn't see one another again?' She couldn't help thinking this was God's wrath for associating with a married man.

'Oh no,' he said, rather too quickly. 'That's not what I want at all. It is only you who is keeping me sane in all of this. I hope we can meet one another again shortly. I do need someone to talk to.'

She nodded, pleased that she hadn't been far from his thoughts. 'I'll be here for you,' she said.

'There is one thing I want to warn you about: the higher ups have read the article in *The Link* and they're none too pleased. Any girl who has spoken to this Besant woman is in danger of being dismissed forthwith. They are going to circulate a statement later that they want all workers to sign.'

'Do you know what it says?'

He nodded. 'Yes. It says that you are satisfied with the conditions here. I'm warning you now, Lottie, and please don't tell the others this, but if anyone doesn't comply they will be sent away.'

Lottie felt her anger rise. The injustice of it all! 'But that's not fair. You know that conditions are bad here!'

'Please keep your voice down. I know that and so do you, but there's nothing I can do about it. Mrs Besant has highlighted the problems and the owners aren't happy about it. The Salvation Army has been quite vocal as well. Things aren't looking too good. If you want to hang on to your job, and for your mother to keep her job at home too, then I suggest you keep quiet and sign the statement. You must say you have nothing to do with Mrs Besant's campaign to bring down this factory.' Oliver's eyes flashed. She had never seen him look so angry or so indignant before. He looked even angrier than the day at the park when that lad had challenged him. But what could she do? Wheels were already in motion, and she did agree with Annie Besant. Conditions were dire. But if she refused to sign the document she and her mother could be left without jobs and then where would they all be? The children would go hungry. They could all end up in the workhouse.

As if realising how upset she was, Oliver stood and drew near to her. He tilted her chin with his forefinger. 'Please don't cry, Lottie. It needn't come to that. All you have to do is sign the document. Don't worry about what the other girls think. Think of yourself, your mother and your family. No one else cares about you here, except for me.'

She swallowed the lump that was forming in her throat before it threatened to choke her. Floss and the other girls must care for her, surely? But when she came to think about it, Floss was all for her own ends. Maybe Oliver was right.

'There's talk, but you mustn't tell anyone of this, that the bosses want to speak to the girl who spoke to Annie Besant and promoted that article in her publication. Would you know who the girl is, Lottie?'

Lottie shook her head, feeling her pulse rise. It would appear that Oliver had no idea that quite a few of the girls had spoken to Mrs Besant. But she genuinely had no idea which girl had prompted Mrs Besant to investigate in the first place and kept her coming back to ask questions. It might well have been Floss but she wasn't sure. She had never admitted to it, she'd only said she'd spoken to the woman, as had Lottie amongst many others, but in this climate of unease, how could she trust anyone? 'What will happen to her if they find out who she is?'

'She'll get an instant dismissal of course, and I very much doubt they will even pay her what she's owed for such a betrayal.'

Lottie felt herself tremble. Was it really worth getting involved in something like this? 'I see what you're saying, honestly I do, Oliver, I mean Mr Steed, but the girls here are paid a pittance for what they do. The workers aren't treated well here at all. There's a lot of truth to the article.' Oliver gave her a stern look and she decided to change tact. 'And I told you about my friend Cassie. She went off with that phossy jaw a few weeks ago and hasn't been seen since. I'm ever so worried about her. She has no means of supporting herself or her family, unless the rumours of the 'hush money' from the foreman are true. Even if she goes into the workhouse, she won't last much longer. It's a killer. It's not like lancing a boil or having a tooth taken out. It's deadly. And the bosses are all too ready to dismiss it's happening. That's what I was trying to tell you Sunday afternoon at the park.'

Oliver's upper lip twitched. She knew he recognised the truth in her words but, like all the other people in charge at the factory, he would never admit to it. He shook his head. 'Mr Bryant wouldn't be happy about hearing one of his workforce talking this way, Miss Perkins.'

'One of his workforce? It's the whole damn lot!' she spat out. There was a new fire in her belly thanks to Annie Besant.

She stood, turned on her heel and left Mr Steed's office. Back at her workstation, Floss looked at her wide-eyed. 'Well, what did 'e want you for?'

'Something and nothing,' she replied, not even trying to hide how cross she was.

Floss narrowed her eyes. 'The gaffer must have called you in there for something or other. Maybe he has designs on you. There have been rumours going around.'

Lottie gritted her teeth. 'People should keep their idle tittle-tattle to themselves.' She stared at her, urging her to shut up.

They hardly spoke the rest of the day, and when it was time to leave the factory, Lottie looked out for any signs of Mrs Besant outside the gates, but there were none. It was now she needed to speak to her more than ever.

Disheartened, Lottie decided to visit Cassie as she hadn't been able to see her for a few days. She'd been asleep every time she called and she didn't want to disturb her. When she arrived at the Bowen house all the curtains were drawn upstairs and down. Had Cassie already passed away? Was she too late to say goodbye to the dearest friend she'd ever had? Mrs Bowen let her in with a solemn expression on her face. Several candles had been lit, their flickering flames casting an eerie glow over the place.

'Am I too late?' Lottie asked.

'No, she's still with us but not for much longer. I've sent Cassie's father to fetch the priest, but I don't think Father O'Connell is going to get here in time.' She sniffed, evidently trying to hold back the tears. 'I think we're nearing the end.'

The sadness that had gripped Lottie's heart was replaced by relief. She was so glad that something had told her to call today on her way home from work. 'Oh, surely not? Shall I fetch the doctor? Maybe he can do something?'

'It's gone past that point, sweetheart. Her breathing is laboured, she's been in so much pain that it will be a blessing that the good Lord takes her from us.'

Lottie swallowed hard. 'Is there anything at all I can do, Mrs Bowen?'

The woman nodded. 'Actually, there is. Come and pray with me, dear. I'd like to think that even if Father doesn't get here in time there will be some sort of prayer said.'

Lottie nodded and squeezed the woman's hand, then they

walked towards Cassie's darkened room. There was a large lighted candle on the bedside table which Lottie felt drawn to, its flickering flame providing her with comfort somehow.

She held her breath as she studied the girl's pale and sallow face as she lay in her bed with her dark hair sprawled out on her pillow. She looked older than her tender years; worry lines etched her pretty face. Lottie suddenly let out a long breath of relief, realising just how much she had been holding her composure until this point. It wouldn't be helpful if she broke down right now. Cassie may even hear her cries, and even though she was no longer able to communicate with them, she might realise the upset around her. No, a peaceful path out of this world was what was needed, Lottie decided.

Both women knelt down on either side of the bed. Realising that Mrs Bowen didn't have the words to pray over her daughter right now, Lottie took over, placing the palms of her hands together.

'Dear Lord, please take the spirit of our dear Cassie into your care.' A tear trickled down Lottie's cheek and she swept it away with the back of her hand.

She looked at Mrs Bowen whose eyes were firmly shut tight, her mouth set in a grim line. Lottie carried on, speaking the words of a prayer which came to her as if she had rehearsed it. She noticed how her voice became stronger as she spoke, and buoyed by the presence of Mrs Bowen beside her, and how much she knew she needed this, she finished the prayer with a heart full of love.

It was almost as though Cassie had been waiting for permission, for the right time to pass. As Lottie reached out and took her hand, squeezing it in reassurance, she felt the girl squeeze back with her own. Lottie looked at her mother to see if she had noticed the slight movement.

'Well, I never,' Mrs Bowen whispered. 'She hasn't responded like this for days.'

She took her daughter's other hand and looked lovingly at her. 'She squeezed my hand as well.' The tears rolled down Mrs Bowen's cheeks, but she was smiling which gladdened Lottie's heart. Then Cassie exhaled a deep, rattling breath and her head rolled to one side.

Lottie sighed, feeling a sharp pain in her gut as she rose to her feet. She bent over the slight form of her friend, and felt for a pulse in her neck.

'She's gone,' she said.

Mrs Bowen wept bitterly, but Lottie, realising she needed to be strong now for Mrs Bowen, patted the woman on the shoulder. 'You stop here, Mrs Bowen, to be with Cassie. I'll watch out for Mr Bowen and the priest, and then I'll make you all a cup of tea when they arrive.'

The woman nodded and Lottie left the room, taking one last look at the best friend she had ever had. She didn't break down until she reached the scullery. She needed her strength to deal with this for Mrs Bowen's sake. Those bosses at Bryant and May needed to be here right now to see what had just happened. Maybe then they'd change their minds about their dangerous practices at that place.

Chapter Eight

The news about Cassie's death had spread amongst the factory girls. Even Floss who didn't seem the sentimental sort, put her arm around Lottie's shoulder and said, 'Don't let on so, me darlin'. Cassie is much better off with the angels.'

But what was upsetting Lottie even more was that, even though the bosses had been informed, there'd been no sign of them offering to pay for the funeral, or even visiting Cassie's family. Mrs Bowen had mentioned that the sick pay – though it was more like 'hush money' – had barely been anything, but enough to keep them quiet. Lottie reckoned they washed their hands of the whole situation even though those very same hands had blood all over them, just like that William Gladstone statue.

Lottie was so angry, and she couldn't help taking it out on Floss. 'Let them go over there now and see the weeping parents and Cassie's empty chair at their table! Will they do that? Of course not! And how will Cassie's parents survive now? Mr

Bowen hasn't had any work at the docks for ages, just earning the odd bit of wage hop picking. Cassie's wage was keeping that house going. I don't much fancy their chances now.'

Later, Mr Steed apprehended her. He'd asked to see her in his office in a very curt manner. Normally she'd have addressed him formally but she was so riled up she hadn't, and didn't even care if she got the sack for it.

'Sit down,' he commanded, something he didn't usually ask one of the workforce to do.

'I understand you were there with Cassie Bowen when she died last night.'

'I was indeed. How do you know that?'

'Never mind how I know. It's very sad but I think it's in your best interests to keep away from that house. It would be far better now if you and the other girls distance yourself from Cassie's death. We don't want this to fall back on Bryant and May.'

Lottie could hardly believe her ears. 'I'm sorry, what did you just say?'

'Believe me, this in your best interests. And especially keep away from Annie Besant. She must not find out about this.'

'She already knows.' It was a partial lie, really. Mrs Besant knew how ill Cassie had been, but was yet to hear about her death.

He looked taken aback. 'But how?'

'One of the girls went to see her last night, I was told.'

Oliver raised his hand to his forehead. 'Oh my goodness, Theodore is going to have kittens about this.'

'Well let him do so. Quite frankly we've all had enough. There is so much unrest on the factory floor and quite rightly so.'

He shook his head. 'Don't go getting involved in all of this, Lottie. It's so much bigger than you are.'

She stared at him in defiance. 'Oh believe me, Oliver. I am already involved.' Then she turned on her heel and left his office. The gloves between the girls and management were now well and truly off.

By the time Lottie arrived home, the kids had been fed and were sitting around the table assembling the matchboxes with her mother. There was no getting away from Bryant and May, even at home. She sighed as she removed her jacket and bonnet.

Her mother looked up from where she'd been carefully pasting a matchbox and smiled broadly. She placed the matchbox on a pile with all the others, while the children continued to assemble them. 'I've left your dinner warming over a saucepan on the hob, Lottie,' she said.

'Thank you, Ma.' She leaned over to kiss her mother's cheek and stood back to gaze at her. Lottie hadn't seen Ma smile like that in a long while, particularly since the death of her pa.

Freddy looked up from where he'd been assembling the boxes, his little fingers working niftily, but poor Davy, who was so cack-handed and needed constant supervision, hadn't noticed her come in. His face was looking more freckled than usual despite the fact there hadn't been much sun during the summer. He had Irish blood running through his veins, all the kids did of course, but none were as freckled as him. Ma always said her own brother had been just the same until the consumption took him. Her brother had been born in the old country, but Ma was East End born and bred, she was as cockney as the bells of Bow and jellied eels.

'You must be starving after a long day at that place,' her Ma continued.

'It's been a gruelling day particularly having to tell the girls about Cassie's death.'

Her mother patted her daughter's hand. 'That must have been so 'ard for you, Lottie. That poor girl's mother, 'eaven knows how she's feelin' right now.'

Lottie nodded. 'She's a strong woman but Cassie was the one that kept her going, At least you have all of us Ma.'

'Aye. I'm lucky indeed, gal.'

'What makes you so chipper today?'

'Well, if you must ask.' Her face flushed red. 'It's—Oh, it's nothing. How about a cup of tea then?' she offered, trying to change the subject.

'I'll make it now,' Lottie said, smiling to herself.

Ma stood and ushered her daughter to the scullery. In a hushed tone, she said, 'I don't want the girls to 'ear us speak – Bessie and Daisy are at that age where they cotton on quickly – but 'ave you 'eard any talk that they might be laying off girls at the factory? I've been told they might be sacking some of them. Is it to do with Cassie's death?'

Not knowing quite how to reply, she answered honestly, 'There is talk of some unrest there, yes, but Cassie's death is only the tip of the iceberg. Why do you ask?'

'Mr O'Hara called with the boxes this morning, as usual, and he stayed for a cup of tea.'

'Oh, he had a cup of tea, did he?' She chuckled.

Her mother slapped her gently, smiling broadly. 'Yes, he did, and we had quite a chat about things. He's promised to get me more work, so there should be a little extra money to go around in future.' Ma seemed very content with herself and smiled at the very mention of his name.

'I would have thought you had plenty to be getting on with already, Ma?' Lottie folded her arms, not knowing how she felt about her mother becoming so familiar with one of the sweaters, let alone the idea of her working at the factory.

'Well, I'd just as well take full advantage of the extra work. He is doing me a favour after all.'

'And is he doing any favours for any other home-workers, do you think, Ma?' Lottie studied her mother's face.

Ma's cheeks reddened. 'I, er, I'm not sure about that.'

'That's a no then.'

Ma turned her face away, obviously embarrassed to be caught out in her affections for the man.

'But, the reason I ask, is that he told me he might be able to get me a job at the factory. There's talk of some girls, well, one in particular who might get fired for having loose lips.'

Lottie nodded. 'Yes, I've been told that, too. It's to do with talking to Annie Besant outside the factory gates and telling her exactly what conditions are like inside.'

Ma's eyes gleamed. 'I've heard of that woman before of course, she was a minister's wife. Seems to get herself fired up to fight for some cause or another. Your father listened to 'er once speaking at Hyde Park.'

Lottie listened with interest as she moved around the small room, getting the saucepan of water bubbling and placing a dinner plate on top. 'And what did Pa make of her?'

'Thought she was great, he did. She was all for the dockers and improving their poor pay conditions. He said she was a friend of William Morris and even George Bernard Shaw!'

'Someone did tell me that,' Lottie remarked, then remembering it was Oliver who had told her, she quickly glossed over it. 'So, Pa liked her then?'

'Yes, 'e did indeed. Now to get back to what I was telling you, if that girl gets sacked, shall I try to get her job? Shamus says she's going to be sacked. They're going to say it's because she refused to use the new cutting machines.'

'No, Ma,' Lottie replied a little too vehemently. 'Don't get involved in things that don't concern you. That lie about the machines will never fly anyhow. No one to my knowledge has refused to use them.'

'Our Lottie, you know something, don't you?' Ma narrowed her eyes.

Lottie sat at the old scrubbed scullery table and her mother followed suit, her green eyes clouding over as she wrung her hands. The sleeves of her old Linley dress were rolled up above her elbows and her hands were roughened and raw, covered in calluses. Lottie felt a pang of sympathy for her poor mother who probably felt it would be a good chance to move up in the world and follow after her daughter into the factory.

'Yes, I know of some things, Ma, but I think it best I keep them to myself for time being.'

Ma let out a long sigh. 'Oh, very well then, but if I get a chance of a job I shall go for it, Mr O'Hara says . . .'

'Oh for goodness sake's, Ma,' she snapped. 'Do you want to end up with phossy jaw or not being able to pee when you want to? That's what it's like! It's not all milk and honey.'

For a moment, Lottie was aware that she had burst her mother's bubble. She stood and leaned over to wrap her arms around her mother's neck and kissed her head. 'I'm sorry, Ma, but I feel caught up in the middle of all of this. Please don't tell Mr O'Hara anything I tell you in case he takes it back to the bosses and uses it against me.'

'I won't, but you can trust Shamus, I've been talking to him a lot lately and, while yes, I did misjudge him to begin with, he's just lonely, that's all, since his wife passed away.'

'Just like you,' Lottie said tenderly.

Ma waved her daughter away with a flick of the hand. 'Aw go on with you, how can I possibly be lonely with you lot around? Go 'ave your dinner before it gets ruined.'

Lottie smiled to herself and released her mother from her embrace. It was good that her mother had some life back inside her again.

As Lottie sat on her own eating her dinner of boiled potatoes, scrag end of lamb, carrots and peas, she thought about how Oliver had been lately. She was shocked that his wife had been so ill, maybe he really did care for the woman after all, especially if he'd wanted to take time off from work to be with her.

The following day at the factory the workers were summoned.

'What's going on 'ere?' Floss said, looking at Lottie who shrugged her shoulders in return.

'I've no idea.'

'You're well in with Steed. 'Asn't he said anything?'

'No, I'm as much in the dark as you are,' she said stiffly, 'and I really resent you making out I'm in with him.' She didn't want anyone knowing of their growing connection or the day in the park.

'Keep yer 'air on gal, I was only joking.'

They were interrupted by one of the foremen who was ushering them over to a table. Lottie could spy Mr Steed sitting there looking very uncomfortable, which meant only one thing. 'Looks like they're asking us to sign something,' she said and they moved forward into the queue.

'Move along now girls,' the foreman was saying. Lottie felt like they were cattle at a market. 'Get that signed if you want to keep your jobs at the factory.'

'What are we signing for?' Lottie asked, looking at Mr Steed who had the pages of the document in front of him. She knew it must be the document he'd warned her about.

'It's a statement issued by Theodore Bryant for you girls to say you have nothing to do with Annie Besant or her campaign to highlight working conditions at the factory. It's very straightforward. All you need to do is sign your name – or for those that can't write, a cross will suffice.'

This was met with a chorus of muttering and a sea of shaking heads. Lottie was appalled to see that some girls had begun to sign the document.

'Well, I ain't signing it!' Floss announced loudly. Oliver Steed glared at her.

'Aren't you afraid of being sacked?' Lottie asked.

Floss jutted out her chin defiantly. 'Nope. I stand up for what I believe in. What about you? Are you going to sign it?'

Lottie hesitated a moment. 'I was going to sign it, but I feel like you do, to be honest. Even the workers who have gone off ill with phossy jaw are treated badly. Cassie Bowen didn't receive a single farthing after they cut off her compensation. It makes me so angry. Her poor mother hasn't even got enough money to bury her child. She'll end up in a pauper's grave.' She'd love to have told Floss about Annie's promise but daren't. But at least Oliver was in earshot and she hoped he'd hear. He'd done nothing to help poor Cassie either.

Steed turned his attention to Lottie as if now in sympathy. 'You're an intelligent young woman, Lottie,' he said in a softer tone. 'Use your influence to tell the girls it's in their best interests to sign, will you?'

She shook her head. 'Sorry, Mr Steed, I can't possibly do that after what happened to Cassie, and she'd still be with us today if it weren't for the working practices at this place, as well you know!'

The foreman drew near with a wooden cane and he lifted it above Lottie's head as if about to strike.

Noticing this, Mr Steed jumped in. 'There'll be no need for that, Mr Baker. We don't want to come over all heavy here. The girls are naturally distressed at the death of a colleague.' Then turning to Lottie he said, 'I'm going to give you more time to think about this, but don't take too long or none of you will have jobs to come back to.'

It was a victory for now at least.

Floss slapped her hard on the back. 'Good on yer, gal! You know it makes sense.'

For the remainder of the day, Oliver steered clear and Lottie wondered whether he'd seen that her signature wasn't on the document still.

''Ere, Lottie,' Floss said, 'whatcha think about 'avin' a meeting about all of this? We could get all of the girls together.'

'After all that's happened here, I think that's a good idea.' Lottie surprised herself at how she was now coming around to Floss's way of thinking. Maybe they should be stronger about fighting for their rights? A few weeks ago she'd never have seen herself taking part in anything like this, but in a very short amount of time, so much had changed.

Floss smiled. 'Good. If yer can get the word out and tell as many as possible we're meeting by the William Gladstone statue after work. Tell 'em we want to discuss that statement they want us to sign and of course what's 'appened to Cassie.'

Lottie nodded. 'I think,' she said, 'it might be best we only approach those who aren't signing the form. I'm not sure we can trust the others.'

Floss nodded in agreement. 'I like your way of thinking!'

When they arrived at the statue at Bow Churchyard, when they would have normally been shattered by their ten-hour day, a state of outrage persisted. Floss had brought an old wooden crate to stand on as the girls gathered around.

''Ow many of you refused to sign that document today?' she asked the crowd.

A shower of hands shot up, except for Lizzie Sharples, a

girl who occupied a station not far from Floss and Lottie's. She stood quietly, her face ashen white.

'Then what the hell are you doing here?' Floss asked. 'Yer either for us or against us. Yer shouldn't 'ave come along!'

'I'm sorry, girls,' Lizzie replied with her head bowed low. 'I felt pressured to sign by Mr Steed. I can see now I made a mistake.'

'You have and all!' one of the girls shouted out. 'Lynch her, girls!'

Lottie was shocked, and not too sure if it was meant as a joke. Yes, they were angry, but she never anticipated how contagious it could be. The group of girls were visibly riled.

'There'll be no lynching by anyone!' Floss shouted them down. 'Lizzie's made a big mistake, but it doesn't mean we can't all walk out of 'ere if we want to.'

There was a long collective gasp. 'Walk out?' Lottie asked.

'Yes, we should remove our labour. They can't treat the workers bad if there are no workers. Spread the word, girls! Tell as many people as you can, but make sure to not let the bosses know what we're up to.'

Lottie didn't feel sure about it at all. 'I think we all need to see Mrs Besant for her advice about this.'

'Look,' Floss said, with fire in her eyes. 'Mrs Besant ain't around all the time. I feel something is going to happen soon. We have to act on it! Mrs Besant has spoken of a proposed walk-out herself!'

Lottie knew this to be true as she'd heard it with her own ears in the park that afternoon Annie spoke to the crowd.

The girls began to cheer and even Lizzie joined in. Lottie agreed with them all, of course she did, but she feared they'd all lose their jobs if they went about things the wrong way.

'Why the long face?' Ma asked later when Lottie arrived home from work. For once Ma was on top of her work and was sitting at the scullery table with the tea pot in front of her.

'Aw, Ma, it was awful in work today. Mr Bryant wants us to sign a statement to say we're having nothing to do with Annie Besant and the things she's saying about the factory!'

'He can't force you to sign that, can he?' She narrowed her gaze.

'I don't think so. Anyhow I didn't sign, nor did Floss nor many others. He's got a right nerve just after Cassie's death.'

'Maybe he intends on making amends for it?'

'I very much doubt that. The bosses are just covering their backs, I reckon. The newspapers would have a field day with all of this. He expects us to cave in as we're so desperate to keep our jobs.'

'Just as well you haven't signed then, gal. It will give the higher ups something to think about. Come on, there's plenty of tea in the pot, go and get a cup and saucer.'

They sat together in companionable silence as they sipped their tea. Lottie studied Ma's face. She seemed to be far away these days almost in a dream world which Lottie had put down to the fact she was working so hard, but now she wasn't so sure.

'Everything all right, Ma?' she asked, setting down her teacup on its saucer.

'Oh yes, everything is more than all right,' she said with a twinkle in her eye.

'Shamus been around again, has he?'

'Why are you asking?'

'Oh, no reason. You just seem to be very happy whenever he's called over here.' She left that remark hanging in the air to see how her mother would respond.

There was a long pause, then Ma said, 'Yes, he does make me happy. He'll never replace your father of course, but he's very good company and he helps me too.'

'Well if you're happy, Ma, then I'm happy too. What about the kids, do you think they like him?'

'You've seen for yourself, Lottie. He makes us all laugh, he's a real tonic.'

Lottie couldn't disagree with that at all.

The next day at the factory, as Lottie and Floss worked together, Floss was summoned away by Mr Steed. Lottie could tell by the look in his eyes that something was amiss. Should she have warned Floss about what he'd said?

An hour later, she hadn't returned to her work so Lottie

asked around the factory floor, but the girls just shook their heads, as clueless as she was. Lottie went in search of Oliver and found him head bent over his desk.

'What's happened?' she asked as he looked up.

'Please close the door behind you and sit down,' he said, sombrely.

Lottie did as instructed. 'So?'

'Floss and two other girls have been dismissed.'

She opened her mouth to speak and closed it again, lost for words. She could hardly believe what she was hearing. Finding her voice, she asked, 'Because they refused to sign that document?'

'No, they're objecting to using the new cutting machines.'

'No, that's not true at all!' Lottie shook her head. 'You may say that's what they've done, but we all know it's about that document. Floss is very good at her job. I can't speak for the other two, whoever they might be, but Floss hasn't made any waves at all.'

'That's not what I've been told.' His eyes looked cold and steely. He was no longer the man who had kissed her at Victoria Park; she was looking into the eyes of a stranger.

'Now hang on a moment, here, Oliver.'

'It's Mr Steed to you,' he reminded.

She gritted her teeth. 'Mr Steed, then. There's more to this than meets the eye. This is to do with Floss standing up for her rights. The other girls too. The thing about the cutting machines is a smoke screen so we don't get to know what the real issue is.'

He narrowed his gaze, then looked her up and down. 'What exactly do you know?'

'N . . . nothing at all.' Deciding she better get out of the office before she put her foot in it, she stood, pausing with her hand on the door knob, then turned towards him and said, 'I think the management's making a big mistake.'

She found Mary and told her to discreetly put word around there'd be another after-work meeting. She told her not to tell the girls what it was about; she didn't want them to risk walking out before they had all composed themselves.

After work, it was Lottie this time who stood on the old wooden crate to address the girls. 'You've probably all heard by now that three girls have been dismissed from the factory, one is Floss herself.'

There was a murmur from the crowd, then one shouted out, 'But what can we do about it? Maybe it will be our jobs tomorrow!'

A roar of discontentment rose up and Lottie waited for it to fade away before speaking.

'What I propose is that we go to see Mrs Besant at her office as soon as possible.'

'But where is that?' Mary asked.

'It's just off Fleet Street. If anyone can help us, she can. She needs to know what's happened here. It just isn't fair. Those girls have done nothing wrong whatsoever. Management are claiming they won't use the new machinery.'

'So, what you're telling us is that the management's using the new cutting machines as an excuse?' Mary folded her arms and jutted out her chin.

'Precisely. I think the real reason is because they refused to sign that document. Mr Bryant wanted to make examples of them all.'

'Well, he's not bleedin' getting away with it!' Mary shouted, raising her fists.

A roar of discontentment rose up again.

''Ere, how do you know about all of this?' Edie Smith, who had been standing quietly at the back of the crowd, challenged. She was a tall gangly girl, who often only spoke when she had something to say.

'I, er, overheard a conversation earlier that I wasn't meant to hear.' Lottie lied. She could feel her face growing hot.

No one questioned her explanation further, so she carried on. 'I think we need to see Mrs Besant as soon as possible, who's with me on this?' A cheer rose up.

Mary intervened. 'I'll put the word around with some of the other girls, the ones I feel we can trust.'

'Good idea, Mary. Management's not going to get its own way a moment longer, Mrs Besant shall see to that. Maybe before we go to see her some of us should speak to the management ourselves?'

'Yes, I think that's a good idea, Lottie. I'll come with you.' Mary nodded, putting herself forward.

'Anyone else want to join us?' Lottie looked at the crowd

of girls who still looked unconvinced. But then one hand shot in the air, then another, and another, until everyone stood as if in formation. 'Good. Meet me first thing tomorrow and we'll go to see Mr Bryant himself.'

The girls nodded.

'Meanwhile, please all take care and be careful who you confide in before this is cleared up. We don't want any more girls getting the sack, do we?'

Now, more than ever, confidentiality was crucial. It was an ill wind that could blow all their jobs out of the factory window and into the hands of others who would only be too glad to fill their shoes to feed their starving families.

As Lottie headed off towards home she found herself behind the muttering crowd of girls. She was glad of their support but worried too in case loose lips caused problems. She planned on speaking to Floss later and find out exactly what had happened in Mr Steed's office.

As she rounded the corner near her home, she felt a hand grab her arm and pull her backwards. Turning, she saw the leering face of Ted, Mrs Munroe's son from next door. As he pulled her towards him, she smelled the beery fumes and it hit her so forcefully that she began to gag.

'W . . . What do you want with me?' she asked, as she trembled with fear.

His bright green eyes glinted with mischief. 'I should think that's obvious, *Miss Lottie Perkins.*' He threw back his head and laughed. It was so out of character for Ted and it unnerved her. 'You've turned into an attractive young lady,' he slurred.

What on earth was the matter with him? She'd never seen him like this before.

As he pulled her closer, she felt her breasts squeeze up against his heavily thudding chest and she was repulsed to feel a hardness between his legs. It was obvious what he was after. With all her might she pulled her arm away from his clutches and slapped his face hard, causing him to stagger backwards until he ended up against the red brick wall of the opposite street in the alleyway.

He looked at her, mouth agape, 'I'm s . . . s . . . sorry, Lottie. I don't know what came over me there.' He was still slurring, but it felt like he had come to his senses.

She was about to say something more when she heard the click of a gate behind her and turned to see Mrs Munroe stood there with a wooden rolling pin in her hand, waving it at her son.

'I don't know what's come over you, lad. Get inside right this very minute!' She practically walloped him with the rolling pin so he had to move quickly. When she'd got him inside and clicked the gate shut, she turned back to where Lottie stood watching. 'I'm sorry.' She said. 'He's been drinking today, by the look of it. See, he was given a bit of bad news.'

Lottie paused a moment to catch her breath, steadying herself by holding on to the wall as she digested what Mrs Munroe had to say. 'I . . . I thought it didn't seem like Ted. I don't think he'd really have harmed me.' In truth, she had been ready to knee him between the legs. But she was shocked at his behaviour because most of the time he was like a gentle giant.

'Yes, a lot of them were given their marching orders today. They're laying people off at the docks, He's devastated. If he does anything like that to you again, please let me know. I'm not having a son of mine accosting decent young ladies in the alleyway.'

Lottie nodded. Although still a little traumatised by the incident, her instincts told her deep down that Ted was putting on the bravado and trying to retain some of his dignity. It was no surprise that he fancied her; he had already grabbed her around the waist in the past, teasing her, but she had never thought of him in that way at all.

'Thank you, Mrs Munroe,' she said, as she pulled the latch on her own garden gate.

Mrs Munroe nodded, but there was a deep sadness in her eyes. Who knew what lay ahead for their family now there'd be no wage going into their home? Ted's father had been disabled by an accident at the docks a couple of years ago. Money had already been tight for them as it was.

When Lottie reached the back door of her house, she smelled the delicious aroma of corned beef stew. She walked inside to see Shamus O'Hara seated at the scullery table – sitting in her father's old seat – head bent over a bowl of stew. He was scooping up mouthfuls with his spoon and savouring every bit by the look of it. For a brief moment, Lottie felt put out the man had his feet under the table, where Pa had once sat. *But Pa is no longer here*, she reminded herself, *and Ma and Shamus are getting on with their lives*. She took a deep breath of composure. It hurt to think that now someone else had come along to replace Pa and it looked like he was going nowhere. She didn't want her mother to remain in widow's weeds forever, she wanted her to be happy, and she had been in a decent period of mourning after all. But still, it was her father she longed to see sitting around the table of an evening, not some sweater from Bryant and May.

'Mr O'Hara is staying for his supper,' Ma announced, looking intently into her daughter's eyes. She could tell she was silently asking for approval – well, she had to give it as the man was in the midst of his meal – but what Lottie really wanted was to tell Ma about her experience with Ted next door. She was sure Ma would be angry with him for accosting her in such a manner but, like herself, would forgive him when she found out he'd been drinking as he'd lost his job.

The sweater looked up from his feast. 'Hello, Lottie.'

'Good evening, Mr O'Hara,' she replied primly.

'I hear there's trouble afoot at the factory.'

How on earth had he got to hear about that? She was going to have to tread carefully. She hesitated before replying, 'Not that I've heard, Mr O'Hara.'

She was hoping that would be the end of it, but he quirked an eyebrow and shook his head. 'Don't worry, lass. I know how to keep things quiet. 'Tisn't in my nature to spread gossip around the place.' He tapped the side of his nose as her mother smiled. She was growing very close to the man and Lottie hadn't yet decided whether that was a good thing or not.

'Well, there's nothing I can tell you, Mr O'Hara. If there is any trouble afoot as you put it, then I'm sure we'll find out about it soon enough.' She removed her jacket and hung it up on the peg behind the door.

'Sit down, Lottie, and I'll serve up your stew. You must be starving by now.' Ma fussed around, slicing bread and ladling the stew into a bowl for Lottie.

It was true, she normally would be very hungry by now as their work breaks were few and far between, but tonight, after the meeting outside the factory, the incident with Ted in the alley, and now finding Mr O'Hara with his feet well and truly under the table, Lottie had suddenly lost her appetite. She was beginning to wonder if the man was a go-between for the bosses and the workers. Maybe he'd been employed to spy on them? She had said as much to her mother previously. What if Ma had unknowingly fed him information that could be used against them? She was going to have to keep a close eye. It was hard to know who to trust at a time like this.

'It's all right, Ma, I'll eat later. I feel a little queasy right now. I'm going for a lie-down.'

'Very well,' her mother said, turning back to the sweater, giving him the extra slice of bread.

Lottie let out a long breath as she headed off for her bedroom. It just didn't feel like home at the moment and she felt she was on shaky ground at the factory, too. She just wanted to feel some sort of normality. Truth was, things hadn't felt normal since Pa had passed away, and might never, ever, feel the same way again.

Chapter Nine

The following morning, a group of the girls marched towards the office of Mr Theodore Bryant, director of the factory.

'Lottie!' Oliver called out when he saw them. 'Where are you going?' He looked alarmed.

Lottie turned to face him, her heartbeat quickening, though this time not out of any desire for her boss – she wanted justice for Floss and the other two girls who had been dismissed. She let out a breath, annoyed to be stopped in her tracks. 'We're off to speak to Mr Bryant,' she said firmly.

He took her arm. 'I strongly advise you not to. You could all lose your jobs, please think about what you're doing here. I've already spoken to Mr Bryant about the issue.'

'It's too late. Wheels are in motion.' She cared not a jot that she had addressed him informally while at work, she had bigger fish to fry.

The sounds of the girls' boots and clogs marching up the

stairs were deafening and other workers looked on to see what was going on.

Mary grabbed Lottie's arm and yanked her away from Mr Steed's grasp. 'Come on, you're needed with us. One of us has to speak up for the rest of us.'

Lottie gulped. As Floss was no longer around, it was going to have to be her.

She looked at Oliver. The whites of his eyes shone with horror. 'I'm sorry, Ol—' then remembering Mary and the others were waiting for her, 'Mr Steed, but this has to be done.'

'Just think about this, will you?' he whispered. 'I don't want something awful to happen to you just because you're getting carried away with something you can't control.'

'It's too late. My decision has been made.'

'Then, on your own heads be it!' he shouted.

His voice still rang in Lottie's ears as she walked away. Although she had feelings for him, the sense of injustice sickened her to the core.

'What did Mr Steed whisper to you, then, Lottie?' Mary asked.

'Oh, nothing.' She felt her cheeks burn red hot. 'He just warned me against doing anything foolish, that's all.'

Mary nodded, placated by Lottie's answer.

When they reached Mr Bryant's office, Lottie hesitated for a moment. *Could they really do this?* she thought. But she looked at the others who were urging her on, bright faces encouraging and hopeful, so she rapped loudly on his door.

'Enter!' boomed a voice from inside.

Lottie trembled as she stepped over the threshold, followed by Mary and a few of the other girls. The remainder waited outside. *There's safety in numbers*, she inwardly reassured herself. *I have to do this for Floss and all the others.*

Mr Bryant looked her up and down. He was well dressed in a gun-metal grey suit and a silver brocade waistcoat with a matching cravat. A silver chain was suspended in a loop from his top pocket, indicating he had a pocket watch. She guessed it was solid silver, though often he wore a gold pocket watch, such was his wealth. This was a man of means. A man who kept his workforce with their noses to the grindstone while they, themselves, earned a mere pittance. He threw away those who were no longer fit for work like spent matches on the pavement outside the factory. Lottie's hands balled into fists at her side. While she was frightened she was also angry, especially for Floss.

'Yes, and who might you be, young lady?' Mr Bryant asked.

She cleared her throat. 'My name is Lottie Perkins, Mr Bryant. I am a cutter from downstairs. I have worked here for more than one year and I used to work beside a girl called Flossie Gittings.'

He perused her with interest over the top of his silver-framed spectacles. 'And?'

'And she has been dismissed forthwith from this factory because she refused to sign the document, the document that said Mrs Annie Besant was a liar. Not only that, but two other girls have been made to leave as well.'

A nerve twitched in Mr Bryant's upper lip and his eyes widened. He snorted loudly and his face reddened in front of her very eyes. 'Young lady, you have quite a nerve coming to my office about this. The girls were troublemakers and, on the advice of the foreman, it was my decision to fire them. Now if you and your colleagues wish to make further fuss about this, then I will remind you that new jobs are difficult to come by and that your boots can be easily filled. I can even bring in the girls from our Glasgow factory to work here to take over your jobs if necessary!'

'But Mr—' she began to protest but his anger was palpable. It was almost as though there was a crackle of electricity surrounding them all – the feeling of impending danger just before a storm was about to break.

He shook his head and pointed to the door. 'I'll hear no more about it, now close the door on the way out and get back to work or your pay will be docked!' He shouted. She had never heard him so hostile or so angry before and it frightened her, but she still wanted to push forward. There was no going back now. And she couldn't believe that Oliver had lied to her either.

'He's not getting away with this, Mary,' Lottie whispered under her breath when they left Mr Bryant's office. 'Pass the word around, there'll be another meeting after work tonight.' The director's bad attitude towards the girls made her more determined than ever to do something. They couldn't just sit back and watch the bosses walk all over them.

'What are you going to do?' Mary blinked, wide-eyed with wonder.

'I think we should all walk out of here and march to the offices of Annie Besant at Bouverie Street, near Fleet Street. She'll help us. We'll do it this afternoon, right?'

Mary winked at her. 'I'll spread the word, no fear, Lottie.'

Lottie found it hard to concentrate on her work after that but as soon as she gave Mary the signal, the girls and women banded together, leaving their work mid-flow to walk out of the factory.

'What's going on, Miss Perkins?' Mr Steed had rushed out from his office. The rumblings of movement and the girls' voices echoed around the factory.

Lottie stood, her chin jutting out in a determined fashion, facing Oliver head on. 'Myself, and the other girls, are unhappy with the working conditions here. We feel three girls have been unfairly dismissed. We are marching to the offices of Annie Besant to see if she can help us as management simply will not listen!' Her heart was beating a mile a minute, but she was thankful that her voice did not falter once while she addressed him.

'Er now, calm down, Lottie. We can talk about this. I did the best I could to talk to Mr Bryant about the girls so they could keep their jobs.'

'I don't believe you,' she said. 'You've had more than enough chances to help out us girls. I asked you to speak to Mr Bryant about moving Cassie and you never did . We will take no more orders from you, nor anyone else for that matter!'

Mr Steed's eyes narrowed and a vein in his neck pulsed. He gulped loudly. When he finally found his voice, he said, 'Please ladies, I beg you to reconsider, think about your jobs here!' The girls jostled past him, nearly pushing him over as he continued to plead with them.

Once outside the factory gates, Lottie and Mary gathered the girls together to tell them what to do.

'Now, ladies,' Lottie shouted, 'we need to stick together and show solidarity here. We will not be defeated!'

'Cor, Lottie, you sound exactly like Annie Besant there!' Edie said in admiration.

Lottie smiled, taking it as a compliment. She estimated there were about two hundred of them in all gathered together. There was safety in numbers.

'Now then ladies, we need to think carefully about this walkout as there might be repercussions!'

'Talk in English, please!' Mary laughed.

'What I mean to say is that our walkout will have severe consequences. I think there are about two hundred of us leaving the factory at the moment. We don't know yet how management will act.'

'I do!' shouted out a girl from the back of the crowd. 'They'll be angry and we might lose our jobs.'

'I'm going back inside!' one of the older women said, turning her backs on them, 'I'm too old for all this 'ere nonsense.' A few of the woman's friends nodded in agreement.

'Nonsense is it?' Mary shouted at her, prompting her to turn back. 'It ain't nonsense, love, it makes complete sense!'

Most seemed in agreement with Mary. The woman's eyes widened, but she stood to hear what was being said.

'Calm down!' Lottie soothed. 'What I want to say to you all is this: if we don't do something right now, here today, then everything we've been through at the Bryant and May Factory will have been for nothing. Nothing at all. Poor Cassie Bowen even lost her life over this place. Many of you have relatives and friends who have been through the exact same thing. The bosses at the factory don't give a stuff whether us girls wash our hands before eating our food. In fact, I'd go as so far as to say the foremen prevent those working with the match dipping machines from doing so.'

'Yes, we're worked like flippin' donkeys!' Mary shouted.

'Now then, three girls have been dismissed, excuses have been made by the management as to why that happened and in my book the story doesn't wash or make sense. I think the girls were used as scapegoats to be made examples of. A warning, if you like, that other jobs might be next!'

A rowdy 'No!' emanated from the crowd.

'Oh yes,' Lottie carried on. To the woman who had been about to leave she shouted, 'Mrs Sharpe, you can leave if you wish, but it might be your daughter, Eliza, who's asked to leave next, or it could even be you!'

Mrs Sharpe's neck shrunk down into the collar of her dress and she hung her head low as if ashamed of herself.

'And you over there!' she shouted to another woman. 'You were nodding your head in agreement when Mrs Sharpe was about to leave. Would you like to lose your job as well? Would you like to be accused of something you haven't done like those three girls were?'

'No, certainly not!' the woman said, meeting Lottie's gaze. 'But what if we lose our jobs as a result of this strike? Who will feed us and our families then?'

'Yes, that's a good point!' Mrs Sharpe chipped in.

'We'll cross that bridge when we come to it,' Lottie said firmly. 'I'm sure Mrs Besant will have some ideas about that. We can raise funds or ask local traders for food; most are very sympathetic towards our cause.'

There was a lot of muttering between the women, all considering the consequences of a walkout. 'Come on, girls!' Mary shouted. 'I reckon if we walk out we'll give the old stuffed shirts something to think about. People need matches, don't they? So they're going to need us back to work at that place.'

'Indeed,' said Lottie. 'We have the upper hand in this game and we have the best cards. So, what do you say, girls? Are you in?'

A show of hands shot up and there were loud cheers.

People standing in the street began to stare, bowled over by the number of women animatedly gathered before them.

'What's going on?' An elderly man stepped towards Lottie.

'We're fighting, sir.'

He removed his flat cap and scratched his bald head. 'But who's fighting?'

'Us matchgirls, we're going to fight fire with fire!'

Another resounding cheer went out as the man shook his head and walked away. 'You lot are all puddled,' he muttered. 'Never heard nothing like it in me life, women fighting indeed? Pah!'

Once organised, they marched several a breast towards the Fleet Street area chanting, 'Annie Besant! Annie Besant!' People in the streets waved to them along the way and shouted their good wishes. People came out of their houses to see what was going on and groups of children tagged along for part of the journey. The men and women in the area knew what was going on and were in support of the girls, and that was all thanks to Mrs Besant for highlighting the poor conditions at the factory.

As they drew nearer to the newspaper offices, the traffic became busier and they had to sidestep costermonger carts, carriages and omnibuses. And there in the distance, standing proud, was the dome of St. Paul's, Lottie drew a deep composing breath – it was quite a sight to behold. Were they doing the right thing? There would be no going back after this. They could all get the sack. She reassured herself that, yes, what they were doing was morally right, it could even save lives. Someone had to stand up for the likes of Flossie and the others.

Lottie glanced up at the window of *The Link* office to see a familiar figure standing there, gazing down upon them. Within minutes, Annie Besant was at the door and had ushered several of them inside.

'What's going on, ladies?' Annie asked, her eyebrows arched in surprise.

'We've been to see management, Mrs Besant,' Mary began, the words tumbling out, breathlessly. 'Lottie told them exactly what she thought and all! Mr Bryant weren't 'aving none of it. He didn't want to know. Told us we'd all lose our jobs if we carried on wiv things. I think he was angry an' all. Might 'ave called the police if we 'adn't left there an' then—'

Lottie took over as she realised Mary might overegg the pudding by embellishing facts, so she made sure she drove her point across. 'We went to see Mr Bryant as we were shocked that Flossie Gittings, who works beside me as a match cutter, and two other girls, were instantly dismissed for speaking to you, Mrs Besant.'

Annie frowned. 'And I'm guessing Mr Bryant wouldn't give you the time of day?'

Lottie huffed out a breath. 'No, he dismissed us all, he told us our jobs would go if we carried on and we refused to sign the document stating what you had said was all lies. He also threatened to bring in the workforce from the factory in Glasgow to do our jobs.'

'Oh he did, did he?' Annie Besant stood with her hands on her hips. 'I've received a letter from him threatening legal action over my article in *The Link*. Well, he's taken on the wrong woman here and the wrong set of girls!'

A cheer went up in support of Mrs Besant.

'You spoke up for us,' Lottie said. 'We aren't going to let you down, Mrs Besant!'

Annie smiled. 'From now on girls, there will be changes afoot. You've done the right thing.'

Lottie hoped she felt as sure as she sounded, else this time tomorrow they could all be out of work, and that might affect Ma's own matchbox making job too.

When Lottie returned home, the full realisation of the day hit her. The majority of the workforce had gone out on strike, and for such a big factory, the sheer feat of it all was astounding.

Her mother greeted her at the door and Lottie was shocked to discover that there was someone waiting in the parlour for her.

He was on his feet and by her side even before she had time to utter a word. For a moment it appeared as though her mother would remain in the room with them, but then she left, tactfully closing the door behind her.

Lottie glanced at the mountain of matchboxes, paste and string that only moments ago Ma and the kids would have been working on and felt utterly ashamed. Ashamed that Oliver had come to her home and witnessed how they lived – the curling old wallpaper on the walls, shabby furniture and threadbare rugs thrown over old wooden floorboards – but he didn't appear to be aware of his surroundings as he took her in his arms, and held her tightly. He rested his chin on the top of her head and she felt his heart beat against hers.

Then she felt his whole body begin to rack with sobs. *What was going on?* She had been convinced he was going to tell her off about the strike and maybe try to convince her to change her mind.

She pulled herself away to stand back and look at him. 'Whatever is the matter, Oliver?'

He stopped sobbing and frowned. 'It's Miriam . . . She's—'

A feeling of dread hit Lottie full force. 'Oh no, it's not— She's not d—'

'No.' Oliver interrupted. 'But it's touch and go, she's been admitted to hospital. They don't know what's wrong with her, she keeps vomiting and losing weight. I fear I will lose her.'

A feeling of guilt took over Lottie for what she had been part of: meeting a married man in the park like that. If her mother found out she'd be so upset and so would the factory girls. They'd see her as colluding with the enemy. She was either one of them or one of *them* – the management.

Lottie blinked several times. 'I think it's best we never meet up alone again,' she said breathlessly. Though that wasn't what she really wanted to do at all, but it seemed the moral thing to do. 'I shall tell my mother you came here to try to persuade me to talk the girls into calling off the strike and returning to their work, understood?'

Oliver's face crumpled. 'But don't you see, Lottie? I need you more than ever now. Let's meet up again on Sunday, I don't think I can get through Miriam's illness without you by my side.'

Lottie studied the worn rug beneath her feet and without meeting his gaze, said, 'But it's not right is it, Mr Steed? I'm only a young girl and you are so much older than me.'

'Look,' he said forcefully. 'I made a promise to your father to look out for you. What would he think of me? I'd be letting him down and so would you.'

She thought for a moment, she had no intentions of letting her dear father down. 'Very well. But I don't think we should be intimate with one another ever again. And please do not let slip to anyone at the factory that we are meeting one another. I shall see you, but it is only to talk and nothing else. I can be a friend to you and no more.'

'You're so beautiful when you talk like that, Lottie.' He took both her hands in his and gazed into her eyes, stealing her breath away.

She was dicing with danger, but what could she do? She

hated to see Oliver this way but she did have feelings for him. Feelings she needed to keep in check.

He raised one of her hands and planted a kiss on it. 'Soon, my lovely, very soon,' he said, then he left her there feeling confused as he walked out the door. She turned to see Ma enter the room behind her.

'Has Mr Steed just left?' she asked, furrowing her brow.

She nodded.

'Well, what did he want? He didn't tell me anything while he was waiting here.'

Lottie paused before replying, 'He just wanted me to use my influence with the girls to call off the strike.'

'Oh, he did, did he?' Ma had a glint in her eyes which Lottie knew meant she wasn't happy about something. 'And to think I gave that man a cup of tea, an' all. He's not the man I thought he was. I always used to like him.'

'Me too,' said Lottie under her breath.

How could she possibly tell Ma that a married man had designs on her daughter?

Someone was hammering at the front door and Lottie hadn't even woken up properly yet. 'Lottie, it's me, Mary, quick I want to talk to you!'

Lottie let out a long groan. Drat! Mary was going to wake the kids up with her yelling and knocking like that. Lottie ran down the stairs, barefoot and in her night gown, to open the door.

'It's hit all the newspapers!' Mary announced proudly, pushing her way in through the small passageway without even being invited inside. 'Apparently, the news editors in Fleet Street are warning people to boycott Bryant and May matches!' She had a triumphant gleam in her eyes.

Lottie blinked several times in disbelief. Could their walk-out really have caused so much publicity? 'You'd better come into the scullery before you wake up the household.'

'My father bought a newspaper on his way home after a nightshift at the docks and he woke me up to tell me the good news! Don't you see? This is great news for us.'

They sat at the scullery table and a huge smile spread over her face as she took it all in. 'I wish we had some kind of champagne to celebrate.' She laughed. 'Will a cup of char do?'

'Yes, please.' Mary nodded eagerly as she unfolded the newspaper. 'It says in the article that Mrs Besant took an interest in our welfare as she'd had her young child removed from her years ago by a Christian organisation. Did you know she's married to a vicar but she left him?'

Lottie spooned the tea leaves into a brown earthenware pot as she waited for the kettle to boil on the stove. 'Yes, I had heard as much.'

'Apparently, they no longer live together and he has custody of their child. I've been reading about her here, she's a member of the Fabian Society and that red ribbon she wears in her hair is in rebellion to the government!'

'Really? I didn't know that.'

'My father told me she proposes to do a lot for the dock workers, didn't your dad work there too before he di—' Mary brought her hands to her mouth in shock at what she'd just been about to say. 'Sorry, I could cut me tongue out of me bleedin' 'ead for saying that.'

'Don't be daft, my father *is* dead. But yes, he was one of the dock workers. He heard Mrs Besant speak on numerous occasions. He believed in all she stands for and would be proud that she's helping us matchgirls.'

'What does your Ma think about the strike?'

Lottie shrugged and shook her head. 'Well, she's none too happy about it as it might affect her work for the factory, but she does understand the reasons.'

Lottie watched the kettle puff out clouds of steam, then, removing it from the hob using a tea towel so as not to burn her hands, she poured the boiling water on to the leaves in the tea pot. There'd be about another twenty minutes or so before Ma was due to wake up, so they had time to chat a while longer. It was good that Mary was on her side, though Lottie realised there would be some at the factory who might try to break the strike.

The girls continued to chit-chat, and some while later, they heard the sound of footsteps above them on the floorboards.

'Ma's rising,' Lottie said, standing up to prepare a cuppa for her mother.

'I'd best go,' Mary said and folded the newspaper to take with her. 'Keep me posted about any developments.'

'I think we need to see Mrs Besant again this afternoon, alone. There were too many there yesterday, we overwhelmed her with our presence.'

'You're right, there. Shall I call for you later?'

'Call about one o'clock and I shall be ready, meanwhile we'd better check no one is going into the factory. I tell you what, let's get over there later. We'll call for some of the others on the way. I'll meet you over there.'

Mary's eyes gleamed. 'I'll pass the word along.' She stood and left the scullery through the back door, just as Ma came into the kitchen.

'Who was that, Lottie?'

'Mary Driscoll. News of our matchgirl strike has hit all of today's newspapers by the look of it. The headline in the paper Mary brought read, "Fiery Matchgirls Walk Out of Bryant and May Factory"!'

'Well I never!' her mother said, as Lottie explained to her what was in the article as best as her recollection would allow. Ma's eyes widened with surprise.

'I've made you a cuppa. I'll be off soon, we're going to stand at the factory gates to discourage any workers from going inside today, there might be some who will try. Not everyone wanted to go on strike, but those are few and far between.'

'Oh, I don't like the sound of that at all. It's one thing to stop working yourselves, but you can't stop others going in through those gates.' Ma's eyes were full of concern.

'I'm afraid we can and we will. We have no other option. Mrs Besant said it should be one out, all out,' Lottie said firmly.

'But what about my job, Lottie, love?' Ma's forehead creased into a frown. It was clear she'd only just considered her own position in all of this.

Lottie bit her bottom lip. 'You must do what you think best, Ma. I don't know if the girls will contest homeworkers: it's the dreadful conditions at the factory they're mainly concerned about. Though of course, as we've all downed tools, it means there will be no more matches to sell, so matchboxes won't be required . . .' She trailed off, knowing her mother wouldn't be happy with that arrangement.

Ma nodded. Then she sat down at the table and cradled her cup of tea in the palms of her hands.

'You take care out there,' were the last words Lottie heard as she went upstairs to get dressed.

A crowd of girls had gathered around the factory gates at Fairfield Road. Rumours were rife, some of the girls seemed to think that workers from the Glasgow factory would arrive at any given moment, while others said the factory was going to close down altogether. They were all just as in the dark as each other.

In the distance, she saw a familiar face striding purposefully towards them – with her long dark, curly hair and freckled face, and that crooked smile, it could only be one person. A cheer went up as Floss herself approached. 'I can't believe yer all doing this for me and those two uvver girls!' she announced.

'We had to do it, love,' Mary said. 'You've been unfairly treated. It's time Bryant and May took a long 'ard look at themselves!'

Another cheer went up.

'I want to take a deputation with me later to see Mrs Besant and find out what we need to do next,' Lottie informed the crowd of excited women. She noticed there were many more bobbing heads in attendance than last time – word had obviously spread like wild fire, no doubt sparked off by the day's newspaper headlines.

'Well, I'm definitely up for that!' Mary said, 'And no doubt Floss being at the heart of all this is, too!'

'You can bet your life on it!' Floss shouted. She smiled, looking around triumphantly as if the victor of all the spoils.

A few others joined in showing their support, raising their hands and shouting out their willingness to engage in strike action. Though it was hard for everyone to hear at the back of the crowd and Lottie noticed some of the women relaying messages on to those stood behind them.

'That's settled then,' said Lottie. 'We'll march over to Mrs Besant's offices again at one o'clock. Meanwhile, have you seen anyone entering the factory?'

'Only Mr Bryant whose face looked as red as a lobster!' laughed Millie. Millie was quite a coarse sort of a girl, who had language like a fish wife, and Lottie greatly enjoyed this comment.

'No doubt he's angry with us all,' Lottie said.

'And I saw Mr Steed,' Mary chipped in.

'Oh?' Lottie looked at her friend for any clue about his manner, particularly after yesterday.

'He looked well put out, looked orf his chump to me. Mad as hell!' Mary laughed.

'Well, he would be like that, wouldn't he?' Floss chuckled.

Lottie felt the hairs on her neck bristle. It was obvious the girls didn't much care for Oliver, but they didn't know him like she did. To them, he was someone who told them what to do – they viewed him as being 'one of the bosses'. But to Lottie he was a kindly, older gentleman, who was doing his best and caught between the devil and the deep blue sea.

As the girls waited at the gate, they noticed a group of women walking towards them, ready to battle their way in. The women, who were probably in their twenties, had their sleeves rolled up as if ready for a fight.

'What yer think you're doing?' Floss asked.

One of the women, who was taller than the rest, with

flaming red hair which she wore loose on her shoulders, showed her gritted teeth. 'We aim to get in there to work, we have babies at home and families that need feeding. It's 'orright for you young 'uns, you ain't got the responsibilities we 'ave.'

'That may be,' Floss said, 'but you go across this picket line and I'm warning you, there'll be trouble.' She pulled herself up to her full height, her chin jutting out in defiance.

Lottie pushed her way forward. 'There'll be no need for anyone to fight today. I just want you ladies to listen to what I have to say and if, after that, you decide to walk into that factory, then we shan't stop you.' She glared at Floss, whose eyes widened with surprise. 'Trust me, Floss,' she whispered under her breath.

Floss took a step backwards.

'Well, what 'ave yer to say to us,' the redheaded woman asked.

'Mrs Besant wants to highlight what's happening to us all at the factory, the poor working conditions, low pay for long hours, and particularly the health risks. I'll give you poor Cassie Bowen who had phossy jaw as an example – the bosses tried to cover that up. She had been ill for weeks, all the signs were there. She got bad jaw ache, headaches and felt so ill. One day she just didn't show up for work and never came back again. Once the bosses discovered she had phossy jaw, they gave her sick pay for a short time only, which was more like hush money if you ask me. Then they washed their hands of her once they realised she wasn't going to get any better and didn't pay her a single farthing after that. Her poor parents have to bury their only child with no financial assistance from the bosses at the factory only with the help of Mrs Besant and us matchgirls. That's why it's taking so long for her funeral arrangements. It's a disgrace if you ask me! She should have had a proper burial by now!

'Does that seem fair to you? The poor practices at Bryant and May led to her painful death in the first place yet no one seems accountable. Do you want that for yourselves? Or your own families? How would your children feel if they saw their mother dying from a cancer, in pain and with no money coming in? There wouldn't even be enough money to bury you, ladies! But don't let that stop them at the factory, if you're quite happy with a painful death, a pauper's grave and your kids ending up in the workhouse, then go ahead and walk through those gates. We've all got to die sometime, after all. But going in through those gates right now will increase your chances of an early death as nothing will have changed at that place for us. Nothing. There'll be more deaths to come, more orphaned children, more weeping parents, more of everything. Now, just go ahead and walk in there, but don't say I didn't warn you and don't come running to any of us if you become unwell.' Lottie pulled her hands at her side into fists. All the emotion of Cassie's death was spurring her on to drive her point home to the group of women who stood before her.

The women looked at one another and began muttering.

Lottie carried on. 'Now, Mrs Besant will be an asset to us, she can help to fight our corner. She has contacts in Parliament and in Fleet Street, if we cave in now and give in to the bosses' demands, things won't get any better for us. In fact, things could get a whole lot worse, we could be punished for this strike action. We *have* to stand our ground. We *have* to stand shoulder-to-shoulder, as one united force!'

'The lass is right!' One of the group said loudly, and even the redheaded woman nodded in agreement. The group began to turn around and walk away. Lottie felt a warm feeling course through her veins. She was so pleased that they listened. Those women had looked as if they were spoiling for a fight.

'Never mind going home, you lot, come and help us 'ere!' Mary shouted after them. But the women pretended not to hear and carried on walking away.

'I do understand their reasons for trying to go into work, though,' Lottie said reflectively. A reminder of how hard this strike was for everyone. 'Mrs O'Malley, there, has a houseful of kids and her husband is out of work. Got laid off the same day as my next-door neighbour from his job at the docks.'

One or two muttered their disapproval. 'It ain't right,' Mary remarked. 'We all need to stick together, one out, all out!'

The girls followed suit shouting, 'One out, all out!' then 'Up With Annie Besant!'

Lottie looked up at the factory to see Oliver gazing down

from his office window at them all and she wondered what he was thinking. The high walls surrounding the factory and the double fronted gates were like a prison. The tall chimney stack usually puffed out clouds of sulphurous smoke, evidence of the work inside, but today there was no movement. In a way, it was a sad sight to see, but Lottie knew that what they were doing was right.

Later, the girls marched once more to Annie Besant's office. Annie decided the best thing to do would be to form a strike committee and call it The Union of Women Matchmakers. She said she was going to get the London Trade Council involved as well. No stone was going to be left unturned if she had her way.

'Girls, please don't alarm yourselves about this strike,' Annie said. 'You didn't start the fire, it was Bryant and May with their petty rules and regulations and poor pay. Soon they are going to get what they deserve!'

A loud cheer went up from the girls and Lottie hoped fervently that Mrs Besant was right.

Freddy and Davy were sitting at the table with Ma when Lottie arrived back home. 'It's the last of the matchboxes,' Ma said sadly. 'Mr O'Hara doesn't think he can get me any more, stocks are running too low. What are we going to do, Lottie?'

'There aren't going to be any matches to fill them for some time so it would be pointless in making them anyhow.'

A look of anguish swept over Ma's face as if she was holding something back. 'It's just that—'

'Yes, Ma? What's wrong?'

'Some of the other out-workers living around here have been approached by one of the managers at the factory.'

Lottie stood with hands on hips. 'Oh, they have, have they?'

Ma ran a hand over her forehead. 'Talk is, and this has come from Mr O'Hara himself, that the bosses want to get the girls and women in to work in the factory instead of you lot.'

'Over my dead body!' Lottie said.

Her mother stood. 'Sssh, come out to the scullery or you'll upset your brothers. Bessie and Daisy are tidying the bedrooms upstairs for me, so keep your voice down in case they hear you.'

'Sorry, Ma,' Lottie said, as her mother ushered her away. She hadn't even had time to remove her jacket and she was getting bad news. Her mother steered her to the scullery table where they both sat. 'You could do with a cup of tea, I've no doubt?'

Lottie nodded. 'It's been hard work out there picketing and sorting things out with Mrs Besant, but we won't give in without a fight. I can see this strike turning folk against one another.'

'How'd you mean, love?'

'There's some that want to break the strike and most that

don't, and some are from the same families and all.' A thought suddenly struck Lottie. 'Please Ma, tell me you're not considering walking in with the other out-workers to steal our jobs?'

Ma stiffened, her expression unchanging. 'What do you take me for, our Lottie? I considered it fer all of one minute, then I thought of the fight you girls have put up this past couple of days. If people walk through those gates before the strike is over, nothing will change – it ain't worth it.'

Lottie let out a long composing breath. 'Thank goodness for that. We're singing from the same hymn sheet, that's what I told the women who tried to get into the factory today and, thankfully, they went back home. You're welcome to join us tomorrow if you wish?'

'Maybe I'll think about it, but for now I have plenty to do at home.' Her mother put the kettle on the hob to boil. 'So, tell me about that nice Mr Steed, did he try to get you to break the strike?'

Thankfully, her mother hadn't as yet sensed her daughter's involvement with the man. 'Well, of course, he'd like to see us return to our stations but I told him, no.'

Her mother nodded. It was going to be a difficult time for them all. 'Ma, how are we doing food wise?'

'I've got enough money for the next few days, but after that, I'm not sure what to do as neither of us will be bringing in a wage. I could offer to take in some laundry for people and maybe even some ironing . . .' her mother said stoically.

'Yes, you might need to do that for now, Ma, to get us over a lean period.

'I could help you when I'm at home but in truth, this strike business will take up a lot of my time with meetings and picketing, and there are demonstrations planned at places like Regent and Victoria Parks. I think Mrs Besant has got something up her sleeve that will eventually involve approaching Parliament!'

'Well I never! That woman never ceases to amaze me. No wonder your father used to like listening to her talks!'

'She's a remarkable lady, Ma. I've never met anyone like her before.'

Lottie had developed a strong sense of admiration for Mrs Besant. She was the sort of person who brought about change for the working classes and wouldn't take no for an answer. She wasn't everyone's cup of tea, though. Lottie was well aware of that. There were many that weren't into her socialist activities, and even *The Times* newspaper was showing its support for Bryant and May by ignoring Annie's claims of 'White Slavery'. The class system in Britain was divided into the haves and have nots, and Mrs Besant definitely gave the latter a voice.

Chapter Ten

Cassie's funeral took place early in the morning. The factory girls lined the street to watch the small procession leave, and Lottie, as her best friend, went in support of Mrs and Mrs Bowen. The girls had managed to help Cassie's parents pay for the funeral with some extra money from their fundraising events, but it was Mrs Besant who had mostly paid for it. It was such a kind gesture, and the Bowens spent the day continually thanking her for her generosity.

As they walked along the streets behind the coffin, which was being led by a horse-drawn black hearse, Lottie heard the slow toll of the church bell. She was pleased that the Bowens had some dignity now, with the financial help from Mrs Besant. The bosses at Bryant and May, well, they'd washed their hands of the whole affair.

Mrs Bowen looked as if she could hardly take another step and Lottie put her arm around her. Mr Bowen walked behind carrying a large wreath of white lilies.

From where they walked, you could see the factory chimney in the distance and Lottie cursed the place. If it were not for that factory, Cassie would still be here right now. An image came to mind of when she had first met her and how she'd marvelled at Cassie's glowing peachy skin and lustrous hair. By the end of her time matchdipping, her skin had yellowed and looked years older, lined and dull, and her once beautiful hair appeared lifeless. The light had gone out of her eyes too. Yes, Cassie had been like a beautiful flame whose light had been cruelly snuffed out due to that place.

Lottie tried to put the matter to the back of her mind. She didn't want to spend Cassie's funeral angry about the circumstances that had led them there. It was supposed to be a happy day, where they could all remember their friend, and daughter, together.

When they arrived at the graveside, the priest spoke about the life of a young woman that had been taken too soon. Lottie had to fight to keep her composure as she blinked back the tears which threatened to fall. She glanced to her side to see Floss wiping away a tear. For all her big talk, Floss was a softie really.

Mrs Bowen was now trembling.

'The Lord giveth and the Lord taketh away,' the priest was saying, and continued to thank the Lord for her all too brief time on earth. When he was finished he made the sign of the cross and several people followed suit.

Lottie watched as Cassie's parents stepped towards the

grave and they each tossed a white lily on top of the coffin. Mr Bowen guided his wife away from the grave's edge, clearly wanting to get her away from the visible reminder as soon as possible. Lottie wondered if he feared she might throw herself down there to be with her daughter. Her whole body shook with grief. Lottie wished she could take their pain away, but she still had her own to contend with.

Cassie, my dearest friend, if anyone deserves to rest it's you. You've gone to a far better place and one day I hope to see you again.

Lottie had to reassure herself that her friend was now a lot better off in heaven than in this cold cruel world, and it made her even more determined to fight the powers that be at the factory. She had a new resolve inside her, fire in her belly and passion in her soul. She wouldn't rest until things changed for the better at the factory and to do that they'd all have to keep on with the good fight, no matter what the cost. They would aim for victory.

A meeting was held the following day. The girls were feeling dispirited after Cassie's funeral, so Lottie decided to speak out.

'I think we need to vote to see who is going to lead us,' she said. Her confidence had grown lately and, buoyed by the advice of Mrs Besant, she needed to take charge of the situation. She didn't mind who led the women as long as they were capable. She suspected the girls would choose Floss or Mary.

'I think I know who the right person is, gals, don't you?' Floss said, turning around to the crowd. Several people murmured and nodded.

'Who were you thinking of?' Lottie asked.

'You, of course!' Floss smiled. 'Yer've got the right voice for this. You speak posher than the rest of us, so you'll be taken more seriously.'

Wanting others to be given a fair chance, Lottie waited to see if anyone else wanted to go for it, and then said hesitantly, 'I'm happy to take on the role, and thanks for the vote of confidence, Floss, but first – does anyone else want the role or if you'd like to nominate someone else maybe?'

They all shook their heads. 'Hands up, gals, who would like Lottie to be in charge?' Floss shouted.

All their hands shot up at once.

Surprised by their insistence, Lottie wondered whether it was because no one else wanted the responsibility, but she didn't mind at all. 'Very well then, I am pleased to be in charge of our fight against the bosses at Bryant and May!'

A cheer went up and a few of the girls ran forward to hug her. For once, she felt accepted by them all. It was a strangely wonderful feeling. Maybe they'd realised she really was one of them or maybe they just realised having manners could help you get somewhere in life.

*

The protests at the picket line were growing in numbers, but also growing in violence. Today had been particularly riotous and even the police had been called in to calm things down. Fortunately, no arrests were made.

'I think we need to hold up some signs when we next picket or go on a march,' Lottie said to Floss as they left for the day.

Floss looked at her with interest. 'That's a very good idea, but where will we get them from?'

'We'll make them of course! Come on, we'll ask around the neighbourhood if anyone has any scraps of old wood and pots of paint.'

They walked over to Lottie's house approaching the back alley, when they saw Mr O'Hara leaving through the back gate.

'What's 'e doing at yer 'ouse?' Floss narrowed her gaze.

'Calling on Ma again I expect.' Lottie chuckled. 'He's all right, Floss, he's one of us. You said yourself you think he's all right.'

Floss visibly relaxed, then nodded. 'Well as long as he's truly on our side. It's hard to know who to trust now.'

'No, he's definitely one of us,' Lottie reassured.

'Hello girls,' Shamus said, as they drew close. 'How are things going?'

'Not too bad, Mr O'Hara.' Lottie smiled

''Cept the police was called in earlier on the picket line, a scuffle broke out.' Floss chipped in, and Lottie elbowed her in the ribs. She didn't want it to get back to Ma so as not to concern her.

'It was nothing at all,' Lottie explained. 'Just a few women trying to cut across the picket line, we soon sent them on their way.'

Shamus nodded. 'Those bosses have got people at each other's throats that's fer sure.'

Lottie paused a moment. 'Mr O'Hara, you wouldn't happen to have any old pieces of wood and some pots of paint, would you?'

He scratched his chin. 'What do you gels think I am? An ironmonger's shop?'

The girls stared at him. Oh dear, had they upset him?

Then he threw back his head and laughed. 'Happen I might now and all. What do you want them for might I ask?'

'We want to make some placards to help with our protest. We can paint on the words we want to say so people will know what this strike is all about,' Lottie said firmly.

He nodded. 'Sounds like a good idea. I'll just nip home and see what I've got in my shed. I know there's some old pieces of wooden boarding there from when I made a fence a couple of years ago. I'll chop those into pieces for you and I think I've got a couple of pots of paint too.'

'As long as we're not robbing you. I wouldn't want you to be unable to paint your fence because of us,' Lottie said.

'It's no bother, 't'will be a way I can help yer girls, it's most unfair what you've all been through. And when yer Ma told me about poor wee Cassie, it fair near broke my heart. She was a little darlin' that one, always had a "Hello, Mr O'Hara!" for me in the mornings, she did.'

Lottie felt a little guilty that she hadn't had much time for Shamus in the past and had doubted his motives on occasion, which made her think of something else. 'Mr O'Hara, was it you who loaned Ma the rent money the other day?'

Suddenly his face flushed, and his eyes widened. He held his index finger to his lips. 'Sssh, don't want your mother hearing, she didn't want to worry you, lass. But yes, it was me. I wanted to give it to her but she's insisting she'll pay it back and just going through a bad patch with the factory closure an' all.'

Lottie nodded. 'Well that was most kind of you, and if Ma says she intends on paying you back, I'd take it from her. She's a very proud lady.'

'Aye, I'm beginning to realise that. Now I'll just nip home to fetch you the wood and paint. When I'm there, I'll ask my next door neighbour, Samuel, if he has some stuff to help as well. He has some old tarpaulins in his garden, maybe he'd let you paint those to use as banners.' He tipped his bowler hat at the pair of them and turned to leave.

'Thank you, Shamus!' Lottie shouted after him, then turning to Floss she said, 'See, I said he was on the side of us matchgirls.'

Floss grinned. 'Well I fink we ought to get some of the uvvers over 'ere to 'elp us then.'

Lottie agreed. 'You go and round them up, Floss, and I'll ask Ma to put the kettle on.

The girls spent the rest of the afternoon in the back yard of Lottie's house, painting slogans on to pieces of wood that Shamus had made into placards. He'd cut up the tarpaulin into long pieces and attached the longest piece to two sweeping-brush handles borrowed from Doris next door.

Floss had managed to get Edie, Mary and Mrs Murphy to join them. She'd had to spell out the words on a piece of paper first to ensure they all spelled them correctly.

Shamus lingered in the doorway, watching while the girls worked, and admiring his handiwork. He winked at Ma when he saw her watching him and she blushed like a school girl.

Ma turned away as if to hide her face and busied herself making cups of tea for the girls, though she still made sure she handed one first to Shamus, who accepted with a big grin on his face and a twinkle in his eyes.

The others seemed to be oblivious to the little romance taking place just under their very noses. They were too busy painting words that they hoped people would take notice of.

Later that day, with the completed placards in hand, the girls walked around the streets holding up them up so everyone could see their slogans: 'Save the Matchgirls!' one said, and 'Bryant and May Must Provide Better Conditions!' and 'Bryant and May Unfair to Workers!' were proudly displayed on others. Some of the girls carried metal buckets to collect money in when they were in the more affluent areas but, even in the poorest of streets, the locals were generous and supportive.

After reading the newspapers, many people were shocked to hear of the conditions the women and girls were working under, and the health hazards and even the deaths at the factory. The girls also related Cassie's story, how one of their own had inspired them to march. Understandably, it caused a level of bitterness and anger, and the public's sympathy lay with the factory workers. The Salvation Army was particularly supportive of the girls' plight, stepping in to campaign for a ban on white phosphorus in favour of using red phosphorus which was far safer, and was the standard practice in many other nearby countries.

'Hey, gals, why don't we try our luck in 'ere?' Floss suddenly announced, gesturing to a pub which stood out on the grimy street.

Lottie guessed that many a man peed his wages up against the wall after drinking in there, much to the disappointment of his poor wife and kids. She shook her head. 'I'm not so sure. They might well be all drunks in there, we don't want any men getting violent with us now, do we?'

Floss smiled as she took Lottie's arm, a mischievous glint

in her eye. 'Aw come on, ducks, where's the harm in it? I want to do me bit after all yer girls 'ave done for me.'

Reluctantly, Lottie gave in and followed Floss inside tentatively, holding the collecting bucket tightly in her grasp. Her ma always steered clear of pubs, had never been in one in her life. They were for bad women she said, so Lottie felt more than a little guilty stepping over the threshold. Floss boldly pushed open the double doors and the strong smell of alcohol hit her full on, reminding her of the recent altercation with Ted in the alleyway. The memory made her stomach churn.

'Pssst, Floss!' She hissed. 'I don't think this is such a good idea!'

But Floss was striding off ahead, her dark curls bouncing on the shoulders of her shawl. Then a shrill voice cried out, 'Well love a duck, if it ain't my favourite niece!'

What was going on here?

'Come on, you silly sausage!' Floss called over her shoulder. 'It's my Auntie Dolly and Uncle Eddie's pub. I wouldn't just go inside any ol' place.' She laughed coquettishly.

Although it was early afternoon, several men stood by the bar supping foaming pints, Lottie guessed they were dockers having a quiet pint following a gruelling shift, but who knew what state they'd be in by the end of the day? Probably staggering their way home after spending half their wages on the sins of alcohol. Lottie shuddered to think about what their families put up with, many a wife trying to hide a black eye after her husband's leisurely drink at the pub turned him into a raging demon. Thankfully, Lottie's pa hadn't been the sort. Oh, he'd enjoyed a quiet pint after work, but he came right home afterwards. He knew when to stop and, if he didn't, Lottie reckoned Ma would have struck him with her wooden rolling pin.

'Come on, Lottie, come and meet my aunt and uncle!' Floss beckoned, intruding into her thoughts. Lottie trailed behind until they settled near the long wooden bar. She'd never been in such a place before and it took a bit of getting used to. Definitely not the sort of place Ma would approve of with its spittoons and dubious-looking women in gaudy coloured dresses, smelling strongly of cheap perfume. Lottie placed the metal bucket at her feet, intending on guarding it with her life.

'Well, if it ain't my dear niece, Floss!' A large lady with a big bosom strode towards the girls, with arms open wide.

Floss whooped with delight and hugged her auntie warmly. 'Where's Uncle Ed?' she asked.

'He's down the cellar changing a barrel, love. My, my, ain't you growing all the time? And who's this young lady?' She eyed Lottie up and down, then wiped her hands on her grimy pinafore.

'This is my dear friend, and fellow worker, Miss Lottie Perkins,' Floss announced proudly trying to imitate her own posh accent. 'And she is a young lady an' all. She has proper manners and such, not like the rest of us!'

Auntie Dolly threw back her head and laughed. 'Aw, you're such a card, Floss! Come on you pair, I'll get you a drink!' She placed either hand on each girl's shoulder and led them further into the fray, Lottie managed to grab the bucket to take with her, no way was she going to leave that unattended.

'Oh, I don't drink alcohol!' Lottie protested.

'No fear, ducks. I had homemade lemonade or ginger beer in mind for you, now which is it to be?'

'You're all doing a fine job, I heard all about the strike from your father, Floss. And anyone who supports a member of this family deserves a free drink here. We'll pass your bucket around later, the men in here are getting paid today, so you should do well.'

'Doubt if they'll give as generously as the toffs!' Floss said, when her aunt had gone to fetch their refreshments.

Lottie nodded. 'Maybe not, but don't forget the story of "The Widow's Mite" from the Bible.'

Floss wrinkled her pert, freckled nose. 'Whatcha mean?'

'Well, although she had very little, she gave all she had, which was really a lot. More than any rich folk gave.'

'I fink I know what yer mean!' Floss slapped her hard on the back, causing Lottie to splutter.

They were in for a surprise, by the time they had downed their second glass of lemonade, the dockworkers were flooding into the pub dressed in their grubby garb, with their oily smudged faces, desperate to down a pint or more, and most dropped some coins in the bucket, so much so, it was beginning to get heavy for Lottie to cart around.

'Now, you girls take care when you leave here with all that money,' Auntie Dolly warned. 'And make sure you share it fairly between the women.'

Floss nodded.

'Thank you so much.' Lottie looked appreciatively at Doll, who gave her a big hug. How wrong could she be about the pub and the people in it?

'How about singing us a song, Floss?' one of the young men near the bar asked. Floss's face flamed and Lottie didn't know if it was because the young man was quite handsome or because she'd been asked to sing.

'That's Charlie, the lad I told you about, the one who took liberties wiv me,' Floss whispered, suppressing a giggle.

Lottie nodded in recognition. 'I didn't know you could sing, Floss?'

'Aye, well, I do sometimes at this pub, been singing here since I was a toddler when Uncle Eddie first sat me on the bar. Apparently, the locals loved what they 'eard and tossed ha'pennies on the bar.'

'Go on, Floss! Sing us a song!' Charlie shouted once more.

'I ain't got time at the moment, darlin'!' Floss shouted across at him. 'But if Auntie Doll and Uncle Ed allow me to,

I might perform in 'ere on Saturday night to help raise money for the matchgirls' fund!'

The young man beamed and tipped his flat cap at her.

'You've got an admirer there,' Lottie observed.

'His full name's Charlie O'Connell, he works at the docks with me da. Had his eye on me for a while and my parents would love to see us wed.'

Lottie thought back to how Oliver had said he wanted to marry her. Was he really serious? Could she become Mrs Oliver Steed? She imagined him and her riding around in their carriage together, him taking her by the arm as they wandered through the park, this time not having to worry about what people thought of them. Oh, if only it were to be so. Sometimes it fair nearly took her breath away just being in his company. She was sure the reason he hadn't backed the girls was because he was scared of losing his job. It had to be. Deep down he believed what they were saying about conditions at the factory.

It was a shame, Lottie thought, that a young girl's aspirations in the East End only amounted to getting wed and in the family way. She so admired Annie Besant for all her convictions. She hadn't bowed to her husband's wishes at all and had done entirely her own thing, though at a cost of her husband having custody of their child.

'That's a great idea about performing to help our fund.'

'Yeah, it's the least I can do after all yer lot 'ave done to 'elp me and the other two gals.'

Lottie patted her on the back. 'And you three got the boot just because you spoke to Mrs Besant. I'm glad no one signed that document the bosses passed around, it goes to show how much support you have in the factory itself.'

Floss's face clouded over, her big eyes brimming with unshed tears. 'I can't stop thinking about poor Cassie Bowen.'

Lottie touched Floss's shoulder. 'It's really hard, I know, Floss. Particularly right now when we're fighting the bosses.'

Floss shook her head.

'At least we gave her a good send-off. She had those lovely flowers and a nice spread back at the church hall.'

'Aye we done the gal proud!' Floss said.

With new determination as she thought of Cassie and her mother, Lottie said, 'That's why we have to keep fighting. For people like her and their families. Come on, let's get that bucket of money safely locked away.'

Lottie smiled as she led her friend through the pub doors and out into the bright sunshine where the other girls were waiting, waving their banners in the street at passers-by.

'Hey Lottie, Floss!' Mary shouted, 'Lots of people have been dropping money into our bucket!'

'That's great, girls!' Lottie said. 'We collected quite a lot in the pub and Floss is going to sing to raise money on Saturday night.' A cheer went up in support of this idea and Floss smiled at them all. She was putting on a brave face, Lottie realised that much. Floss was usually so held together, today had been the first time she had seen her show signs of weakness. It must have rocked her to the core losing her job like that. It was a good thing that she was getting involved in all their efforts, to keep her occupied. And her idea to sing on Saturday night was a great one.

Lottie met Oliver near the fountain at Victoria Park as arranged. This time he did not appear to be so upset, but she could tell something was amiss as he walked towards her.

'Oh, Lottie, it's so good to see you after everything that's been going on at the factory – and my home life too.'

She stepped forward and he took her white gloved hands in his. It was a shame she still had to wear her same Sunday best dress as the last time they'd met, but she had no other. Though she brightened it up with a new blue ribbon her mother had sewn on to her straw bonnet which matched the blue bow of her dress.

'What's happened?' She looked into his eyes, but he seemed guarded, suspicious even.

'Come this way. I should not be seen talking to you.' He led her by the elbow to an area that faced the lake yet was well shadowed with tree branches, and sat her down on a bench. 'Mr Bryant is bringing a libel case against Mrs Besant. He says she is out to besmirch his good name and the reputation of Bryant and May. He's very angry, Lottie.'

Lottie nodded. 'I quite understand, he's bound to be angry, but so is Mrs Besant and all the matchgirls for the way they've been treated. None of us will back down.'

He nodded. 'I do understand all of that, of course, I do. But you have to understand that you may not have jobs to go back to. Theodore will not take this lying down, you know. Now you must not tell the others of this, but I think there are plans to try to get the out-workers into the factory to work, which could mean your mother will be asked.'

Of course, Lottie already knew this but she didn't want to show Oliver. So she shook her head. 'No, my mother will not work at that place,' she said firmly.

'She might if the strike goes on for months and there's no food in the house,' Oliver said soberly.

Lottie thought for a moment. 'Well, hopefully, it shan't come to that.'

Oliver nodded. He took her hand in his. 'Dearest Lottie, I always knew you had fine breeding, you're not like the other girls at that place. You know how to conduct yourself properly – it won't be much longer, and we can be together for good. Always.'

A shiver ran the length of Lottie's spine. 'I . . . I don't understand?'

'My wife's condition worsens by the day, I fear she's dying.'

The blood in Lottie's veins turned to ice. What prompted him to come to the park when his wife was at death's door?

'Then why are you here with me? You should be with her and your children.'

She felt him tense and he removed his hand and put his head in his hands and began to weep. After some time, he raised his head and said, 'It's the only way I can cope, Lottie. Look, I have an idea, there's a lodging house I know just down the road, if you would come there with me and just speak to me where we can't be overheard by anyone passing in the park, it would make me feel so much better. I have a little something I'd like to give you when we're on our own.' He sniffed.

That was so thoughtful of him. But still a little voice told her it was wrong to be alone with a married man, especially indoors.

Lottie bit her lip. 'Oh, I don't know, I don't feel right about that at all, Oliver. Your wife is still alive and it wouldn't be seen as proper to go to such a place with a gentleman. It would give me a bad name.'

He looked at her intently, 'But I want you so much, Lottie. You are such a beautiful young woman. I swore to your father I would take care of you, you have my word on that.'

Hearing him mention her father sent a pang of guilt coursing through her body. 'I'm sorry, Oliver, maybe I am being selfish.'

'Look, we can just have a cup of tea. I know the lady who runs the establishment; she'll allow us to chat in the parlour.'

That didn't sound too bad. There would be a lady around. What could go wrong?

'Very well then, we can chat without being disturbed.' She hoped she was doing the right thing, but he looked utterly bereft, she couldn't deny him his chance to pour out his feelings in private.

Oliver stood and held his hand out to help her up from the bench. She felt protected when he was around, something she hadn't felt since Pa had died.

When they arrived at the rundown house on Queen Street, Oliver stood on the pavement, digging into his trouser pocket. He produced a rusty-looking key.

'You have a key? How is that?'

'I've paid up already,' he said, smiling, then pushing open the door, he waited for her to step inside.

She looked up and down the grimy street that stank to high heaven of manure and, she suspected, maybe even human waste.

Once inside the house, Lottie looked around her. The dank hallway smelled strongly of damp and the wallpaper was peeling off the walls, there was no carpet on the floor. The place felt cold, uncared for and empty. He locked the door behind him with the key and a shiver ran up the length of her spine.

'I don't understand,' she muttered. 'Where's the landlady you told me about?'

'It's all right, she had to pop out to go shopping I expect, come with me.' He took her hand and led her into a room where there was a single bed. Although the room was dusty, the bedding looked reasonably clean. There was also a small table and chair and a wardrobe.

'But I thought you said we'd be in the parlour for tea?'

'And we will be later when Mrs Marsh returns. Meanwhile, please sit on the bed with me, Lottie.'

He sat on the bed and patted the counterpane beside him. Gingerly, she sat down beside him. The springs creaked heavily as she sat as if it had received much use.

'This is what I have to give you, Lottie,' he whispered. He reached into the top pocket of his waistcoat and pulled out a silver chain with something on the end of it and he handed it to her.

She gasped as she gazed at it in the palm of her hand, delicately running her fingers over the small, heart-shaped silver locket. 'It's beautiful, Oliver.'

'It's only what you deserve, my love. Here I'll put it on you, lift up your hair.'

She handed him the locket and lifted her hair from her neck with both hands, just as he had asked. She could feel his trembling hands as he fastened the clasp and his warm breath on the back of her neck.

'There, all done, my sweet. A token of my love, an early engagement present, if you like.'

She dropped her hair and looked into his eyes. 'Thank you

so much, Oliver, you're so good to me.' The gesture made her feel like he really cared for her, but before she had a chance to take it all in, he pushed her backwards on to the pillow and was kissing her heavily. She could barely breathe. His lips clamped down on hers, far more forcefully than his tender kisses at the park the first time he'd ever kissed her. He was putting his full weight upon her and she felt trapped. She tried to push him off, but he was too strong.

'Oh Lottie, my body is on fire for you.' His voice sounded thick with lust and she felt his hardness against her leg.

She let out a little yelp as she felt his hands beneath the skirts of her dress and she realised what he wanted. She hoped she had not led him on by coming here. She only ever wanted to take tea with him.

'Come on, we're as good as engaged,' he said, noticing her reluctance.

'Please Oliver, this isn't what I want, I'm a virgin,' she cried, but it only seemed to make his passion more fervent. 'Come along now, Lottie, you know you want to,' Oliver coaxed. 'Why else would you have come to a place like this unchaperoned?'

He was pulling away at her drawers now and the tears were rolling down her cheeks, how foolish she had been, now her life was about to change forever if she didn't put a stop to it. The best thing she could do, she decided, was to pretend to go along with it.

'Y . . . yes, I'm just scared the landlady might come back

and catch us, that's all, Oliver.' Her breaths became short and shallow as she tried not to panic.

'No fear, my sweet.'

Breathlessly, she said, 'Then if we have time, I'd rather remove all my clothes, so you can see my body, every inch.' The words felt as though they were not her own, she was an actress playing a part. A part she needed to play so she could get off the stage, unharmed.

Oliver's eyes widened, and he nodded and smiled, then released her from his embrace. Slowly, she rose to her feet, and facing him, began to unbutton her jacket and flung it on the table. 'I'll need some help undoing the back of my dress, can you help me please?' Her heart was thudding its own rhythm and she feared she might faint from the stress of it. She felt like a baby deer caught in the jaws of a lion who was about to devour her.

Oliver stood and, as he approached, she could feel his warm breath on her neck; he trembled as he undid the first button. 'You're so beautiful, Lottie, I can't wait to ravish your young body.' He kissed the back of her neck and then stepped away.

As anger consumed her, she turned and stamped heavily on his foot with her boot. He yelled out in pain and she took the chance to run for the door which unlocked easily. But when she reached the front door she was perturbed to find it was locked. Fortunately, the old metal key was in the lock. She just hoped she had time to open it before he caught up with her.

'You little bitch, you'll pay for this!' He called after her, his loud footsteps echoing around the passageway.

The palms of her hands were perspiring – it was harder to turn the key than she thought, and it was very rusty which made it all the more difficult. She heard him making to come after her. One final try. She breathed slowly and tried to focus her trembling hands on the lock in front of her. Her heart still pounding, she finally managed to turn it, and then she was out on the street. But he was quick even though he was limping and appeared by her side in a matter of moments. He grabbed her by the hair, pulling tightly.

'Oh no, you're not going anywhere, you little madam!' His eyes seemed huge and bulging, and his teeth gritted in anger.

'Ouch, you're hurting me!' she cried out. He was trying to drag her back in the house, still holding her by her hair. The pain seared through her as he pulled at the roots. And just as she thought that he was going to succeed in getting her back inside, she heard a voice behind her.

'And what on earth is going on here, might I ask?'

She turned to see a face she immediately recognised. It was the lad she'd seen that day at Annie Besant's rally in the park. What was he doing here?

Oliver released Lottie's hair from his grasp and pushed her roughly away, which caused her to stumble and fall on the pavement. She landed right in front of the stranger who immediately shielded her from Steed, who in turn made off running up the street, without even a backward glance.

Her rescuer knelt down to help her to her feet, suddenly recognition showed as his eyes widened.

'You're that girl from the park!' he said. She nodded. He had the warmest brown eyes she'd ever seen and looked a couple of years older than herself. 'It's all right. You're safe now,' he reassured, as he took her hands, helping her to her feet. 'That fellow was giving you grief that day I saw him, too. Who is he?' He turned to watch Steed's retreating back, as his figure became a blemish in the distance.

'He's my manager at the match factory,' she panted, taking a ragged breath.

He studied her face for more answers. 'You ought to keep away from him. What was he doing to you?'

Lottie felt too ashamed to say the truth. 'I think he was annoyed with me as we're all on strike.' She fibbed.

The door to the house was still ajar and she realised she'd have to go back in there to retrieve her things. 'Will you come in with me please? I've left my jacket behind,' she asked the man.

He nodded and gestured for her to walk in front. It was such a gentlemanly show she thought she might cry with relief.

'I don't even know whose house this is,' she explained, as she led them to the bedroom where she'd left her jacket.

'I do. It belonged to an elderly lady who died recently. It's been up for sale for a couple of weeks.'

'He told me it was a lodging house.'

'Unfortunately, some men will say whatever they need to get what they want.' The young man shook his head in disgust, and then caught himself and quickly said, 'Not that I would, of course.'

'Thanks,' she said, and then cried out in frustration. 'I'm so ashamed of myself!' It had all got too much for her and she broke down in tears.

The young man placed his arm around her shoulders. 'What did he do to you? Here, sit down.'

Lottie stared at the crumpled sheets on the bed and shivered from head to toe. Just the thought of what Oliver had tried to do to her. 'I . . . I can't. He tried to have his way with me. I got away by tricking him.' She looked up at him through glassy eyes.

'Well, you're quite safe with me. Please allow me to walk you home. He may return or try to come after you,' he said softly.

She nodded gratefully. 'Thank you. I don't even know your name . . .'

He smiled a smile that lit up his eyes. 'It's Tom. Tom Harking. I work at the dockyard. That's why I was listening to Mrs Besant at the park that day, she's very much in support of us dock workers.'

Lottie brightened up at hearing of the docks. 'Then you might have known my father.'

Tom's eyes rounded, and he smiled broadly. 'Possibly. What's his name?'

'He died a few months ago, his name was Albert Perkins.'

Tom's eyebrows shot up as if in surprise. 'Was he usually called Albie?'

'Yes! That was him!'

Tom shook his head, sadly. 'I was sorry to hear he'd died. He was a lovely man, he always looked out for me.'

Lottie thought for a moment. 'Then you would have known Mr Steed, the man I tried to get away from. He used to work at the dockyard with my father.'

Tom shook his head. 'Sorry. I've never set eyes on that man in my life. Only that day I saw you both at the park.' A feeling of dread swept over Lottie. Noticing this, Tom asked, 'What's the matter, you've gone as white as a sheet.'

'I've been so very foolish. Mr Steed told me he used to work with my father and that he told him to watch out for me.'

Tom blinked several times. 'He did that to gain your trust, do you think?'

How could she have been so foolish to believe his lies?

'Yes, and now when I think back on it, he offered to meet me one Sunday for an afternoon out at Vicky Park with his two daughters, but when I arrived, they weren't there.' Suddenly, Lottie began to feel breathless with anxiety.

Tom stopped walking mid step. 'Did he harm you in any way?'

Lottie felt her cheeks flame with embarrassment. 'He kissed me in the park, and then later said his wife was dying and he'd marry me some day.' Realising how silly she'd been, she lowered her head. 'It all sounds so desperate and foolish now, Tom.'

'Now, look here, miss, sorry, please may I know your name?'

'It's Lottie.'

'Now look here, Lottie, that man from what I could see of him, is a lot older than you and he tried to take advantage. I have no doubt he's been cheating on his wife for a while. By my reckoning, you've had a lucky escape. And please, don't be so hard on yourself, you're still grieving the death of your father. It's understandable you'd become attached to a man who gives you kindn—' Tom stopped himself as he realised what he was saying and Lottie blushed. 'It sounds as if he used his position of power at the factory to spin the situation to how he wanted it. You don't deserve that, Lottie.'

Lottie huffed out a long breath. Tom was speaking sense and this was a real wake-up call for her. Though it hurt to hear the truth, it was all for the best. It was as if someone had thrown an ice-cold bucket of water all over her. She could finally see sense. What was real and what was not? She looked at Tom with fresh tears in her eyes. 'Thank you for being there today, Tom.'

He cocked a cheery smile as he doffed his cap to her. 'My pleasure, m'lady.' She appreciated his attempt to cheer her up.

Then he offered his arm so they could link arms and they walked off down the street together.

Her mother had told her many years ago that she thought it was destiny that brought her and her dear Albert together. Else otherwise how would their paths have crossed? He was from a wealthy family and she the poorest of the poor. He'd been her Prince Charming until his family found out and cut him off altogether.

Lottie thanked her lucky stars that Tom had been there to rescue her. It was almost as though they were destined to meet. Who knows what would have happened otherwise?

Chapter Eleven

Over the following days, Tom became a regular caller at the Perkins family home. Ma and the kids were really taken with him, especially when they were told he had worked with their father. If Freddy and Davy weren't clambering all over him and asking him to kick a ball, then Bessie and Daisy were asking him to tell them stories. He had a quick, creative mind, and told them all sorts of tales about hobgoblins.

'You ought to write those stories down, Tom,' Lottie said enthusiastically.

He cleared his throat. 'I have. I've submitted a couple to the newspaper.'

'Really?' Lottie was astonished at his candour.

He smiled nervously. 'I don't suppose I'll ever get to see any in print.'

'Well, you never know. Is that what you'd really like to do? Be a writer?'

He nodded. 'A writer of sorts I suppose, I'd love to be a newspaper reporter.'

Lottie thought about it a moment. 'Maybe I know just the right person to approach about it all.' Annie Besant was the person with contacts all right and she printed her own newspaper.

Tom's eyes widened, and he smiled broadly. 'Lottie Perkins you never cease to amaze me.'

'Annie Besant is the person you need. She can put you in touch with who you need to speak to. I'll have to introduce you to one another – her offices are on Bouverie Street.'

'Thank you,' he said, as he embraced her warmly.

Tom reached out and squeezed Lottie's hand. He was so different to Oliver Steed: here was a genuine person, who really wanted what was best for her. She was beginning to see the difference between someone of her own age, hardworking and trustworthy, and someone a lot older who had duped and manipulated her for his own ends. How very foolish she had been.

Each day there were still some women that defied the pickets, mostly out-workers who had been told they could get work inside the factory. Her ma still had not officially been approached, thankfully, but Lottie couldn't help but suspect that it was maybe Oliver Steed who was persuading the women to try their chances of getting into the factory. Consequently, scuffles happened regularly at the gates. A couple of times, the police were even called in as tempers flared from both sides.

One lady, Molly Murphy, had turned up at the picket line with two black eyes, to the shock of the women around her. It turned out that her husband had got drunk the night before and ordered her to return to work or else. He wanted his dinner on the table. With the help of the other women, she managed to procure some rotting vegetables and stale bread that night which was enough to stop her from getting roughed up again. Lottie and the others worried about Molly and, considering her circumstances, said they wouldn't blame her if she tried to cross the picket line. But Molly refused and, defiantly, she had carried on with the strike.

'T'will take more than a black eye to make me break the strike!' she announced.

But today was Saturday, and not a day for worrying. It was the night Floss would be singing at the Dog and Bone to help raise money for the girls. She'd asked Lottie if she'd play the piano and, even though she was a little rusty as it had been a long time since she'd tinkled her fingers over the ivories, she knew it was a good cause, and wanted to support Floss in every way she could. She hadn't played since before her family fell out, when she would go to her aunt's grand house, which had its own piano, so she asked Floss if they could rehearse that morning.

It turned out that Floss had the voice of a song bird and

Lottie was tremendously impressed. Her speaking voice was a little gruff and the amount of expletives she used would put any fisher wife to shame, but when she opened her mouth to sing, it was a different matter.

They rehearsed three songs. The first was a popular song called, 'The Boy I Love is up in the Gallery'. That song went down a storm at the music halls. It had been written for the music hall star, Nelly Power, who sadly had died the previous year. Poor Nelly had died young of pleurisy and the newspapers reported her of having a very large funeral when she died, so great was her stardom. Lottie's pa had told her he'd never seen so many people lining the streets in all his born days. Sadly, he'd died himself not long afterwards, another one taken too soon.

The second song was a favourite of Floss's, 'The Rose of Tralee', as it reminded her of family back home in Ireland. Floss's family were proud of their Irish ancestry. As there were so many Irish living in the area, sometimes Lottie would walk on the streets and, hearing the many shades of Irish dialect, she would swear she wasn't in London at all, but in Tipperary or Cork. It was something she sometimes envied, that Floss had such a connection with her ancestry, whereas Lottie's own family history was one she often felt she needed to hide.

The final song was a new song to Lottie called, 'Where Did You Get That Hat?' Floss said she'd heard it sung on stage recently and had memorised the words and tune in her head.

Since they didn't have money for sheet music, Lottie had to do her best to play the song by ear, which was difficult at first, but gradually she was able to get the hang of it by listening to Floss singing and adding a few chords here and there. It was a comedic song and Floss borrowed an old floppy hat from her Auntie Dolly to heighten the humour. Dolly had sewn fancy coloured feathers on to the sides and it had a large artificial daisy sprouting out of the top. Floss did look a picture. And, as they rehearsed, the way she performed the song, holding on to the hat and lifting her skirts at the same time with her other hand, made Lottie roar with laughter.

A notice was put up in the pub window that the matchgirls would be putting on a benefit concert and word soon got around. A couple of the other girls agreed to join in as well: Edie and Mary performed a double act as dancing girls, and Tom agreed to help the matchgirl fund by telling one of his ghost stories. It turned out he was quite the performer, as well as an excellent storyteller.

Funds were now running a bit low so Lottie hoped it would all go well. Instead of dividing the money up, it was agreed they'd get the best price they could for leftovers and scrags from the market, so at least they had something to take home to cook. It was hard for some of the older workers as they had husbands and kids to feed, and many of their husbands had lost their jobs at the docks. They were doing as best as they could under the circumstances.

That night, people in the area flocked to the pub in their droves, and those that couldn't get inside the doors stood outside to listen with the doors and windows open, and even they asked to drop a donation in the bucket.

There were few of what Lottie would have described as 'ladies' present. Apart from some matchgirls themselves who preferred to stay outside rather than risk the wrath of their parents, the only other women were the performers themselves, Doll, and a couple of notorious ladies of the night.

As Floss took to the stage – a few stacked wooden pallets covered by an old red curtain – the men cheered. Charlie's jaw slackened when he saw Floss in her bright blue gown that Doll had loaned her.

'Close your mouth lad, or ye'll be catching flies!' Doll joked and chuckled heartily to herself.

You couldn't hear a pin drop during Floss's performance of 'The Boy I love is up in the Gallery'. Lottie noticed Floss look directly at Charlie from time to time and he returned her gaze by beaming with delight. At one point, she strode through the crowd to tickle his chin, which immediately caused mates to ruffle his hair in jest. His cheeks reddened profusely which only encouraged them.

By the time the set was over and Lottie had played her last note, the crowd were in good spirits. They whistled and applauded in appreciation and Floss took a little curtsey before stepping down from the makeshift stage. 'Where Did

You Get That Hat?' had gone down particularly well, people were really impressed as it was a new music hall song that Floss had brought to them in the East End that they'd never heard before and they greatly enjoyed her antics, chuckling and cheering along.

Someone at the back had shouted, 'You ought to be on the stage for real!' which caused others to shout out in agreement.

Lottie thought it a good idea herself and as they were packing up to go home, she brought it up. 'Have you ever considered that, Floss? Going on the stage for a living?'

She shook her head and said matter-of-factly, 'No, not really.' She shook out her heavy, curly mane and picked up her jacket ready to leave.

'Well, if you want, I'll help you visit the music halls. I could play for you while you sang. If they heard you sing and how good you are they might give you a break.'

Floss tossed back her dark curls and gave a non-committal laugh.

'I'm serious, Floss! It would be better than working for Bryant and May at any rate.'

'You're right there, you are. Anything is better than working for those slave drivers.' She laughed and then her tone grew serious. 'But we're fighting for a better workplace. Who knows, it may not be so bad soon . . .'

Tom helped Lottie carry the bucket of coppers back to her house. It was very heavy and he was worried someone might try to rob the girls. He was taking no chances. Charlie and Floss also walked some of the way with them, and the men took it in turns to carry the heavy metal container between them. Charlie didn't want Floss to walk on her own after they parted ways, but Lottie suspected there was much more to it than that and that he wanted to spend some time with her.

The girls had been surprised and pleased to find out that Charlie and Tom both knew one another from the dockyard, and in fact were quite good friends.

'The trouble with our jobs,' Tom was saying, 'is that we don't earn much for our work, anything from three to seven shillings a week.'

'That's not a lot,' Lottie said.

'No, it isn't. It must have been hard on your father having a family to support.'

Lottie nodded. 'It was. That's why I went to work at the factory as soon as I could. Though Pa was one of the lucky ones, he got regular employment at the docks.'

Tom sighed. 'There's trouble afoot about our pay and working conditions too, mind you. Ever since you girls went on strike, there's been talk of us trying the same thing. We're very much in support of you all.'

Lottie smiled. 'That's very good of you. Pa would be so pleased to hear that.'

'The conditions at the factory sound much worse of course – at least we're not working with that dangerous phosphorus stuff like you lot are – but we struggle to know whether we'll earn enough money each week. We just turn up on a day-to-day basis to see if we're needed.'

Lottie felt his sadness radiate through his words. 'How does that work?'

Tom frowned. 'We get steered into a shed and the foreman walks up and down to decide which men he wants that day. Of course, in our eagerness to work we'll accept anything. There are always fights. I see family members and best friends fall out with one another. It's horrible. And it's almost as if we're cattle. With big iron bars either side of the shed, we're treated no better than cattle at market! The foreman selects his best cows from the herd.'

'Oh Tom, and I thought we had it bad at the factory.'

He stopped a moment to look at her and then placed both palms of his hands on her shoulders protectively. He gazed into her eyes and whispered, 'But you do have it bad at the factory, Lottie. One of the men said his daughter was coming home with pains in her jaw, and when they turned out the light at night her face was glowing. Glowing! He knew there was something wrong then, but over time she became really unwell.'

'I know, Tom. Several have left the factory because of it.'

'The surname was Bowen, I think. It's awful that they let that happen.'

'That would have been Cassie! She was my best friend.'

Lottie was so full of joy to hear that Tom knew of her friend, she briefly forgot how the whole sorry situation had turned out. All the feelings of sadness suddenly rushed back to her and it was as if she was learning the news of her death afresh, and she fought to hold back her tears. 'She died. Very recently.'

'I didn't realise she'd died, Lottie. I'm sorry to hear that news.' He pulled her into a hug and, as he held her tight, whispered consoling words into her ear. As the tears began to subside, Tom pulled back and said, 'Her father hasn't been down the docks lately, we thought he'd started to go hop picking again. Every time he showed up for work he never got selected for a day's work. Poor Alf didn't stand a chance. You see it with so many of the older men, or the weaker men. They just stop showing up. Alf was a good worker though, all the same . . .'

'That's why we're fighting this fight. It's for the likes of Cassie Bowen. And also all the girls who got dismissed for speaking out, like Floss did.'

Floss and Charlie caught up with them. 'Did I hear me name being mentioned?' she laughed.

'Yes, but in a good way,' Lottie said. 'Let's all go back to my house for a cup of tea. Ma will have put the kids to bed by now.'

Lottie heard the copper jingle-jangling in the bucket as Charlie took his turn carrying the bucket containing the fruits of their labour. She realised just how well they'd done for themselves and the other girls that night, and she felt proud of their achievements.

The following day, they counted out the takings on the scullery table in front of Ma and Mr O'Hara. Their eyes widened when they saw how well the girls had done.

'I've been thinking,' Ma said. She seemed in an excitable state as her green eyes glittered with gold flecks. 'Instead of you just doling out food to everyone, how about I set up a soup kitchen here? It would be my way of helping out the strikers. Now that I've no work to contend with unless I break the strike, I could put together a tasty stew with a hunk of bread and butter every day to ensure the girls and their families have a decent meal.'

Lottie thought about it for a moment and looked at Floss. 'What do you think?'

'I think it's a grand idea, Mrs Perkins!' Floss said enthusiastically. 'You'll have to have some extra out of the money though for coal to keep the range going.'

Mr O'Hara nodded at them all. 'Yes, you don't want to be put out of pocket, Freda.'

Lottie chewed her bottom lip. 'I don't know, it would be a lot of work for you though, Ma.'

'Well, I could help her if you like.' Floss stood up.

'Me as well.' Mr O'Hara joined in. 'I could take my horse and cart to market to get the best prices on the meat and veg.'

Ma turned to him. 'Oh, Shamus, I don't want you getting in trouble with the bosses on account of me.'

Mr O'Hara smiled. 'No, don't you worry about that. You poor gals have been treated unfairly at that place, that's for sure. Will be a sad day if that Mr Bryant tries it on with Shamus O'Hara!' He held up his fists and they all laughed.

Eventually, they all came to an agreement that making some sort of soup kitchen might well work.

And so over the following couple of days, word got out to the workers and their families and before long everyone knew that there was a constant supply of bread and stew at the Perkins' household. Mr O'Hara kept to his word and brought in daily supplies and Annie Besant had generously set up a special fund to keep the girls going during the strike, so Ma always had enough to buy more bread and ingredients for the stew.

It was good to see Ma so passionate about something, and together with her growing friendship with Mr O'Hara, it looked as if things were starting to look up for her Ma, what with all the troubles the family had been through in the last year.

At Mile End, Lottie, Edie and Floss looked on in awe as Annie Besant voiced her feelings about the matchgirls.

'And I'm telling you, people, you don't know the half of it, these poor girls get a clout from their foreman if he feels like it, if they accidentally spill their matches on the floor they get their pay docked, if they turn up late for work they are locked out for a half a day . . .'

There was a lot of jeering towards the treatment endured by the girls. 'Are you with me on this?'

The crowd cheered.

'And so, Theodore Bryant is threatening legal action, he wants to try putting me in my place, does he?' The crowd laughed as she raised a fist. 'Well, I'll tell you what I'm threatening . . . a march to Parliament where the matchgirls can put their case forward!'

There was an even louder cheer than before.

Floss, Edie and Lottie all looked at one another and whooped with delight. Their pleas for fair treatment would be finally heard by those that could do something about it.

'The government needs to be addressed,' Mrs Besant carried on, 'it is they who are allowing white phosphorus to be used in our match factories, it has been banned from use in certain countries, they opt to use red phosphorus instead. Why can't the British government follow suit?'

Edie whispered behind her hand to the other two. 'I've heard that the Salvation Army is thinking of setting up a new match factory and using that red phosphorus instead. Maybe we can work there, girls? I bet they'd pay us better wages an' all.'

Lottie nodded. 'It will take time for them to sort all that out though, get the right building and equipment. But we can't sidestep the issue. We still have to work for what's best for us all.' The girls could hear more cheers going up and turned to listen to their heroine once again.

Mrs Besant continued, 'Bryant and May's managing director, Frederick Bryant, another from the Bryant family, claims his loyal workforce are liars! He says working conditions are excellent. Well, I'm telling you now, here today, the only liars in all of this are the bosses at Bryant and May, not their workforce! Are you all with me on this?' The crowd cheered for her proudly.

When the cheering had died down, Mrs Besant said, 'I was at a meeting of socialists at Hampstead in June. Bryant and May had announced monster profits with dividends of twenty-two per cent which severely contrasts with them paying out wages of between four and eight shillings to workers per week! Well, they can try to sue me all they like but I only speak the truth! So, I intend to take the girls and women with me to Parliament so they can air their grievances for themselves.' Then much to their surprise, Mrs Besant called the three girls forward. 'These girls here have been instrumental in this strike. Please give them three cheers!' A rowdy cheer rang out, the loudest Lottie had heard so far.

There was a massive round of applause as people punched the air, the amount of support was phenomenal, and it gladdened Lottie's heart.

When the crowds had begun to drift away, Edie said, ''Ere gals, why don't we go over to Vicky Park?'

Lottie wasn't so sure, she was extremely tired, but Floss spurred her on. 'C'mon, ducks, we all need to relax a bit more, we've been working hard over this strike business, ain't we?'

Lottie nodded, and the three girls linked arms to walk to the park.

Once inside the park gates, they bought some penny ices, but this time there was no sign of the young flower seller that Oliver had bought the rose from, and Lottie hoped that all was well for the girl. There was so much poverty around that sometimes young children were forced to sleep on the streets, putting their lives at risk in all kinds of ways.

They strolled around the park, buoyed by the successful and lively rally Annie had led, enjoying the lovely day. But then Lottie spotted a well-known face pass close on by, which caused a shiver to course down her spine and tentacles of fear plague her heart. It was Oliver Steed with his daughters and his *wife*. Mrs Steed was smiling and looking up at him adoringly as his daughters ran off towards the lake. This was not the figure of a dying woman. What a fool she'd been to fall for his pack of lies! Although she did look rather pale and thinner than Lottie recalled.

With her heart beating madly, she strode over to where the couple were about to seat themselves on a wooden bench. Oliver saw Lottie coming and his eyes widened in trepidation, he made to usher his wife away until Lottie called after him, 'Mr Steed, haven't you forgotten something?'

Mrs Steed tried to catch her husband's attention, completely oblivious to the fact that the two already had a connection, and quite a connection at that. Lottie marvelled at the coincidence that she would see the two together here in Vicky Park of all places!

Mr Steed turned to stare at Lottie, and asked, 'What is it you want, young lady?' making out as if he didn't know her at all.

Lottie seethed with anger and, as she balled her hands into fists at her side, she used this anger to spur her on. 'It's nice to see that Mrs Steed is now fit and well, I think you'd forgotten to tell me that?'

'Oliver, who is this young girl? What have you been telling people about our business?' Mrs Steed's neat eyebrows drew together in puzzlement.

'Nothing, my sweet.' He patted her white gloved hand. 'I've never seen that girl before in all my life.'

Lottie stood now with hands on hips. She couldn't tell his wife what had happened between them, it was just too unfair on the woman, who was an innocent in all of this. Instead, she turned to her and said, 'I'm Lottie Perkins, a worker at the match factory, your husband is my manager. And he did tell me you were ill.'

Oliver shook his head.

'Is this true, Oliver?' Mrs Steed looked troubled.

'No, of course it's not.'

At that point, Edie and Floss turned up at Lottie's side. ''Ere what's going on?' Floss asked.

'It's Mr Steed here, Floss, he's denying that I work at the match factory.'

'Is that so?' Floss and Edie flanked Lottie either side.

'I also work there.' Edie chipped in. 'Lottie isn't a liar.'

A look of alarm swept over Oliver's face as his wife said to him with a snarl, 'Not again, Oliver? You've always had an eye for the young ladies, shame on you!' She strode off in search of her daughters, leaving Oliver looking shamefaced.

'What did you have to upset my wife for?' he said curtly, and then ran after her calling out apologies.

'Cor! What was all that about?' Floss wanted to know.

'Something and nothing,' Lottie assured her.

'Didn't look like nothing to me,' Edie added.

Lottie let out a long sigh of exasperation. 'All right, but if I tell you something both of you, promise you won't tell the other girls?' She drew in closer to them.

'Cross my heart and hope to die,' Floss said, making a cross sign over her heart with her index finger and Edie followed suit.

Lottie lowered her voice to a conspiratorial tone and filled them in on the happenings of the last few weeks, how Mr Steed had lied to her about knowing her father, about the date in Vicky Park that Sunday and how he'd kissed her. She even told them about how he invited her to a lodgings house and tried to have his way with her, although she brushed past this quickly, the memory still being too raw for her to think about in too much detail.

The girls were visibly astonished. Edie listened in silence as Lottie told her tale while Floss interrupted with further questions for more detail, and chipping in with her own opinions on what had happened.

After Lottie finished, Edie cleared her throat and spoke. 'I don't know how to tell you this, girls, but he tried the same thing with me a few months ago.'

A shiver skittered down Lottie's spine. 'Oh no, Edie. Do tell us what happened.'

Edie drew a deep breath. 'He kept cornering me at work.'

'That rings a bell,' Floss said cuttingly.

'There was always an excuse for me to be called into his office for something, I felt like he was singling me out from the rest of you. If I'm honest, it made me feel special.'

'Yes, that's what he did to me,' Lottie said, placing a hand on Edie's shoulder. 'He didn't get his way with you, did he?'

Edie's face flushed red. 'N . . . no, not quite, he reckoned his wife didn't love him any more and arranged to meet me at the park, but thankfully he was called away on business that time. He was needed in Manchester for something important, so it never happened.'

'Do yer think if he hadn't been called for, he'd have taken yer virginity?'

'To be honest with you girls, I was head over heels with him, I never told anyone just like you, Lottie. It could well 'ave happened. He got around me by saying he'd get jobs here for my younger sisters but that never 'appened.'

'The rotten beast!' Floss raised her fist in the air. 'It's like with Lottie. He used both of you for his own ends and he could have got you both up the spout an' all. You were dead lucky.'

Lottie and Edie both nodded.

Floss put an arm around Lottie. 'Are you all right now though, Lottie?' and then gave a look to Edie. 'And are you all right, as well? You poor things having to keep it to yerselves.'

'Yes, I'm fine now. Luckily Tom was there and looked after me once Mr Steed had scarpered.'

'I did wonder how you knew Tom.' Floss shook her head sadly. 'I've known Charlie and Tom for ages, but had never seen you talk to him before, you should've said.'

Lottie lowered her head. 'I was embarrassed to say anything to any of you. You'd have thought me bad for fraternising with Mr Steed in the first place when I knew he had a wife. And he was going to help me and Ma get better jobs. I didn't want you both to hold it against me.'

'I don't really know what that big word *fratter* something means but it sounds serious. But I get it. Come on, gals, what do you say we get out of 'ere before that Steed and 'is wife walk back this way?'

To this Edie whispered, 'She's right, hold your head up Lottie Perkins, yer've nothing to be ashamed of and nor have I. He accosted us with a view to satisfying his evil lusts. We were like two flies in a spider's web.'

Lottie looked up and smiled at her two friends.

'Yer pair were dead lucky,' Floss added. 'At least with the strike on he can't try it on with any of the other girls.' Lottie was thankful for this at least.

All three left the park linking arms, and it was a huge weight that had been lifted off Lottie's shoulders.

Chapter Twelve

Lottie had butterflies in her tummy. She was expecting Tom to call at any moment and, wanting to make sure she looked the best she could, she checked her appearance in the wardrobe mirror, pinching both her cheeks to make them pink. They'd spent a lot of time together recently but this time he'd said he wanted to take her on a date. 'You could do with a good night out!' he'd said and this made her all the more nervous. She was about to turn and leave the room when she heard a knock at the front door.

'I'll get it, Ma!' she shouted.

'Where's the fire!' Ma shouted as Lottie rushed down the stairs. 'Yer'll do yerself an injury there!' But Ma had a twinkle in her eyes knowing how excited Lottie was for Tom to be calling on her.

Lottie took a deep breath, patted down her hair and opened the door to find Tom stood on the doorstep with a cheeky grin on his face.

He gave a low whistle as he looked her up and down appraisingly. 'You look lovely, Lottie.'

'Don't leave Tom on the doorstep, invite him in,' Ma chided.

Lottie was mesmerised for a moment, her mouth dry, heart pounding. This wasn't like the crush she'd had on Oliver Steed, it was as if it was the first time she'd realised this could be a real relationship.

'Where are my manners, Tom? Please come inside.'

He removed his cap and followed her indoors.

Ma insisted they both have a cup of tea before leaving, though Lottie longed to get going so she could be alone with Tom. It was as if Ma realised it was what her pa would have done: checking him out, asking questions about where he lived and was he good enough for his daughter? Now Ma had to be both father and mother to them all.

Lottie linked her arm with his as they left the house and walked out on to the street. She looked behind to see Freddy and Davy with their heads beneath the lace curtain, pressing their noses up against the window and making funny faces.

Tom turned, saw what she was looking at and burst out laughing. 'They're a pair of cards those brothers of yours!' he said, waving at the boys. He turned back towards Lottie.

'I suppose so, it's nice to see them in such good humour. We all went through so much when Pa died.'

He nodded thoughtfully. 'It makes such a difference to a family when the head of the house dies, doesn't it?'

'It sure does. If it wasn't for the fact I'm working at the factory and Ma homeworking for the firm, then we'd be done for and end up homeless. I do worry about that, you know.'

'I bet you do.'

They fell into step together and walked in silence until Tom said, 'A penny for them, Lottie?'

'I was just thinking about my Aunt Dorothea, my father's sister.'

'Oh?'

'She's very wealthy and so would my father have been if he'd not met my mother, she was from the wrong side of the tracks as far as my father's family were concerned.'

'What happened then?'

'When they first met, my parents would have to meet in secret, only Aunt Dorothea knew. But once his parents found out they forbade the romance to go on any further so my father ran off with my mother and settled here in the East End.

They kept in touch with my aunt who was a regular visitor to my home while I was growing up. We went to see her fairly often. But then one day my mother fell out with her, very badly. I never discovered why.'

'That's a sad tale if ever I heard one,' Tom sympathised.

'I miss her so much. I haven't seen her for so long and even then it's just from afar when we're both at church together.' Lottie took a deep breath and sniffed. 'Well there's no use moaning about it, that's just how things are.'

'I suppose they are, but let's think of finer things. How about we go to a magic lantern show or the theatre tonight?'

'Oh, I couldn't possibly expect you to pay for me, Tom.'

He shook his head. 'Of course you can. You're my girlfriend now, Lottie.'

Girlfriend? She liked the sound of that.

He took her hand and led the way. He wasn't afraid to show his affection for her, not like Oliver, and it felt good.

They opted for a magic lantern show as Lottie insisted it was cheaper than going to the theatre. The hall was packed when they arrived as they were a little late, but they managed to find two seats at the very back of the hall, and when the lights dimmed, Tom took her hand again. They watched a story of a young woman's tale of unrequited love. It was mesmerising and Lottie could have watched her for hours. When it was over, Tom insisted on buying her a bunch of violets from a flower seller standing outside. 'For you,' he said with a big smile.

Holding them to her face, she inhaled the sweet perfumed fragrance. 'Thank you so much, Tom.'

'It gives me so much pleasure to see your face light up, Lottie.' He gave her a peck on the cheek and she felt an inner glow spread inside. Taking her by the hand he said, 'Let's go and have a little stroll around the park.'

It was just beginning to get dark as they arrived and the gas lamps were already lit, reflecting yellow pools of light. When they neared the lake, Lottie trembled, remembering how Steed had taken her out on the boat that day.

Mistaking her shaking for being cold, Tom offered her his coat. She nodded, as she realised she did in fact feel chilly so he stripped off his jacket and draped it around her shoulders.

'Tom,' she said, 'why are you so kind to me?'

'Think nothing of it. I just like to treat people well and I respect women.'

'How come, though? A lot of lads I know of your age don't know how to treat a lady.' She thought back to those two lads who had teased Floss outside the factory gates and mocked her.

'I suppose it's down to my ma. She's a strong lady and worked hard to bring us all up. She gave me my values in life.'

Lottie nodded as she watched the lights reflected on the lake. It was quiet here in the evening and she felt like they were the only two people in the whole wide world.

The spell was only broken when Tom said, 'Now let's head to the refreshment rooms before we go to get the omnibus back home. A cup of hot chocolate should warm you up a bit, my love.'

Tom intended getting her back home at a reasonable hour. He was the best boyfriend ever, not a letch like Oliver Steed; in comparison he wasn't fit to tie Tom's shoe laces.

*

The reporting in many of the newspapers favoured the match-girls' plight and spoke out against their employers, tagging them with names such as 'Slave Drivers' and 'Slave Masters'. Lottie was delighted to see that people had begun to boycott any products by Bryant and May, choosing matches by rival companies instead. Lottie continued to speak out in support of the workers at demonstrations and marches.

People cheered in support of the matchgirls almost everywhere they went. An elderly woman at the back of the crowd at the Mile End Waste stepped forward and announced, 'Here we are, girls!' dropping two pennies into their collection bucket from her gnarled, spindle-like fingers. One of the other girls had later heard her say the pennies were all she had but she had to support the girls, appalled at what they had to endure at the match factory. Later, when the strike fund was being distributed out amongst the workers, a woman, of around Ma's age said, 'Few people can fail to be touched by the way you girls are determined to stand together . . . in every direction girls can be seen plotting how they can help one another on until Bryant and May do the right thing.'

The lady's husband punched the air. 'How can them bosses sleep at night, I'll never know! They're crooked as the day is long!'

'Thank you all for giving us your time and support today, ladies and gentlemen,' Lottie concluded. 'In a couple of days' time, we shall be marching all the way to Parliament to speak with MPs who we're hoping can help us.'

People patted her on the shoulder, others shook her hand. It was good to know there were so many on her side. As the crowds dwindled away and Lottie said goodbye to Edie and Floss, she turned and felt a shiver run down the length of her spine knowing a familiar figure stood behind her. He seemed to tower above her, and the evening sunlight from behind him made it hard to see his face, but she knew it was him. Even the sounds of his ragged breaths gave him away. She squinted to see his face, holding the palm of her hand over her eyes to shield them from the sun.

'O . . . Oliver . . .' She trembled.

'Do not ever use my Christian name again.' He growled. 'Not after what happened in the park the other day.' His breaths were still heavy as he drew towards her.

She took in a long, composing gulp of air and let it out again. 'Don't worry, *Mr Steed*, I don't wish to become that familiar with you ever again. You truly misled me.'

'As you misled me, also, you little madam!'

'Utter poppycock!' she spat.

'You led me on, missy. And if anything else gets back to my wife about this you shall pay dearly. I shall tell people how you led me on so I could marry you. I shall damage your reputation once and for all.'

Lottie's jaw slackened. 'You mean to tell me that time your

wife was sick it was just *me* leading *you* on believing you wanted to marry me'

He nodded, his eyes now glazed and his voice slick with venom. 'For your own ends, yes. My wife isn't interested in me in the bedroom department any more.'

'And you did the same thing to Edie as well!' Lottie spat. 'Men like you should be locked up!'

He threw back his head and laughed. 'You factory girls are easy meat – I've had a few of you.'

'Not me, nor Edie!' Lottie said in indignation.

'It would only have been a question of time with Edie, she was panting for it!'

'You vile beast!' Lottie shouted, and he stepped forward so he could grab her in his arms, locking her into his embrace.

'With you it was different though . . . I was doing it for you, for us, Lottie. My wife isn't the lovely young thing she once was, she has borne me three delightful children, but she no longer cares to allow me my husbandly pleasures. She looks so matronly. But you, you're young and untouched. I finally felt young again. We could still have it all. Just relent and give me every part of you.'

She could feel his warm breath on her cheek, his breaths rapid and shallow. She felt ensnared and struggled for breath.

'You're such a tease. If you were to succumb to me I will make sure your mother gets a job at the factory and you don't lose yours.'

Lottie worried there was to be no escape this time, it would soon become dark as dusk descended and there was no one around that she could see. The people from the talk must have all left by now.

He dragged her into an alleyway and pushed her up against the craggy red bricks. Having her pinned down, he lifted her skirts and yanked at her drawers, ripping them from her as her naked flesh was exposed beneath her clothing.

'No, please, no!' she shouted, tears rolling down her cheeks, but he was too strong for her. She felt his hardness against her thigh. He intended taking her here and now, she had got away from him once, but now he was back for more. She tried to scream out but he placed his hand tightly over her mouth as his other hand roamed up her leg. She was struggling to breathe and her heart was pounding heavily with fear.

'You're going to get what's coming to you, you little bitch!'

Then quite suddenly, she heard the click of a gate in the row and voices drifting towards them. A man and a woman. They were heading in the opposite direction but still Steed took a step back. It was as if he'd just come to his senses.

Lottie's eyes were full of tears, but that didn't bother him. Instead, he dropped his hand from her mouth and lifted her chin with his thumb and forefinger, squeezing hard. 'There now, you see, I can take you whenever I wish. Don't you worry, we'll be together soon enough. This isn't over. Come on, I'll walk you home . . . I'll be back when the time is right.'

She couldn't go home like this. She didn't want her mother or her brothers and sisters to see her. Where could she go? She trembled all over, feeling dazed and confused.

Lottie was numb inside, shocked at what had just almost occurred, it was worse than that day he'd taken her to the unoccupied house. Noticing her torn drawers on the cobbled ground, she stooped to retrieve them and stuffed them inside her skirt pocket. She felt defiled. No way did she want him to walk her home.

'I can find my own way home!' she said, trembling all over as she turned to walk away. To her surprise, he remained where he was.

How could she have ever felt she loved someone like him? She swallowed to hold back the tears as she tried to put as much distance between them as possible with each step she took.

Chapter Thirteen

Lottie found herself running in the opposite direction of home. Oliver called something after her in a mocking tone, but she couldn't hear him. She blanked out everything connected to him and focused on scurrying through the familiar – and some not so familiar – back lanes until she found the home of Aunt Dorothea.

The house was much bigger than some in the area, though high-walled and surrounded by trees. She managed to unfasten the large wrought-iron gates, close them behind herself and stagger up to the front door, all the while trying to glance over her shoulder to ensure Oliver wasn't following her. Other people who looked like she did would usually have had to use the servants' entrance, and she was sure if anyone saw her they'd be taken aback.

Panting, and her legs feeling boneless, she rapped the heavy brass door knocker, and tried to compose herself. After a moment, the door swung open to reveal a maid who Lottie did not recognise.

The girl looked a little younger than herself and gave her a disapproving look. 'Sorry, the lady does not want to buy anything today, and in any case you should be calling around the back entrance.'

'I'm not here to sell anything – I'm here to see my Aunt Dorothea,' Lottie explained.

The maid shook her head as if she didn't believe her and was about to close the door when Lottie heard a familiar voice from within.

'Who on earth is that at the door?' her aunt asked.

'Auntie, it's me, Lottie!' she cried out, then became aware of her aunt all dressed in navy bombazine heading towards her and embracing her in her arms. The soft lavender scent she remembered so well, it had been such a long time.

The next thing she knew, she was laid out on a chaise lounge in the drawing room as the maid waved a small bottle of smelling salts beneath her nose.

As her aunt's face came into focus, she asked, 'I'm pleased to see you again, of course I am, but what brings you here, dear?' She dismissed the maid so as to give them both more privacy.

Lottie sat up on her haunches and her aunt pulled her close to her bosom.

'Auntie, something awful has happened to me this very evening, I was taken by force by a married man.' She broke down in tears and cried huge racking sobs until she could cry no more.

Aunt Dorothea dried Lottie's eyes with her lace handkerchief and made soothing noises, before crossing the room to pour out a glass of sherry from a decanter on top of the piano.

'Here, sip this slowly,' she advised, and handed it to her.

The warm liquid seeped into Lottie's bones, comforting her. She had only ever tasted sherry once and she liked the feeling it gave her. 'Now tell me, who is this fellow? Who would do that to you?'

'He is Mr Steed, my boss at the match factory. He told me that he had known Pa at the docks and that he'd promised he'd look out for me – untruths on both counts.'

'I'm sorry, what did you say? "*Had* known"?' Aunt Dorothea blinked.

Sadly, Lottie shook her head – she didn't want to be the person to tell her aunt that her brother had died.

After she'd finished explaining what had happened, her aunt sat there motionless, her knuckles white as she clenched her wooden walking stick.

She swallowed hard and took a few sips from her glass of sherry. 'I am so sorry to hear that news, Lottie. I never knew or else I would have attended his funeral, but as you know, your mother and I do not see eye-to-eye. But this is not the time to speak of such things. I need to know more about this awful event you describe.'

Lottie told her aunt everything about how she'd been duped into meeting Oliver at the park, the lodging house, how he claimed his wife was ill and the attempted rape. It felt good to open up to an adult.

'We need to report this to the police of course,' Aunt Dorothea said.

'I'm sorry, Auntie, I don't know if I can do that, it will besmirch my character. I just don't want anyone to know!' She began to sob.

'There, there. I quite understand, Lottie. But if you don't report it the beast will go unpunished and who knows which young girl he will attack next.'

Lottie knew her aunt was making sense. 'I'll think about it,' she conceded, wiping the tears on the back of her hand.

'Look, I think it's best you have a bath and stay the night here, then decide tomorrow. You can't go home looking all upset and especially with that man still out there somewhere. We can send a message to your mother. She might not like the fact you are staying here but at least she'll know where you are.'

Lottie nodded gratefully and closed her eyes for a few brief moments. Her insides were churned up and her arms felt sore from where Oliver had pinioned her against the wall, something that she'd never experienced before in her life. 'Thank you, Auntie,' she murmured.

Aunt Dorothea instructed the maid to fill a bath full of hot water, and as she stood in the elegant room where the bathtub lay, Lottie felt safe again.

The maid looked at Lottie intently. 'Would you like some of your aunt's special fragranced soap, miss?' she asked thoughtfully. The girl was only about thirteen years old, and Lottie could sense she was trying to be helpful. She probably felt bad for assuming she was a servant girl.

'Yes, please,' Lottie said, and then added, 'What's your name?'

'It's Alice, miss. I've filled the bathtub with some pails of hot water and some cold, but I've left a pail of cold water beside it in case it's too hot for you. I've left some towels on the chair for you as well, and if you need me to 'elp you get dressed then just call out, I won't be far away. Your aunt left you a fresh nightdress and dressing gown, and she says she can loan you a day dress for the morning.'

Lottie winced, her head was pounding from the stress of the evening, and her bones felt stiff. 'I can manage from here on in, thank you very much, Alice.'

Alice bobbed a curtsey as she left the bathroom. No one had ever curtsied to her in her life and the poor girl probably came from a similar East End background to herself. She undressed, tossing her clothing on the floor, then gently lowered herself into the warm water and laid back, closing her eyes for a moment. It couldn't be true, could it? That only an hour or so ago, she had been violated by a man old enough to be her father. A thought suddenly struck her. Was Oliver the man who had got one of the other girl's pregnant at the factory? They'd been so sure it was the foreman but it all suddenly started to make sense. It was all just a game to him. He'd have told the naïve, unsuspecting girl that his wife was ill to gain her sympathy. She couldn't believe that he'd done the very same thing to Edie that he'd done to her. The man was a dirty, rotten scoundrel.

As she immersed herself in the water, its temperature thankfully being just right, she thought of Alice and realised that, no, she wasn't really like the girl at all. Pa had come from a wealthy family. If things had been different maybe she would be living in a luxurious place like this house. And tonight would probably have never happened as she wouldn't have had to work at the factory. The thought was bitter. But then she reminded herself that if things were different, it would have meant that Pa would never have met Ma in the first place and he'd have married someone else from his own social standing, and she and her brothers and sisters would not exist at all.

Lottie had dried herself and put on a fresh nightgown when her aunt arrived. 'I've asked Alice to bring you a tray of food with a glass of milk. Now then,' she said kindly as she sat on the bed beside Lottie. 'What's your mother up to these days since your father died?' She reached out and pushed a strand of hair that was in Lottie's face out of the way, tucking it behind her ear.

'Oh, Ma's all right. Well, I say she's all right, but of course now she has no job as she was making matchboxes, and now the factory's gone on strike, it's difficult for her: she's been taking in folk's washing and ironing while setting up a soup kitchen for the workers who are on strike.'

Aunt Dorothea arched an eyebrow, then nodded as if understanding how dire the circumstances were. 'I don't suppose your mother earns much at Bryant and May?'

Lottie shook her head. 'No. She earns tuppence-farthing for each gross of boxes and has to pay for her own string and the paste, too. But we're lucky, Annie Besant has been helping us girls. She's set up a fund for us and we're also trying to raise funds ourselves.'

Auntie settled herself back in an armchair beside the bed and crossing one hand over the other, said, 'I've read about Mrs Besant. She's a remarkable woman, indeed.'

Lottie brought up her knees beneath the counterpane and rested her chin on them. 'She's a great lady fighting for our cause. There is so much deprivation in the East End.'

'I do understand, really I do, Lottie. If there's any way I can be of any help, please let me know.'

Her auntie stood, then leaned in to place a swift kiss upon

Lottie's cheek. She smelled of lemon and lavender, it was a familiar fragrance from the days when Lottie came to the house for piano lessons. She realised in that moment how much she missed her aunt and wished there had been no family feud to deal with. Ma was a proud, headstrong woman.

'Now after you've eaten, try to get some sleep and we'll have a think in the morning what we're going to do about this situation, I'll send a letter over to your mother explaining you have stopped over the night. I'll get the livery man to deliver it.'

Seeing the look of alarm on Lottie's face, her aunt said, 'Don't worry, I won't put in the letter what happened to you, you can tell her yourself face-to-face when you see her.' Auntie shook her head sadly. 'Now, try to get some rest, things will look so much better in the morning.'

But Lottie slept hardly a wink that night, she tossed and turned and when she did finally fall into a fitful sleep, she woke up sobbing as she was reminded in a dream what Mr Steed had done to her.

Chapter Fourteen

'If you won't go to the police, Lottie, I'm going to see Mr Steed myself, his wife needs to know what's going on,' her aunt said stoically. They were seated around the breakfast table and Lottie was playing with the thick slice of toast on her plate. Normally, her stomach would have been growling with hunger, especially on seeing the melted golden butter that her aunt had given her to soak up the bread with, but there was a sickness inside her stomach after Steed's attack and a lump in her throat she found hard to swallow. Auntie Dorothea's breakfast table was groaning with food that could have fed an East End family of four for a couple of days. A waste, Lottie thought. There was a large tureen of porridge, a silver platter of sausages, bacon, scrambled egg and mushrooms, various jars containing jams and marmalades, two types of bread – one a seeded wholemeal and the other a white bloomer loaf, and a pot of hot tea in a pretty china teapot adorned with pink tea roses, not like her Ma's cracked brown earthenware teapot at home.

'Please, Auntie. I don't think you should do that,' Lottie pleaded.

Her aunt looked at her with kindness and compassion in her eyes. 'If we don't go to see Steed's wife then we have to report it to the police before it happens to some other young girl.'

A shiver coursed along Lottie's spine, she hadn't wanted to consider that. What if she said nothing and some other young girl was actually raped? He could have taken away her virginity if he hadn't been disturbed – it was something she intended keeping for the man she married.

Slowly, she nodded. 'All right, if it helps to save someone else. There is one other thing . . .'

'Oh?' Aunt Dorothea arched her brow.

'Mr Steed told me his wife was ill with a sickness, I have wondered if somehow he made her ill on purpose. I wasn't sure he's speaking the truth about her illness after what's gone on but when I saw her in the park the other day she looked like she had lost a lot of weight, she was a shadow of her former self.'

'Surely not? But then again I have heard of that kind of thing before. A man I once knew was poisoning his wife using hemlock, but luckily she became suspicious and called the doctor, who confirmed her suspicions. He'd been chopping it up and adding it to her food each day. Perhaps we need to mention your suspicions about what Mr Steed might be up to to the police?'

Lottie hesitated for a moment, mulling things over in her

mind. She'd never forgive herself if she omitted that information in case Mrs Steed died at the hands of her own husband. Her aunt was right. 'I suppose we should.'

'Now finish your breakfast, then you're going to get dressed and we'll pay your mother a visit before calling in at the police station.'

Lottie swallowed hard. Ma and Aunt Dorothea hadn't spoken in years and now they were going to discuss something so intimate. It wasn't going to be easy.

Aunt Dorothea loaned Lottie one of her floral day dresses. It was a little grand for Lottie to wear and a little long for her, so Alice had taken it up with some needle and thread.

'I know you feel too dressed up in that frock, Lottie, but it's too small for me these days and your waist is nice and trim. I'll loan you a woollen shawl if you feel overdressed?' Her aunt smiled.

Lottie nodded as she studied herself in the long walnut mirror in the hallway. 'I really like it, it's so kind of you. What did you do with my clothes?'

'Now don't you go worrying about those, I've packaged them up to show the police as evidence as your undergarments were damaged and blood-stained.'

Lottie swallowed hard, she had some scratches on her upper thighs where he'd torn away at her undergarments, the blood must have come from those. It was going to be difficult talking about such matters to the police.

Auntie's livery man, Bill, got her cab ready and the pair got in to head towards the police station. But first, they had to stop off to see Lottie's ma along the way.

When Ma saw it was Dorothea walking up the back path to see her, she took a step back. She had been in the middle of hanging out some bed sheets on the washing line that she'd taken in for neighbours.

Her hands flew to her mouth and, for a moment, Lottie feared Ma would tell her aunt to leave the property.

'Cat got your tongue, Freda?' Dorothea asked, with a gleam in her eyes.

Lottie watched Ma's reaction carefully – would she run back into the house? Or get angry with her sister-in-law? But, instead, she stood her ground even though she looked a little anxious. 'D . . . Dorothea, I'm so sorry, I should have told you about Albert's death, please forgive me.' Her bottom lip quivered as though she might cry at any given moment and there was a catch to her voice.

'That matter's not now, Albert is dead and buried and there's no more we can do about it. I am here though to speak about more pressing matters. Can we talk inside?'

Ma dropped the sheet she had been in the middle of attending to, back in the wicker laundry basket. 'Yes, of course, where are my manners? I'll make us all a cup of tea.'

The three of them settled around the scullery table, Lottie trembled from head to toe. What would Ma say when she realised her only daughter had almost lost her virginity to a man who was old enough to be her father? And indeed, what would Pa have thought himself? No doubt, knowing her father, he'd have been prepared to lambast the brute.

As they supped their sweet brew, the whole sorry tale came out and Ma's eyes began to fill with tears.

'Oh, Lottie, my dear child, what has that beast done to you?' She hugged her warmly.

'What we need to do,' Dorothea said gently, 'is to go to the police station immediately. We have some evidence that something happened by the state of Lottie's undergarments.'

Ma nodded. 'He won't get away with this, make no mistake! Bryant and May are hard taskmasters and he's one of those sorts.' She stood and stared at her daughter. 'But Lottie, how did this 'appen in the first place? Were you cavorting with the man? That's what I'd like to know.'

Lottie looked up at her mother through glazed eyes. 'I'm sorry Ma, he paid me a lot of attention.'

Her mother folded her arms and tapped her foot impatiently. 'So, that's why he came here recently to see you? And I bet that time you lied about being over at Floss's house that Sunday afternoon, you were with him?'

Lottie nodded slowly. 'I was, yes. He took me to Vicky Park.'

'And you couldn't tell me, your mother, any of this? You shouldn't have lied to me!'

Lottie sat there, speechless. Ma looked so hurt. 'I'm sorry, Ma. I didn't mean to keep anything from you . . .'

Her mother shook her head. 'I can't even trust me own daughter. If Floss hadn't called looking for you, I wouldn't have 'ad a bleedin' clue to your whereabouts, my girl! I've been waiting for you to trip yourself up!'

'Come on now, Freda,' Dorothea soothed. 'It's not the girl's fault, she's at an impressionable age and it sounds to me like the man duped her. Also, there's something odd about his wife's illness. We think he might have been drugging her and making her ill.'

But there was no getting through to Ma when she was in this sort of mood. It was obvious that she thought this was Lottie's own doing and she seemed to have little sympathy for her.

'If the neighbours should ever find out about this and, God forbid, if your name becomes blackened, no man will want to marry you.'

Dorothea stood. 'Look, Freda, you need time to digest this information. I do stress this is *none* of Lottie's doing. She's a good girl. I'm going to the police station with her right now. Won't you join us?'

Freda shook her head. 'The only one who had duped anyone is that girl. Albert would be so ashamed of 'er if he was still alive.'

Lottie could not believe what her Ma was saying. And for her to speak about her as if she wasn't there!

'Then there's no more to be said,' Dorothea said stiffly. 'I shall take the girl back home to stay with me until you've calmed down. Come on, Lottie.'

Without waiting for an answer, she strode out of the scullery and, too shocked by her Aunt's decision to say anything further to her Ma, Lottie followed her down the path.

'Thank you for support, Auntie.' Lottie sniffed once they were back in Dorothea's carriage.

Her aunt smiled and passed her a lace handkerchief to wipe her tears on. 'As your father's sister, I owe you this support and far more, it's the first thing I can do for my dear brother,' she said. 'Now, we'll go to the police station and tell them what's occurred. Do you think you can cope with that?' She studied Lottie's face.

Lottie nodded as she dabbed her eyes, then her aunt reached out and patted her hand. 'Good girl, I'm so proud of your bravery. And don't take any notice of your Ma. It's me she's angry with really. We never made up after that row and we caught her unawares today.' She popped her head out of the carriage window and called out to Bill, 'Please take us to the police station, the one nearest the match factory,' then she settled herself back down against the leather squabs and closed her eyes as the carriage rattled along the road. Lottie watched as several children ran excitedly after it: they didn't often get to see such lovely carriages in their neck of the woods. Normally, she'd have felt excited for them but as the tears spilled down her cheeks, she rested her head against the window and closed her eyes to blot out the pain.

When they arrived at the police station, the main reception desk was in uproar. Several women in gaudy coloured dresses, smelling strongly of a mix of gin and cologne, were in the throes of being manhandled towards the cells by two burly police constables.

'I think we've chosen the wrong time to show up here,' Lottie said, doubtfully.

Aunt Dorothea shook her head and pursed her lips. 'Look, don't let this lot put you off, my dear girl. We should be attended to, even if the police force has less man power than it used to.' She sniffed loudly, catching the attention of the desk sergeant, whose mutton-chop whiskers engulfed his small round face.

'Can I help you, Madam?' he said, though the word came out more like 'Modom'. He was clearly affecting a posh voice to impress her aunt who, in her well-cut clothing, stood out amongst the roughened, shabby people filling up the vestibule.

Auntie cleared her throat and straightened her damask cape on her shoulders. 'We need to speak to someone about an incident that occurred early yesterday evening. In private, if you please,' she stressed.

The sergeant nodded. 'If you could please take a seat,

modom, miss, I'll see if there's someone available to speak to you both.'

Auntie glanced at Lottie with a gleam in her eye and then back at the sergeant. 'I'm sure you'll do your best for us, Sergeant er . . . ?'

'Carter, Madam. Someone will be with you in a tick.'

Down the corridor, several shouts could be heard from the women who resisted being handled into the cells, and one even appeared to proposition one of the constables, her raucous laugh echoing off the walls. Lottie surmised they must be prostitutes and it sent a chill down her spine.

After far more than a tick – more like a quarter of an hour to be precise; Lottie's eyes had remained fixed on the clock – a gentleman in plain clothes appeared. He wore a brown tweed suit and sported a well-trimmed moustache. He smiled broadly when he saw them.

'Miss Perkins,' he intonated, 'how lovely to see you again.' He took both of Auntie's white gloved hands in his own, seemingly genuinely pleased to see her.

Puzzled, Lottie followed the pair as they arrived at a small room. It contained a walnut desk, large leather chair and two wooden seats, next to which was a tall filing cabinet and three shelves containing various leather-bound books and ledgers.

'What can I do for you both?' His face held a serious expression.

'First, Gerald, let me introduce my niece, Miss Lottie

Perkins.' She turned to Lottie, 'Lottie, this is Gerald Simpkins. He's a detective inspector here.'

Gerald smiled once more, gazing at Lottie. 'You must be Albert's daughter!'

'Yes, sir.'

'Well, I never, I knew your father well and was sorry to hear of his passing.'

'Thank you.' Lottie smiled politely though she did wonder how this man could possibly have known her father.

Auntie draped an arm around Lottie. 'I must explain to you that Gerald and I were friends as children. We've known one another's families for years; Gerald and your father were best friends as children.'

'I see,' Lottie replied.

Gerald smiled broadly. 'And your aunt is being very modest too, Lottie. She is very generous towards the police and often donates to charitable causes in the area.'

'Please sit down both of you, now what can I do for you?' Gerald asked, seating himself behind his desk.

'Lottie, tell Gerald what you told me,' Aunt Dorothea urged, placing a hand on Lottie's forearm.

Taking a deep breath, Lottie let the words tumble out, 'I work at the Bryant and May factory, and as you would be well aware, we are currently on strike . . .'

The detective nodded.

'Well, anyhow, we had a meeting at the Mile End Waste

area yesterday evening, I was the last to leave, and when . . . I . . . I . . . d . . . did so . . . I was accosted by a man.'

The detective's eyes flashed. 'And do you know this man, Lottie?'

She shifted uncomfortably on the hard, wooden chair, it was a hot day and it felt airless in the office. She ran her finger under the starched lace collar of her dress. 'Yes, I do, sir. It was Oliver Steed, one of the managers at the factory.'

'And what exactly happened next?'

There was a lump in her throat.

'It might be an idea to give Lottie a drink of water,' her aunt said.

Gerald stood and poured a glass for Lottie from a glass pitcher on the cabinet behind him. He offered one to Dorothea too, but she declined with a wave of her gloved hand.

Lottie was parched, and she took several sips before placing her glass down on the desk. 'Sir, he manhandled me, though I tried to get away. He forced himself upon me, but fortunately was disturbed by a man and woman nearby, else I would have been raped!'

'It's an abominable disgrace!' Auntie said fiercely.

'So, to clarify,' the detective continued without showing much emotion, though Lottie guessed his job made him like that, it wouldn't do for him to get hysterical and begin showing fits of pique, 'you weren't raped?'

She shook her head. 'No, sir. But it would have happened

if he hadn't been disturbed. It was obvious what he was about to do.'

'And we have some evidence here of Lottie's undergarments. They've been damaged during the attack,' her aunt added.

The detective nodded, and then there was a long pause as he mulled things over. 'Were there any witnesses at all?' he asked, looking intently into Lottie's eyes.

She shook her head. 'The couple who disturbed him were walking in the opposite direction so, unfortunately, they didn't witness anything. They left their house a few doors up the street, so it was too far away for them to see or hear anything, but it disturbed him, Steed I mean. It put him off what he was doing. He was like a man possessed.'

'He was probably scared of getting caught out, I expect,' the detective said, rubbing his whiskered chin. 'I'm afraid it's his word against yours. Don't get me wrong, I can get him in here for questioning, but it's doubtful he'd admit to it. And I do understand that it was very distressing for you, Lottie.' He looked at her with a great deal of sympathy in his eyes.

'There was talk of another girl being made pregnant by one of the managers though,' Lottie added.

'I'm afraid I can't help with that unless the girl comes forward. If you could ask her to come in, that might help,' Gerald said.

Auntie handed him the brown paper packaging containing

Lottie's clothing. 'Here are the garments I spoke of, Gerald. I only hope now that brute doesn't catch up with my niece and impregnate her!' She shook her head in disgust at the whole sordid affair.

A sudden wave of fear engulfed Lottie. In all of the aftermath, it hadn't been something she had honestly considered. What if he came back, like he had threatened, and got her pregnant? She fought to hold back the tears. This time yesterday all had been well, they'd had a successful day campaigning, speaking at various meetings and collecting funds, and she'd also been on good terms with her own mother. Now, she'd been almost raped, fallen out with Ma and having to live elsewhere. Could things get much worse for her?

As if sensing Lottie's dismay, the detective looked at her and said, 'Don't worry, Lottie. We'll bring Steed in for questioning and see if he cracks. I believe what you're telling me, it's all about whether the court will or not.'

'The court? I hadn't even considered that.' Lottie trembled.

Her aunt laid a hand on her shoulder. 'You're not alone, dear child. I shall support you every step of the way.'

As they left the police station, Lottie realised she needed to speak to Floss and the girls, she had to warn them about Steed. Auntie was right. What if he did it to someone else? And what about Tom? How could she possibly tell him what she'd been put through? Would he believe it a second time? He might think she'd been leading Steed on.

'What are you thinking, Lottie?' her aunt asked as they walked towards her carriage.

'I need to warn people about that man, I need to speak to Floss.'

'And who is this Floss?' Auntie peered down at her over her gold-rimmed specs.

'Flossie Gittings, her family come from Tipperary, though she was born over here. She worked next to me on the cutting machines on the factory floor. It's her getting fired that sparked off this strike in the first place.. We're not too far away from her house, could we go to find her right away?'

'Yes, let's do that. We'll take her back to my house for luncheon, shall we?'

Lottie realised her aunt would be in for a huge culture shock when she met up with Floss. It was one thing that Ma was quite down-at-heel, but Floss was something else entirely.

Floss's mouth was agape with surprise when she saw Lottie alight from the carriage on the grimy street. Thankfully, Aunt Dorothea remained inside the carriage, but Lottie caught her sniffing at the strong odour. The smells of the factory and the horse dung in the streets was so much stronger in summer.

Lottie turned back to her aunt. 'Are you all right, Aunt Dorothea?' She'd noticed her gagging slightly and she was now searching in her reticule for something. Lottie noticed her take out a lace handkerchief and hold it to her face.

'Yes, I'm fine. I've suddenly the need for one of my scented handkerchiefs, that's all. Go and talk to your friend, please.'

Lottie turned back to Floss.

Floss's eyes grew large with excitement. 'Cor, Lottie, I always said yer were a lady, fancy you getting out of that carriage! Where yer bin to? I came to call fer yer this morning and your ma said you weren't in, but she wouldn't tell me where yer was?'

Lottie took in a deep breath and let it out again. She was used to the sights and sounds of the East End, unlike her aunt. She looked up and down the street to ensure no one was listening. The street was quiet, save for a cat curled up on the pavement on the opposite side of the road. Floss's street was one of the poorest in the district, packed with Irish dockers' families and a few other cultures as well, mainly from Eastern Europe. Lottie took Floss aside to explain to her what had happened.

'Yer poor thing,' Floss said, once Lottie finished speaking. 'That man ought to be 'orse whipped and I'd be just the one to do it an' all. I reckon he was the one who put the boot in fer me with the bosses. Are you 'orright?'

'I'll survive, I suppose. Speaking of which, do you remember there was a rumour going around a few months back, how one the bosses got a matchgirl pregnant?'

'Yeah, Lottie. I reckon it was Steed who did the deed there.'

'Do you know who it was he got pregnant?'

'I fink she lives at the end of the next street over. Ain't seen her in ages though. She'd left the factory before you joined us. I can take you to 'er 'ouse, if yer like? Her name is Cynthia Goodall but me ma thinks she might 'ave moved away.'

'Maybe they moved away due to the shame of it all,' Lottie suggested. 'Anyway, we wanted to invite you to luncheon at my auntie's house.'

'Me? You want me to come to your posh auntie's home?' She blinked in astonishment.

'Yes, you, Floss. She'd like to meet you.'

A big grin spread over Floss's face. 'I'll just get inside, wash me face and hands as I bin cleaning up the yard, and put on me best frock!' she said brightly. 'I ain't never met a lady before! Let alone been to 'er 'ouse!' she squealed with excitement.

Aunt Dorothea arranged for the girls to have a ham salad with plenty of slices of bread and butter, followed by a Victoria sponge that Cook had made the day before. If Cook and Alice were surprised to have another guest, who looked even more like a street urchin than Lottie did, then they weren't saying so.

The table was laid with a clean, embroidered white linen cloth. There was a small brass pot containing some pretty coloured sweet pea flowers in the midst of it and next to that a china cake stand, containing slices of the sponge and scones. Beside that, there was a small jug of fresh cream and a matching bowl of strawberry jam. The best silver cutlery, and bone china cups, saucers and plates were employed for the occasion.

Floss's eyes widened. 'Cor, Lottie. I feel like royalty being invited 'ere today!'

Lottie smiled. She would have felt like royalty herself if circumstances had been different and she wasn't sore from the bruising Oliver Steed had inflicted.

Noting her discomfort, Floss wrapped her arm around Lottie. 'Never you worry, gal, that man will 'ave his comeuppance soon enough and make no mistake about it!'

Lottie had told Floss all about her encounter with Steed on the carriage ride to the house, with Floss opened-mouthed. There were just too many shocks for her to digest. Lottie forced a smile, but felt her stomach churn inside. Meanwhile, Floss and Aunt Dorothea chatted easily with one another.

They had discovered they shared a talent for singing and Dorothea was regaling tales of how she'd wanted to sing as a young girl and had seen the finest artistes on stage at various theatres. Floss was hanging on to her every word and Dorothea was relishing in the attention. Everything here was so classy and she knew Floss must be both astounded by the elegance and confused to why Lottie had never mentioned the full extent of her background.

It had been a long time since Floss had eaten so well or drank her tea from a pretty china cup with a matching saucer. Floss was lucky to get a cup of tea from an old jam jar back at her house and then she had to share it with her brothers and sisters. Lottie was so pleased that Floss could enjoy all of this and get treated like a lady, even for a short while.

Lottie still felt so raw from what had happened and did not feel as if she were good company, so she made her excuses to leave the room.

Once in her room she could keep it in no longer and she ended up bawling her eyes out on to Dorothea's luxurious bedspread. It had been a tough day visiting the police station and she was exhausted. But, after having wiped her eyes, she felt it would only be courteous as a host to return to where her aunt and Floss were enjoying dinner.

She tried to compose herself and head back towards the dining room when she heard voices from across the landing. Auntie was allowing Floss to try on one of her old ball gowns.

'Here put this on, Floss. I'm going to take you to see someone I know in the music business.'

The cornflower blue satin gown skimmed softly over Floss's curves, making her appear every inch a lady and not a young girl any more. Her long dark hair, which usually fell loose on her shoulders, was now pinned up on her head, with soft tendrils framing her face. Her eyes sparkled from happiness. She looked like a completely different girl.

Auntie pinned a white rose she'd plucked from the vase behind her to Floss's neckline.

'That looks perfect,' Auntie said. 'Now Alice can attend to your hair and properly pin it up for you. She's a little treasure, and I'll also loan you a cape so you'll look the part,' she said proudly.

Lottie stood for a couple of minutes as she watched Floss twirl around, viewing herself in the mirror and admiring her reflection. Then Floss turned suddenly, having caught sight of her friend.

'Whatcha think, Lottie?' she asked, with a faint blush to her cheeks from the fun she had been having. 'You've not said much.'

'I think you look just like a real lady,' Lottie said.

That made Floss's day as she practised walking in front of the mirror. There was no changing her accent though, but Auntie insisted, there was no real need for it anyhow. Floss was the type of girl the public would love, just like Marie Lloyd.

Chapter Fifteen

Auntie Dorothea insisted Floss stay the night to keep Lottie company, which Lottie thought very kind of her. It wasn't until they'd bathed and were both safely tucked up in bed that Lottie allowed her feelings to spill out. 'I can't believe I'm spending the night under another roof and not my own home,' she said.

Floss nodded. 'Won't your mother worry about you though?'

'Yes, most probably but I know how angry she'll be. Ma's the sort who won't let things go. She's very headstrong whether she believes something is right or wrong and won't back down in an argument. Poor Aunt Dorothea has discovered that. Life is too short to hold a grudge against someone else.'

'So how did you come to get involved with Mr Steed in the first place? I never understood how that happened?'

'I was so very foolish, Floss, I thought Oliver was in love with me,' she whispered, fearing Auntie might wake up in the room next door. 'He kept saying I was special to him, he singled me out from everyone else.'

'Aw don't blame yerself, ducks. It can be a very consuming feeling when an 'andsome older man fancies you. And he did lead you on. It was wrong what 'e did making you fink that first time you met him at the park that his daughters would come along as well.'

Lottie nodded. 'Yes, I suppose so.'

'There's no suppose 'bout it. He lured yer and 'e lied to yer saying 'e knew your pa and he'd asked 'im to keep a watchful eye on you.'

Lottie sighed loudly. 'But I should have been more careful and not allowed him to kiss me in the first place.'

'Well maybe so, but 'ow were you supposed ter feel? You haven't long lost your pa. You were looking for love, Lottie, but in the wrong place. Now Tom, 'e finks a lot of yer.'

Lottie let out a long breath. 'Well, he won't any more when he finds out I'm soiled goods, now, will he?'

'Don't be daft. It ain't as if yer've got loose morals, it was all against yer wishes. And in any case, yer not soiled goods at all. Yer were lucky to get away from that pig!'

'Yes, I think I must have a guardian angel up there somewhere.'

Floss murmured in agreement. 'Maybe it was your pa, looking out for you. And let's 'ope the police throw the book at Mr Steed an' all.'

Lottie hoped that would be the case, but somehow she doubted it. 'Nothing seems to stick to him, Floss. I can't believe I got involved with him in the first place.'

'Well at least you've met Tom since and he's a good sort, ain't he?'

Lottie nodded while her mind focused on the young man who had come to her rescue. She knew where she stood with him and how he'd never do anything to compromise her values or beliefs. How she missed him but she could never face him right now. She felt thoroughly ashamed of what had happened to her.

By the following morning, word had been sent to Auntie from Gerald Simpkins that Oliver Steed had been taking in for questioning. As Floss eagerly tucked into several rashers of bacon and two fried eggs, Lottie felt unable to eat a thing and instead she nervously chewed at her fingernails. What would happen now? Would he deny it all? What would his family think of him being taken off like that by the police?

Aunt Dorothea glanced at her niece above her spectacles. 'Stop doing that, Lottie, you'll ruin your nails. Justice shall be served on that man at last.'

Lottie grimaced. 'It's not that, Auntie, I, above all people, would like to see justice for myself and any other young girl he's duped, but I fear for his family. His wife and daughters, how they will feel when he's carted away.'

Auntie snorted loudly in a most unladylike fashion which was unusual for her. 'The brute should have thought of that before he did what he did to you. He wasn't thinking of his wife and family then, was he?'

'I suppose not.'

'Now eat up, Lottie, we're going to take Floss around the theatres today and then I'll have a word with Mr Simpkins to see what's happened at the police station.'

'But I'm needed to picket with the girls today, so is Floss!' Lottie protested. 'I've already lost a day yesterday, they'll be wondering where I am.'

'Then Floss shall get out of the carriage and explain that both of you can't possibly help today and I shall hand her a donation to give them – that should appease them all.'

Lottie wasn't so sure, and she also worried whether, now she'd fallen out with Ma, she would stop feeding the girls at her home soup kitchen.

Floss swallowed loudly and went to snatch another piece of bread and butter.

'Mind your manners, Floss,' Lottie said, looking at Auntie.

But Auntie just smiled, 'Leave her be, it's probably a while since she's feasted like this.' Floss had melted Dorothea's heart, that much was evident, and as she'd never had any children of her own, it was obvious she saw something of herself in the girl, the part that loved to sing, dance, act and perform, and behave in a rebellious fashion – something that had been quelled by Dorothea's own father.

After visiting a group of girls at the picket line outside the factory and explaining that both Floss and Lottie would be back tomorrow, the girls reluctantly agreed that this once they were allowed time off. Lottie felt bad that she couldn't tell them the real reason behind it all, that she needed time to recover and might have to be called back to the police station for another interview about the assault.

Edie looked both girls up and down at the gate, then narrowed her gaze. 'Yer both looking posh, what's going on and whose carriage is that?'

'It's my auntie's,' Lottie replied.

Edie gulped. 'I can't understand you having to work at the factory if you come from a bit of money,' she exclaimed. 'No wonder people were calling you, "Lady Lottie"!'

''Er family fell out.' Floss butted in. ''Er Ma doesn't like 'er Auntie and now 'er pa is dead, there's no family money.'

The girls looked on as Lottie's eyes filled up with tears, but the real reason wasn't the family feud, it just reminded her being stood here that evening when she'd been speaking at the Mile End Waste and Steed had shown up. Things would never be the same again.

Mary's face clouded over and she chewed on her bottom lip.

'What's wrong, Mary?' Lottie asked.

'It's your Ma, Lottie . . . I don't know how to tell you this, but she tried to cross the picket line this morning with a couple of other women. The bosses have got through to her. She told me Mr Steed had called to her home and offered her some money to go into work and do our jobs.'

Dread seeped through Lottie's veins. How could Ma do this when she'd told her what the man had tried to do to her? Her heart was racing. 'Oh, no, not Ma, please don't say she's gone in there to work?'

'Nope,' Edie said with a big grin on her face as she slapped the palms of both her hands together. 'We gave all the women and girls who dared try getting into that place short shrift, and fair play, they listened to us an' all and turned back around for home, two of 'em have even joined us. They're all home-workers like yer ma. She asked if any of us had seen you, Lottie. Why aren't you staying at home, anyhow?'

Lottie let out a long sigh, deciding to give a version of the truth for the moment. 'I can't tell you everything, but Mr Steed is being questioned by the police and I think I'll be called to give evidence at some point, it's nothing to do with the factory – well it is in a way – he's been making advances towards me.'

Edie nodded knowingly.

''Ere, he better not have molested you!' Mary raised a fist.

Before she could have the chance to reply, Floss jumped in

and handed the girls an envelope of money, 'This is from Lottie's Aunt Dorothea for our cause,' she said forcefully.

The girls were so intent on seeing what was inside the envelope that Steed and his involvement with Lottie were forgotten for the time being. Lottie heaved a sigh of relief as she and Floss turned and both clambered back aboard the carriage. 'Thank you, Floss,' she said, as they seated themselves beside a very proud-looking Aunt Dorothea. 'If it hadn't been for your quick thinking then I'd have been bombarded by questions.'

'Fink nothing of it, me old duck!' Floss said, with a big grin on her face.

All Lottie could think about was her own mother trying to cross that picket line, after all she'd told her about how hard they'd all fought. Why would she do something like that? Unless . . . A thought occurred to her: maybe Oliver Steed had called around to the house and tried to win her mother over? Who knows what information he might have fed her. She was desperate to make ends meet and there was little money in the house now the strike was on. They lived day-to-day and only their fundraising helped the girls and women to survive.

Oh Ma, how could you? I trusted you.

Feeling betrayed she went to close the door when she heard a voice calling her name. Turning, she saw Tom standing before her, his eyes shining.

'Where are you going and where have you been?'

She shook her head as her eyes filled with tears. 'Tom, I can't speak about this right now. I have to go, I'm sorry.'

He made to grab hold of her hand, but she pulled away. How could she tell him about Oliver's attempted rape? He'd think her so foolish. In any case, she didn't have the words right now.

She left him standing there as Dorothea made the gesture for them to start moving.

'Why wouldn't yer talk to Tom?' Floss asked as Lottie sat back in her seat.

'I just couldn't. I am thoroughly ashamed that I got myself in a position of vulnerability with Oliver once again. Tom rescued me the last time. He will think I'm running after the man.'

'You nitwit,' Floss said. 'Tom likes yer a lot. He'd never think that.'

Maybe Floss was right. Lottie turned her head towards the window and thought she'd wave to him, but he was no longer there. Maybe he'd given up on her now altogether and she couldn't blame him if he had the way she'd just tried to push him away.

Still waiting to hear from the police, they made a stop off at Wilton's Music Hall, in the Whitechapel area of the East End.

'I remember this area well,' Auntie said, when they drew up outside. 'My mother and father didn't like me coming here as they thought of it as a very poor area indeed. There used to be a pub in this spot called The Prince of Denmark Tavern, it was reputed to be the first pub in the whole of London to have mahogany fixtures and fittings. It was very swanky for this area.'

'But how would you possibly know that, Auntie?' Lottie's eyes narrowed suspiciously.

Auntie tapped the side of her nose. 'Let's just say there were ways and means of getting my way about performing without my parents ever knowing about it! There was a concert room built behind the pub where I used to perform. I had my fans, of course, and even had to pretend I was a proper East Ender, I suppose it was like enjoying a secret life.' For the first time ever, Lottie noticed a faint blush spread over Auntie's face.

'Cor, yer had a beau, didn't you, Dorothea?' Floss exclaimed excitedly.

Dorothea blushed coquettishly, much like a younger woman would, then her face clouded over. 'I did indeed, but my parents found out about him. Arnie was killed in a fire here and the place had to be rebuilt. I'm afraid I never got over losing him and that's why I never married in all these years.'

'I had no idea,' Lottie said.

Dorothea smiled. 'Why would you? I doubt your father would have mentioned it. He knew very little about what happened, only that our parents ensured I kept well away from this place.' She took a white lace handkerchief from her reticule and dabbed away at her eyes.

'Who was Arnie, then?' Floss asked.

'One of the other performers.' Auntie sniffed. 'He was so funny, he could make anyone laugh.' She had a wistful look in her eyes, so Lottie changed the subject.

'So, you think Floss could get an audition here?'

'No,' Auntie said sharply, causing both girls to look at one another in amazement. 'This is soon to be converted into a mission hall, I'm afraid, its music hall days are over, but the manager here has contacts.'

Lottie blinked as they entered the hall in all its splendour with its crystal chandeliers, marble busts and paintings of cherubs on the ceilings. She'd never been inside a music hall before, but she could well imagine how exciting it must have been for her aunt in her younger days.

'Cor, Dorothea, it ain't 'alf nice in 'ere!' Floss exclaimed as she twirled round and round, staring up at the ceiling.

'Indeed,' Dorothea agreed, as if she'd been suddenly transported back in time.

A loud cough alerted them to someone stood beside them. Auntie turned and said, 'Wilfred, I'm glad you're here there's someone I'd like you to meet: Miss Floss Gittings. Floss, this gentleman is Mr Townsend.'

Floss made a mock curtsey at the man, who was well

dressed in a black suit, crisp white shirt and cravat, causing a big smile to emerge on his bewhiskered face. 'Pleased to meet you, sir!' she said, proffering a white gloved hand.

Wilfred took Floss's hand and kissed it, causing her to flush with embarrassment as she was unused to such treatment.

'Ah, Dorothea, are you bringing this young lady here as a prospective act?' Wilfred asked.

'I am indeed, Wilfred. I know this place is closing soon and will be converted into a mission hall, but you have the right contacts. Is there anywhere she could audition? I know how you always know the comings and goings of the theatre world . . .'

'I do indeed, Dorothea. I'm glad we've managed to keep in touch all these years.' He turned to the girls. 'We both walked the boards here in our time . . . Dorothea had the voice of an angel.'

'And the mischievous spirit of a little devil!' Auntie hissed behind her white gloved hand, making the girls chuckle.

Wilfred pointed to a piano at the side of the stage. 'Well first, young lady, I'd like to hear what you have to offer before I consider touting you around various music halls.'

'Understandably,' Dorothea said, holding both of the palms of her hands together as if in silent prayer.

'Shall we?' Wilfred asked.

He seated himself at the walnut encased, upright piano. 'Have you any sheet music, young lady?' he addressed Floss.

She shook her head and looked at Lottie for assistance,

who said. 'It's all right, Mr Townsend, I know the songs off by heart, if you'd allow me to play?'

Wilfred stood and allowed Lottie to take his place, as the girls ran through their entire repertoire, the one they'd used at the pub for the fundraising event.

Lottie watched Wilf's reactions nervously, but he wasn't giving anything away. At the end, he began to applaud. 'A splendid performance from both of you. I particularly loved that song, "Where Did You Get That Hat". It's such a catchy number. You have so much talent, well both of you do, but I take it only one of you wants to go on stage?'

'That's correct,' said Lottie. 'Floss is amazing, don't you agree?'

He rubbed his chin a moment and nodded. 'I think I know just the slot for her at the Paragon Theatre in Mile End. Young lady, if you could accompany me there later this afternoon, that would be a good start.' He glanced at Floss who nodded her head vigorously.

Aunt Dorothea beamed at Wilfred. 'Thank you, so much, Wilfred. I hope to return the favour someday.'

Wilf smiled. 'You have nothing to repay me for, dear Dorothea.'

Lottie wondered what he meant by that remark but said nothing of it to her aunt.

'I shall take the girls out for luncheon and return. Would you care to join us, Wilfred, if you have the time?'

Wilfred's eyes shone, making Lottie feel that he held her aunt in high esteem. 'I should like that very much, but you must allow me to foot the bill. You are, after all, doing me a favour by bringing this young lady here, as well as a favour for her. If she wins employment, then I shall be handsomely rewarded as her agent.'

'Cor!' Floss blinked. 'I've got meself an agent! Only the other week I was cutting matches and earning a pittance.'

'Believe me, young lady, you shall earn more than a pittance if I can get you a slot somewhere. That act of yours will go down a storm. You have a wonderful voice and comedic timing. You remind me of someone,' Wilf said, his eyes turning towards Dorothea.

Before Lottie had the chance to question their obvious friendship – they certainly seemed close – Dorothea explained, 'Wilfred is Arnie's brother. They had a double act together before the fire.'

Wilf nodded and smiled, but a wistful look swept over his features.

'They were known as The Townsend Twins. They went down a storm with the audience, too—'

'What 'appened the night of the fire?' Floss chipped in.

Lottie shushed her, but Wilf spoke sombrely, 'It was late afternoon and we were called off stage for a break. I'd hardly had time to drink my glass of lemonade before someone in the corridor shouted that there was a fire. I did as instructed and we all assembled outside, but when I turned to look for Arnie, he wasn't there. Later, I was to learn that he had perished in the fire along with another lad. They'd run towards the fire thinking they could help put it out I suppose, but they never made it back out.'

'And the worse part of it all,' said Dorothea, 'was I had fallen over in the rush and Arnie had helped me out of the building, then he ran back in to help.' She turned away and Wilfred held her in his arms to comfort her.

'Sssh now,' he said gently. 'Let me take you all to lunch, there are some powerful memories for us both in this place.'

Lottie nodded. 'I think that would be an excellent idea, Auntie, and later we can watch Floss audition at the Paragon, that's if you don't mind, Wilfred?'

He smiled. 'I should be honoured for such beautiful ladies to accompany me there. I can't make any promises mind, but I shall put in a good word for Floss.'

Floss grinned and Lottie noticed, behind her back, Floss was crossing her fingers on both hands. She smiled. This could be the chance of a lifetime for her.

Chapter Sixteen

When they arrived at the Paragon, Lottie heard Floss draw in a deep breath as she stepped down on to the pavement from the carriage, overwhelmed by the grandeur of it all. Wilfred was there to greet them at the foyer.

'Ah ladies, I'm glad you could make it on time.'

Lottie noticed that he gave Dorothea a long lingering look and she smiled back at him with a faint blush appearing on both cheeks as he took her gloved hand and kissed it.

Floss was wearing Dorothea's blue silk gown with a matching blue cape and silk bonnet and looked splendid. She was every inch a lady.

Lottie gasped as she drank in the décor inside the music hall. It was Oriental in character, draped in rich dark maroon velvet. In the alcoves were blue porcelain flower pots containing large fern plants. The main ceiling of the theatre had a huge gold dome, elaborately decorated with suspended brass gasoliers in all four corners of the ceiling.

As her eyes swept downwards, she took in the stage area which was very large with decorative scenery and props, framed by burgundy, velvet sweeping curtains, edged in gold brocade. It was all so very grand and breathtaking.

Wilf introduced them to the theatre manager, Mr Pemberley, a stout looking man with a bald head and black twirled moustache. Despite his austere appearance, he was very warm and welcoming.

'So, this is the young lady, I've heard so much about.' He greeted them with arms open wide.

'Yes, this is Miss Flossie Gittings,' Dorothea said, taking his outstretched hand and allowing him to kiss it. 'She has a fine voice. And my niece, Lottie, shall play the piano for her during the performance.'

'Very well,' Mr Pemberley said. He took a seat beside Dorothea and Wilfred in a row a few seats back from the stage to watch Floss perform.

Floss sang her usual routine as they thought it would be foolish to try to change something that worked so well.

Floss flaunted herself around the stage as Lottie played. Auntie had loaned her a floppy hat for 'Where Did You Get That Hat?' on which Alice had stitched a large artificial daisy.

At the end of the performance, after Floss had sung possibly the best she ever had, there was total silence. Floss and Lottie looked at one another. Lottie's heart pounded madly in expectation. What was the manager thinking? Did he like Floss's performance?

She heard some mumbling, and she looked over to the trio.

'Well done, young lady. Well, both of you,' Mr Pemberley said. 'Miss Gittings, I'd like you to start here next Monday, but you'll need to come to rehearsals beginning tonight. How does that sound?'

Floss nodded eagerly. 'Thank you, Mr Pemberley.'

For once, she was at a loss for words. Stunned into silence. Lottie rose from her piano stool and rushed over to Floss's side where she gave the girl a hug. 'Floss, I'm so pleased for you. Well done, you'll never have to return to that factory ever again. You have so much talent, the footlights are your future now, not the factory!'

Floss had tears in her eyes. 'I don't know what to say, 'onest I don't,' she said, which was more to herself than to the others.

'I'll get a contract drawn up,' Mr Pemberley said, 'which will be for three months to begin with, then reviewed pending how well you perform with regards to future work here.'

Floss nodded, she was over the moon. Afterwards, Wilfred took the three of them to a swanky restaurant in the West End where the food was delicious and the wine free-flowing. It was a dream come true, at least for one of them.

*

The following day, Lottie was back on the picket line outside the factory explaining to the girls how Floss was destined for stardom thanks to her lucky break.

'Cor! Knock me down with a feather!' Edie exclaimed, her eyes rounded like two saucers.

'Never mind about Floss, what about poor Lottie?' Mary Driscoll snapped, as if she was jealous of the girl's success.

Lottie hesitated a moment before replying, 'My auntie is calling to the police station today to see what happened yesterday when Mr Steed was brought in for questioning.

'If yer ask me I reckon they should lock that man up and throw away the key!' Edie countered. 'I got many a cuff around the ear 'ole from him! And he helped to throw away good staff like spent matches when they got that phossy jaw!' Lottie could tell that the anger was coming from what he had done to her, but she didn't want to tell the others about that. Only Floss and herself were privy to that particular information.

Mary nodded in agreement. 'What about you, Lottie? Did he ever wallop you?'

Lottie shook her head. But what he'd done to her in that alleyway was far worse.

Wanting to change the subject to ease the pressure on Edie, Lottie asked, 'Anyone tried to get over the line this morning before I arrived?'

There was a murmur amongst the girls that concerned Lottie. Then Mary said, 'If yer talkin' about yer ma, she ain't been back and don't worry about the soup kitchen neither, she is still keeping it going for us, but she says she's 'ad a word with them at the church hall and they've agreed she can set up there and they'll help her while we're all out on strike.'

Lottie smiled.

Mary studied her face. 'What's happened with you and yer ma, Lottie? You never told us why you're now living with your auntie.'

Lottie inhaled deeply and let a long composing breath out again. 'It was all over Mr Steed. She's got the impression I'd been leading him on.'

Mary's jaw slackened. 'Surely not? 'Ow come she'd think such a thing, anyhow?'

'He called to the house to see me the other day, and there was the time I lied to her saying I was at Floss's.'

Mary narrowed her eyes suspiciously. 'And where was yer during that time?'

'At Vicky Park.' She turned towards Edie. 'Remember, Edie? I told you and Floss how Mr Steed told me his daughters would be there, but when I arrived, they were nowhere to be seen.'

Edie nodded. 'She's telling the truth, Mary. A while later we were at the park after listening to Mrs Besant, and Steed showed up there with his wife and daughters. You should have seen his face when he saw us. He was like a scalded cat!'

Mary nodded, seemingly placated for time being.

Edie tugged on Lottie's sleeve of her jacket. 'I think we need to see Mrs Besant to find out when the march on Parliament will be taking place.'

When Lottie popped back to her aunt's home, she found the place in uproar. Alice was cowering in the kitchen and Cook was attempting to placate her. In the distance, there was the sound of some sort of crockery smashing against a wall.

'What on earth is going on?' Lottie looked at Cook for an explanation.

'I don't really know what's going on, miss. The mistress has been all of a temper, since she arrived back home this afternoon.'

'Leave it to me,' Lottie said. 'I'll sort it all out.'

She marched into the drawing room to see her aunt's face red with rage, her bottom lip trembling and a pulse on her neck throbbing. Her best china cake stand was smashed at her feet. She held both hands stiffly by her side, her fists clenched so tightly that her knuckles were white.

'What's wrong, Auntie?' Dorothea gritted her teeth. 'Please calm yourself down.'

Lottie turned to see a pitcher of water on the table and poured a glass for her aunt, which she handed to her.

Aunt Dorothea took several sips of water, before setting her glass down on the small wooden table beside her.

'What's wrong?' Lottie seated herself on the small leather pouffe in front of her aunt.

'You're not going to be happy about this, child. I've just returned from the police station. Mr Steed has been released without charge. They say they have nothing to charge him with, he was free to go. I'm so very sorry, Lottie. I did try my best.'

Lottie put her head in her hands. She'd been so hopeful that Steed would be put away and now nothing was going to happen at all. He had got away with it. Oliver Steed was a snake. Nothing seemed to stick to him. She looked up at her aunt and clenched her fists. 'This is so unfair. Goodness knows what he'll do next. At least I was able to get away, the next girl may not be so lucky.'

Dorothea looked at her niece with a great deal of sympathy in her eyes. 'I know, Lottie. And you're right, it is most unfair. I'm trying to think if there's anything else we can do about it all.' She shook her head.

Lottie looked at her auntie. 'I really don't know what to say. He'll do it to some other unsuspecting girl. We can't risk that.'

At that point Alice walked into the room. She bowed a curtsey at Aunt Dorothea. 'Cook said to let you know dinner will be a little late this evening, ma'am.'

Lottie wondered if this was due to her aunt's sudden outburst and smashing of the crockery, but wisely didn't say so.

Dorothea nodded. 'Thank you, Alice. Could you please bring us a pot of tea meanwhile?'

'Certainly, ma'am.'

Lottie watched as Alice departed. For the sake of young girls like poor Alice, she decided something needed to be done about a predator like Oliver Steed and she thought the answer might be staring her in the face. 'I think we need to pay Mr Steed's wife a visit. What do you think?' Auntie immediately brightened up.

Later that day, Lottie and Floss joined Edie and Mary and some of the other matchgirls and they marched to *The Link* office. Annie Besant's assistant served them cups of tea while Annie herself doled out slices of fruit cake.

'It won't be much longer now girls,' she enthused. 'The powers that be at Bryant and May have threatened legal action against me. They went to the press, writing to my newspaper to defend their factory and its conditions, saying that the dismissed girls were liars and had been brainwashed by socialist outsiders – meaning me, of course. But we have so much support that I think they'll back down by the time we get to Parliament tomorrow.' She turned to Lottie. 'What's wrong? You look as though you're worried about something. You missed one of our meetings the other day. I was expecting you to stand up and speak on behalf of the girls. It has more impact coming from one of you than it will from me.'

'I'm sorry, Mrs Besant, truly I am.' Lottie recounted how Mr Steed had assaulted her.

Annie Besant studied her for a while. 'I'm so sorry to hear of this, Lottie. Are you all right?'

'Yes, miss. I've got a few cuts and bruises, but I managed to fight him off, and my honour, thankfully, is still intact.'

Annie's eyes were full of genuine concern. 'And have you been to see the police about reporting what happened?'

'Yes, Mr Steed was arrested and questioned yesterday, but nothing came of it. So, my aunt and I are going to pay his wife a visit so she will know what's been going on. We're so disappointed that the police let him go.'

'That's preposterous!' Annie Besant said. 'Would you like me to have a word with them? I can vouch for your good name and how you'd been speaking on behalf of the girls that day.'

Lottie bit her bottom lip. 'I think maybe not for the time being, Mrs Besant. My aunt has some influence with a senior detective at the station and even she couldn't sway the situation.' The truth was Lottie didn't want to make things worse for Annie than they already were. There was a chance that she and some of the matchgirls could get arrested if they weren't careful. Some of their previous demonstrations had been quite fierce and involved scuffles in the street with the police. The last thing they needed was for any of them to be arrested, particularly now as they had the opportunity to address some members of Parliament.

*

Floss turned up at Auntie's house just before they were due to take the carriage to speak with Mr Steed's wife, the gleam in her eyes testament to how excited she was.

'I wasn't expecting to see you, Floss. I thought you'd be in rehearsals. What's brought you here?' Lottie asked.

'I was, and I am and lovin' every minute. Ain't life grand?' she enthused. 'I got a break before tonight's performance and brought you this letter from Tom.' She pushed a white envelope into Lottie's hands.

'You saw Tom?' Lottie looked hopeful, but then remembered why she was keeping her distance. 'You didn't say anything to him about what happened to me, did you?'

'No, 'onest I haven't. He came over to me house early this morning. He's worried about you. Says 'e hasn't seen you for days and yer ma won't tell 'im where you are.'

'I just don't know what to say to him, Floss. I honestly I don't.'

'Look, just tell him the truth. You ain't done nothing wrong, gal. You told me he'd already seen Steed off that time when he took you to that house that was up fer sale. He knows what the man is capable of. He could even go to the police and tell them what 'e saw that time when Steed manhandled you.'

That was something Lottie hadn't thought of. She immediately brightened up. 'Thanks, Floss. Stay and have a cup of tea, will you, while I answer this letter and maybe you can pass it on to Tom for me?'

Floss nodded, a beaming smile on her face. 'It will be a pleasure, m'lady!' she bobbed a mock curtsey, and both girls laughed.

*

Lottie knew where Oliver Steed lived as he had told her where it was, describing it as 'the largest in the area'. Whether he had been boasting or one day intended her to call there, she just didn't know. But when they arrived at the house at the end of a lane, surrounded by high privet hedges, she felt a pang of guilt at the thought of upsetting his family. Auntie just patted her hand and told her it needed to be done. Steed's wife had a right to know.

They left the coach in Bill's capable hands while they walked up the path and rang the doorbell. They waited for several moments until finally the door was opened by a young maid, who blinked several times when she saw them both stood there. Lottie had no doubt if she'd arrived alone she might not have been allowed access, but Aunt Dorothea looked like a woman of means in her fine attire.

'Can I help you?' the maid asked, furrowing her brow.

'We're here to speak with Mrs Steed,' Dorothea said, in a cordial fashion.

The young girl's eye began twitching suspiciously and said, 'I'll just go and check to see if Mrs Steed is expecting you. Who are you?'

'No, she is not expecting us. I am Miss Perkins. I have

come to see her on a personal matter, which should be of great interest to her.'

The girl nodded and turned to speak to her mistress. A couple of minutes later she returned. 'She says to come this way.' She led them into what looked like a drawing room. The house was nowhere near as big as Dorothea's home, but it was a lot bigger than most in the area.

Mrs Steed stood framed against the window and she turned as they entered. 'Please sit down, ladies,' she offered. If she was surprised by their visit then she wasn't saying so, and she showed no recognition whatsoever of Lottie since their last encounter, which she put down to the nice clothes she had got from her aunt.

'Tea?' she offered, but Dorothea dismissed the idea with the wave of her hand.

'No thank you, what we have to say to you is of more importance than a cup of tea.'

Mrs Steed quirked a quizzical eyebrow then said, 'Please do sit down, ladies.'

Dorothea and Lottie exchanged a glance and seated themselves on the sofa while Mrs Steed chose to sit in a flowered armchair near the fireplace. The fire wasn't lit as the weather was so warm.

'And how can I help you? I've already donated to two charities this week.' She patted her mouth with the palm of her hand as if stifling a yawn.

'I'm sure donating to various charities must be tedious for you,' Dorothea began, 'but let me tell you, we are not after any money.' She cleared her throat. 'We've come to tell you about your husband, Oliver.'

Lottie noted how much thinner Mrs Steed appeared and wondered if it was due to the suspicions she had that Oliver was poisoning her. The woman stiffened in her chair and narrowed her gaze at the pair of them.

'I can assure you that what my husband does is no concern of *yours*,' Mrs Steed answered sharply.

'Oh, but it is, when it involves my niece, Lottie, here.' She kept eye contact with Mrs Steed, then raised her voice a notch. 'Did you know, Mrs Steed, he has been wooing her and telling her you were about to die? He's her manager at the factory and he's been behaving in the most inappropriate manner.'

'Outrageous.' she replied with disgust. 'Oliver would never do such a thing and with a factory girl of all people. So, you're one of the girls we saw at the park that day?'

Lottie nodded. 'I am, ma'am, yes.'

'There's more.' There was no stopping Dorothea now. 'The other evening he cornered her in an alleyway at the Mile End. He tried to have his way with her.'

Mrs Steed stood. 'Get out of here the pair of you with your pack of lies!' she spat, pointing to the door. 'My husband is a good man. I will not believe it. I shall get a solicitor on to you both!'

'Would you believe me if I told you I have a suspicion he might be poisoning you . . . making you sick . . .' Lottie offered.

For the first time, a look of doubt swept over Mrs Steed's face. 'Nonsense. I have been ill, yes, but—'

'No, I don't believe you have,' Lottie said firmly. 'He wants you out of the way. He has designs on me, and I'm not the first young woman to turn his head, either. By the way . . .' Lottie reached into her pocket and brought out the silver locket that Oliver had gifted her, dangling it in front of the woman's eyes. 'Do you recognise this?'

Mrs Steed narrowed her eyes. 'Where did you get that?'

Realising what she had to say was going to hurt Mrs Steed, but needed to be said, she took a deep breath and said, 'Your husband gave it to me as an engagement present.'

The woman's jaw dropped. 'An engagement present? That's the locket he gave me for my birthday last year, it went missing a while ago.'

'And that's because he obviously stole it from you and gave it to me.'

'Well if he did so, why would he give it to a commoner like yourself?'

Ignoring the woman's slur, she said, 'Because he said he wanted to marry me. He told me you were going to divorce him, but now "you're dying" and "there's no more that can be done for you".'

Mrs Steed let out a loud, piercing scream that brought

the maid running from the hallway, and she collapsed on the floor with a heavy thud.

As the maid attended to her, kneeling on the floor and fanning her down with a newspaper, she looked up at both of them with accusing eyes and said, 'What have you both said to her?'

Lottie dropped the offending locket and they beat a hasty retreat out of the house and down the path to the awaiting carriage with Auntie holding on to the bottom of her skirts to stop herself from tripping over, her bloomers on full view, it should have been a comical situation, but Lottie found it sad and upsetting, nevertheless.

'Let us get out of here,' Auntie said. 'At least the woman knows the truth now.'

'She knows it all right,' Lottie said, 'but whether she'll believe it is quite another matter.'

Maybe Mrs Steed had no idea that her husband had been arrested by the police at all, it certainly seemed that way to Lottie.

Chapter Seventeen

Annie Besant took the deputation of fifty of the girls to march on Parliament the following day. Even Floss came, despite her not having to worry about finding work at the factory any more. The girls marched arm-in-arm across the embankment towards the House of Commons and they chanted things like 'Rights for Matchgirls!' and 'A Fair Wage for a Fair Day's Work!'. The mood was one of, almost, jubilation and Lottie was relieved; finally their voices were about to be heard and listened to by people who could actually change things for them. They passed people along the way who wished them well, stopping to shake their hands or pat them on the back. At the back of Lottie's mind though were the poor girls amongst them who weren't so jubilant, their heads lowered and covered by scarves, and she realised how difficult it must have been for them to attend today.

Once inside the Houses of Parliament, they got to speak to three MPs – one was Charles Bradlaugh, who had previously spoken about the matchgirls in Parliament, as well as Samuel Montagu and James Bryce.

Bradlaugh, who Annie pointed out to them, was very clean shaven and middle-aged looking, Lottie noticed. His skin seemed very smooth and his hairline was receding a little. He wore a black neck tie and had a serious manner about him, but then again this was a very serious matter. What could this man from a different, more privileged background, do for them all? Lottie wondered. She'd heard of him before but not the other two members of Parliament.

Annie ushered the girls to seat themselves on wooden benches before she addressed the issues involved in the strike, her role in it and the matchgirls' demands.

'When I wrote "White Slavery in London" and it was published in my newspaper, Bryant and May threatened me. They wanted to sue me for libel. They were most affronted by this story as it brought to the public's attention a matter they were oblivious to. After all, who would have thought a young woman may have died simply to give you the right to strike a single match?

'It was easier for that lot at Bryant and May to turn their anger on the girls rather than address the real issues here. The powers that be at that factory set up a smoke screen to cloud the real issues at stake!' She held her chin high in a determined fashion. This was a woman who was used to public speaking. A woman who could give a voice to those that had no voice of their own. Lottie admired her so. She took in a breath and let it out again, her heart beating madly as she settled down to listen to what else Annie Besant had to say. She continued, 'That's why we are here today. We need to negotiate! Although we've had the support of Mr Bradlaugh and he's been an intermediary of sorts, we need to sit around a table and speak with the management at Bryant and May.'

Floss looked at Lottie and whispered. 'Cor! What a woman! Go, Annie! Go!'

'Sssh,' Lottie said, though secretly she felt exactly the same way as Floss. It was exciting to hear the woman speak. She was a social activist of her time. A woman who got things done and things changed as a result.

'Mr Theodore Bryant would probably agree to a meeting as I know him to be fair-minded,' offered Bryce, who had spoken for the first time. 'What does he have to say about this issue to you all?' he addressed this to the girls.

'Nothing!' Edie snorted. 'He ain't said a thing, we heard nothing at all from him!'

'Well, what would you like him to do for you, ladies?' Mr Bryce continued.

'We need to be able to breathe properly for a start,' Mary replied. 'The fumes from the phosphorus are so thick – that's the reason some girls become unwell. They get headaches and jaw aches an' all.'

Annie continued. 'The problem is, gentlemen, these girls

have to eat in the same place they work, often eating the food they have brought with them at the stations they work upon. Often if they wish to wash their hands before eating, the foremen will prevent them from doing so. The white phosphorus is being ingested with their food. And if any of the girls complain about the pain in their teeth which are rotted from the phosphorus, they get lambasted by the foremen who rough them up. A cuff around the ear is quite normal practice at the factory. The girls aren't even allowed proper toilet breaks, and they get their wages docked for the most trivial of errors.'

She summoned one of the girls over from the bench by wagging her index finger. A girl of around fifteen years old wearing a headscarf, who had been sitting quietly, until now, rose to her feet and walked to Annie's side. Her movements were slow as she shuffled her feet, head lowered. Annie Besant continued. 'The poor girls who carry boxes on their heads are becoming bald as their hair is worn away like Emily, here, who has been brave enough to come to Parliament today to show you the result of working for Bryant and May.' Annie looked at the girl and nodded.

Trembling, the girl undid her scarf, revealing an almost bald head, apart from a few sparse tufts of hair on her crown. There were audible gasps from the MPs. The shock induced had the desired effect. They appeared highly uncomfortable by the girl's presence.

'Thank you, Emily.' She glanced at the girl and smiled, and she left to join her friends on the bench, retying her headscarf as she walked slowly. The other girls were used to seeing such sights but the MPs were not. 'Would any of you like to see your own young daughters with bald patches on their heads?'

The three MPs glanced at one another, mumbling. Annie carried on driving her points home. 'You see, gentlemen, they've learned to keep quiet about what goes on at that factory and to not complain to management. Because if they complain, they get even worse treatment than before. We need Mr Bryant to stop listening to his foremen and meet with us instead!'

A ripple of applause and cheers went up from the girls in the gallery.

When it had died down, the MPs conferred amongst themselves. It was impossible for Lottie to make out what they were saying, but there was a lot of nodding and shaking of heads.

Finally, one of them spoke. 'The company's actions are insufferable!' Bradlaugh exclaimed. 'No one should be subjected to these conditions. You ladies have the support of the public and from my understanding are very well regarded. Your industry is a crucial one; people will always need matches. Mr Bryant cannot afford to lose his whole workforce. Neither can he afford to lose the support of the general public,' he said with solid conviction. There were murmurs of agreement amongst the girls and Annie was nodding her head. None of the matchgirls had ever been inside an intimidating environment such as this to witness a Parliamentary debate before. Only Annie had been here previously. It was exciting beyond belief to behold.

Mr Montagu, who had been listening to the proceedings quietly throughout, spoke, posing a much larger question, 'You have brought some distressing conditions to our attention today here at Parliament. A legal bill can take a long time to pass through Parliament. What is to be the answer to this? A socialist revolution? I am aware of your close involvement with William Morris and others, Mrs Besant.' He peered at her over his spectacles. Was he expecting another 'Bloody Sunday'? Lottie wondered.

'If Mr Bryant refuses to meet with us, we will take the right course of action appropriate towards the situation,' Annie replied passionately. 'After all, it is better to remain silent, better to not even think, if you are not prepared to act. But we will not be battered into silence, hence we are all prepared to act on this issue. Every last one of us here today. I don't think the girls are asking too much to be able to eat their meals away from their workstations, to be able to wash their hands regularly without being hit by the foremen. Nor do I think it too much to allow the girls to be able to return to work who were fired after only speaking the truth, who did so to give a voice to those who didn't have a voice of their own. They are all brave young women in my book, and it is our duty to look after their welfare!

'The girls tell me they would like to be able to go directly to management with any complaints they have in the future, without a need to see a foreman first, where they are most likely silenced with slaps. If their complaints had been acknowledged to begin with, many would have been saved from the effects of phossy jaw, and they would all still be alive to tell the tale! Unfortunately, young Cassie Bowen died after succumbing to the condition and the powers that be turned their backs on her plight, not even offering to pay for her funeral! If it wasn't for her friends' fundraising attempts, her parents wouldn't have been able to bury their own child!'

'And without your help too, Mrs Besant!' Floss shouted out, then slunk down in her seat, realising she should keep quiet. But Annie just looked at her and nodded with a smile.

She lifted her arm in the air and the girls cheered loudly, causing the MPs to look at one another in wonder once more. They'd never encountered a woman like Annie Besant before, that much was obvious. She was a fierce flame to be reckoned with.

Annie then turned her back on the MPs and marched towards the girls, who had been hanging on to her every word. She turned to face the men on the other side of the room. 'Today, we fight for the health of these girls and women, but tomorrow, we want to see fairness for all. Tomorrow we'd like to see a common room, which can be a refuge for those who have never had a proper home to begin with.

Somewhere where there is a welcoming atmosphere and camaraderie. Trolleys to transport the boxes of matches so the girls don't have to lose their hair by carrying them on their heads. If necessary, gentlemen, we are ready for a revolution! What else do the poor have to lose when they have absolutely nothing to begin with? I still hold out hope there will be a gradual improvement at the Bryant and May Factory. I propose a peaceful path to set the slaves free from bondage and that the girls get a chance to change the world. That they go about setting up a movement where we all care for one another and where we give rather than take. A better place for these girls and that should begin right now!'

The applause in the chamber was spontaneous from all as it echoed off the walls. Mr Montagu ran his finger under the stiff looking, starched collar of his shirt. Annie had obviously made a big impression. The matchgirls had a voice at last and, most importantly of all, their concerns had been listened to and understood.

*

Lottie reflected on recent events as she walked away from Mrs Besant's office. In total they'd been on strike for three weeks, though it had seemed more like three months. Mrs Besant had said the London Trades Council had met with Bryant and May and big changes were afoot. At that meeting, the company had given in to almost all the women's demands: there were to be no more petty fines or deductions from the women's wages and, best of all, the women would have a rest room where they could rejuvenate and relax while on a work break. Something many of the women didn't get to do at their overcrowded homes. Also, they would not need to eat at their stations any longer, thereby lessening their risks of contracting phossy jaw. Trolleys to transport the matches were also employed so the girls didn't need to carry heavy boxes on their heads. Obviously, Annie's mention to the MPs about their own daughters' hair had hit home.

'Cor, Lottie. This has been a triumph for us gals!' Floss announced proudly. Seeing her friend's face, she continued. ''Ere what's up, duck? You look like you lost a penny and found a farthing?'

Lottie twisted her lace handkerchief in her hands. 'I know I should be jubilant like the rest of you, but it really gets my goat that I've fallen out with Ma over Mr Steed and the brute has been allowed to get away with it all.'

'Yer won't rest until something is done about it, I can see that,' Floss said, as she put her arm around Lottie's shoulders.

Lottie shook her head. 'No, I won't.'

'A couple of good things have come out of this, Lottie, mind. You're now reunited with that lovely auntie of yers and I've now got a job on the stage, which is all I've ever wanted.'

Lottie smiled and she hugged her friend. 'I am so pleased

for you, Floss. You'll never need to walk back through those factory gates ever again!'

They continued to walk in the direction of home, and as they turned the corner, Tom came hurtling towards them.

''Ere hang on, Tom me old son, where yer going in such a hurry?' Floss asked.

His face reddened when he saw she was with Lottie. She wondered what he really thought of her.

'Sorry. I've got an interview for a job at *The Star* newspaper. I took your advice, Lottie, and sent them a couple of my stories.'

Lottie had never seen him look so excited. His eyes gleamed with hope and expectation. 'I'm really pleased for you, Tom,' she said. But somehow, she couldn't find the words to tell him the real reason she had kept away from him.

'I called over to your house a couple of times to see you, but your ma said you weren't in. I thought you'd have got back to me by now, especially after the letter I sent you, your reply told me nothing at all – how you were or anything, only that you were fine and staying with your auntie.' He studied her face for any answers that might be forthcoming.

Lottie lowered her head. 'Sorry if my reply was short, Tom, I've had a lot on my mind lately.'

'For 'eaven's sake you pair, yer need to chat to one another. Arrange to meet up somewhere later!' Floss rolled her eyes.

'Yes, how about it, Lottie? I won't be long at the interview, if you want to wait in that coffee shop there?' He pointed. 'I should be with you within half an hour.'

Lottie looked at Floss for confirmation. 'What yer waiting for, gal?' She turned to Tom. 'Us matchgirls have got something to celebrate today, Tom. Bryant and May has accepted all the conditions we laid down. Up the workers!' she cried, punching the air with her fist.

'I'm so pleased for you girls,' Tom said, grinning broadly. 'So, how about it, Lottie?'

Lottie smiled. 'Yes, I'd like that, Tom. And good luck with your interview.'

He pressed some coins into the palm of her hand. 'Order yourself a coffee and a sticky bun or something, whatever you fancy. You're going to bring me luck. I just know it.'

She nodded. Then she watched as Tom went off with a spring in his step.

'I need to get back to the theatre,' Floss said. 'Hope you have a nice time with Tom and don't do anything I wouldn't do, will yer?' She laughed heartily.

'Bye, Floss.' She kissed her friend on the cheek and made off towards the coffee shop, uplifted at having encountered Tom.

She crossed the busy road, which was peppered with costermonger carts, carriages and the odd omnibus here and there. As she weaved in and out of the bustling crowds, she located the coffee tavern Tom had mentioned. She peered in through the misted window to see there were several sets of tables and chairs inside, each laid with a pretty linen table cloth with a small vase of flowers in its centre. To the other end of the tavern was what looked like a long, wooden counter. She took a deep breath and entered the steamy room, which smelled strongly of coffee beans and cinnamon.

A lady wearing a black high-necked dress with white frilled collar and white starched apron approached her. 'Can I help you, miss?'

'I'm looking for a table for two, please,' Lottie said nervously, never having been anywhere of the kind before. 'Someone will be joining me shortly.'

'I see, miss. Would you like a table by the window?'

'Yes, please.' Lottie could see it was an excellent spot to view the world passing by, so many people busy doing their own thing. Being cooped up at the factory all day long she hardly, if ever, got to see this side of life.

The waitress took her jacket and then returned to the table to ask if she'd require something while she waited. She had never even tasted a cup of coffee before, tea was customary at home, or sometimes her mother brewed ginger beer, but apart from those drinks and the odd drop of milk if there was enough to go around, and water, this was something totally new. There were a lot of coffee taverns springing up due to the influence of the Temperance Movement, who encouraged people to abstain from the evils of drink.

'I think I'll have a cup of coffee, please.'

'Which sort would you like, miss? We have Brazilian, Costa Rican, French . . .'

In her ignorance, Lottie didn't know there was more than one type of coffee. 'I think I'll try the French please.'

'Is it the first time for you to try a cup of coffee, miss?' the waitress asked kindly, as if realising how confusing it must be for her.

Lottie nodded, shyly.

'I won't make it too strong for you then, it is an acquired taste. There's demerara sugar on the table – that goes well with it.' She winked at Lottie.

Behind the counter, Lottie heard a loud whirring noise and realised the waitress was grinding the coffee beans. It produced a most delicious, pungent aroma, like nothing she had ever smelt before.

She heard an overhead bell tinkle, and three men wearing bowler hats and pin-striped suits, swept in, speaking in an excited fashion. The other waitress, who was a younger woman, seemed to know them and directed them to a table not too far away from Lottie. She heard them say the words, 'The Scoop of the Year' and 'justice'. Then one of them went on to speak about 'the factory' and she realised they were talking about Bryant and May and the fact the powers that be had given in to the Matchgirls' Union, and Annie Besant had been the driving force behind it all. It was evident that these were newspaper men from Fleet Street.

Before Lottie had the chance to hear any more, the waitress brought her tray to the table. It contained a high-necked, cream-and-brown earthenware pot with a long, curved spout and a matching cup and saucer, with a small jug of cream. The pot was similar to the teapot used at home but a different shape entirely.

The waitress smiled as she left the table. Lottie wondered what she thought of a naïve East End girl frequenting this part of London. Gingerly, she poured the coffee into the cup, not knowing whether she should have put the cream in first or not, but it seemed more sensible to add it last of all, so she did. She leaned over to inhale the delicious aroma.

She took a sip and immediately recoiled. It wasn't what she expected at all, it was much stronger than the weak straw-coloured tea her mother served at home. Then she remembered what the waitress said about the special sugar and she spooned two teaspoons into the cup and stirred well. She took a sip and this time was satisfied with the taste. She was just about to think what she could do about contacting her mother, when the overhead bell tinkled again and Tom came marching in, his eyes lit up and alive.

'Well, did you get the job? You weren't long – the waitress has only just brought my coffee to the table.'

He drew out a chair and seated himself opposite her. 'Unfortunately, not. Well, not as yet. I was given an assignment by the editor that I have to complete before tomorrow morning. It could possibly go out in the evening edition of the newspaper! He said it will be better than any interview. He likes my stories, but he wants to see if I can write non-fiction.' He shook his head. 'All that time I spent walking here thinking I was going to get some interview and he immediately gives me an assignment and not long to get it ready for copy at that!'

'Well, if you ask me it sounds as if you already have the job, Tom.'

He smiled. 'Maybe. But what on earth can I write about, Lottie?'

'Please don't tell me you can't think of something, Tom, when we matchgirls have just had the most marvellous news?' She leaned in to speak to him in a conspiratorial tone. 'See those men on that table just over there?'

He nodded. 'What about them?'

'I think they are newspaper men from Fleet Street the way they're talking. They came in here in a state of excitement about "The Scoop of the Year". They mentioned Bryant and May and the matchgirls.'

'By Jove, Lottie, I think you're on to something there. If you wouldn't mind, I could interview you and maybe Floss too. Didn't the whole thing kick off with her and two other girls to begin with?'

'Yes, that's right. And don't forget, you could say you were an on-the-spot-reporter too as you saw us raising funds in

Floss's aunt and uncle's pub. There are loads of things you can say.'

'Wonder what I can headline the article with, though?' He tapped his chin as he mulled it over.

'How about something with "flames" in the title?' Lottie suggested.

'Yes, that's an excellent idea, Lottie.' His eyes gleamed at her idea.

At that point, the waitress arrived at the table. 'I see your young gentleman has joined you,' she beamed at them both, causing Lottie's cheeks to burn with embarrassment. Tom had never been referred to as her 'young gentleman' before. She glanced over at him to see he was also smiling, not worrying one jot how anyone perceived them. 'Now, what can I get you?'

'I'll have the same as *my young lady*, please.' He grinned at Lottie, who shyly looked away.

'That's French coffee then, sir. Anything else?'

Tom glanced over at a glass display unit at the counter containing several sorts of cakes and pastries. 'What cakes do you have on offer, please?'

'I've got custard slices, Chelsea buns, jam tarts, apple pies on today.'

'How about a custard slice, Lottie?'

She brought her gaze to meet with his, he was teasing her with his eyes. 'Yes, please.'

'I'll have two of those then, please.' The waitress nodded and went off to see to the order. 'What were we saying, yes, you said to mention the word "flames" in some way. How about, "A Fierce Flame Burns Brightly"?'

'I really like that, Tom. How about adding to it, "The story of Annie Besant and the East End Matchgirls"?'

'So, it becomes, "A Fierce Flame Burns Brightly: The Story of Annie Besant and the East End Matchgirls"?'

'Yes, I like that.'

'Me, too.'

'And don't forget if those hacks at that table over there are going to write their own stories about it by tomorrow, they won't have the same inside knowledge as you!'

Tom looked at her intently, 'Oh Lottie, you are such a clever person. I could kiss you right here, right now!'

Lottie's heart almost skipped a beat. Tom had only ever pecked her on the cheek up until now.

They spoke excitedly about Tom's non-fiction article for several minutes until the waitress brought Tom's coffee pot, cup and saucer, and the custard slices topped with drizzled icing over to them on a silver tray. Before even pouring his coffee, his brown hazelnut eyes clouded over. 'Please, Lottie.' He reached across the table and took her hand in his. 'What's wrong? Why did you stay away from me?'

She swallowed and to her horror, felt tears prick the back of her eyes. 'I . . . I . . . haven't been . . .'

'Take your time, dear Lottie. I didn't mean to upset you.'

She swallowed again as he topped up her coffee cup and poured one of his own, adding cream to both cups. He offered her the sugar bowl and she heaped a couple of spoons into her coffee and then he followed suit.

She stirred it and took a sip, then set down her cup. 'It was the evening I spoke to the crowd at the Mile End Waste site . . .'

'Go on,' he urged.

'I was about to leave, everyone had packed away and we were in the process of going home, when I felt a presence behind me. It was Oliver Steed . . .'

'The man you had the altercation with on the pavement when he took you to that unoccupied house, right?'

She nodded, lowering her head. 'I'm afraid so. I had avoided him ever since then, but I had no way of knowing he had been watching me. No doubt hiding amongst the crowd and he chose his moment to pounce carefully. This time he was more antagonistic than ever. He pushed me up against the wall and tore at my clothing . . .' To her horror she felt her shoulders shudder as she convulsed with grief at what had occurred.

Tom extracted a clean white handkerchief from his top pocket and handed it to her. 'I am so sorry, Lottie, but did he—'

'Rape me, do you mean?'

He nodded, his eyes full of concern for her plight. 'Yes?'

She shook her head. 'No, I managed to fight him off

before he almost got his way. It scared me to death even more than the time you caught him manhandling me, as this time he had torn off some of my underclothes.'

He squeezed her hand. 'You poor thing. Have you been to the police?'

'Yes, my Aunt Dorothea took me. They brought Steed in for questioning, but they released him. They said they didn't have enough evidence to nail him.'

'Then what about mine?' he asked. 'I could go there and make a statement about what I saw happen a few days before.'

'Would you?' Tom's face appeared misty before her tear-filled eyes. But for the first time in ages, she felt hopeful.

'Yes, of course. We'll go there after we finish here.'

She lowered her voice. 'Have those men behind me noticed I've been crying?'

'I very much doubt it, Lottie. They're too full of *bonhomie*, back slapping and congratulating one another to notice their surroundings. I have to make sure that article is a good one that gets *The Star* noticed. It's a relatively new newspaper and if I could do that, it would make a good impression on the editor. It looks as if that lot over there want to claim the glory for whichever paper they work for.'

Lottie guessed it was either *The Times* or some other well-established broadsheet. She dabbed at her watery eyes with the handkerchief and went to hand it back to Tom, but he held up the palm of his hand and shook his head. 'No, you keep it, a little gift from me.'

She studied the edge of the handkerchief. 'But it's got your initial embroidered into it, T for Tom, it belongs to you.'

'From now on, whatever I have belongs to you too, Lottie.' He took both of her hands in his. 'You're not alone in this, once we've finished here I'm coming with you to the police station.'

'But what about your newspaper article?' she protested.

'No problem there, I'll interview you on the way. I've seen a lot of what you girls have accomplished anyhow from the picketing at Fairfield Road to the soup kitchen your ma set up. The street demonstrations, the talks, everything. I'm going to make it the best story of my life!'

Lottie turned around in her seat and looked at the three men behind her, wondering if they realised they had such competition. Tom was up and coming. The world was his oyster if he could get in with *The Star*.

They ate their pastries and finished their coffees. Lottie needed to use the toilet and was pleased there was one in the yard at the back of the tavern, which even had one of those new modern flushing systems. Some of the public toilets in the area were highly questionable and stank to high heaven. Afterwards, Tom insisted on hailing a hansom for them to get to the police station.

'I feel guilty you're spending all this money on me, Tom.

How can you afford to?' He tapped the side of his nose. 'Let's just say I've got a mystery benefactor.'

Lottie had no idea who he was referring to, but decided to say no more about it, then on their journey to the police station, Tom asked her plenty of questions which he noted down in a small leather-bound notepad.

'My word, you're like a real newspaperman, Tom,' she said proudly.

'That's me, Lottie. Tom Harking, Reporter for the People!' He announced with a big grin on his face.

By the time the cab had weaved in and out of all the traffic and arrived at the police station, Tom had got all the answers he needed. When they alighted, he helped her down from the cab and escorted her into the police station.

When they got to the reception desk, it was empty. Tom called out, 'Hello, is anyone there?'

A uniformed sergeant appeared at the desk. 'Anything I can help you with, sir, miss?'

'Yes, my good fellow. We would like to speak to . . .' He turned to Lottie. 'Who did you say the detective was, Lottie?'

'Gerald Simpkins,' she said, and waited respectfully. She felt Tom was being a little too lighthearted and almost mocking the desk sergeant.

He cleared his throat. 'I'll just go and have a word with him now.'

Lottie turned to Tom when the policeman had vacated the desk. 'Why are you speaking to him like that?'

Tom chuckled, 'They need to remember their station.' He chuckled. 'Pardon the pun! Besides, if I was like a little church mouse I wouldn't have nabbed that interview at the newspaper, now, would I?'

Lottie supposed not.

A couple of minutes later, the sergeant returned with Gerald at his side. 'Ah Lottie, it's you. Would you both come through to my office?'

They followed the detective into his room and took a seat each opposite his desk. 'I'm glad you called as I have some excellent news for you,' he said, seating himself. He took a quick glance at Tom. 'Are you going to introduce us?' It was as if he was gauging whether Tom should be present while he discussed official matters with Lottie.

'This is my friend, Tom Harking, Mr Simpkins. I am happy for him to be here.'

'Very well.' The detective cleared his throat. 'A young woman has come forward claiming that Oliver Steed accosted her in the alleyway the other evening. She was unharmed, but thankfully, recognised him from the match factory. This will add weight to your case.'

Lottie sat twisting Tom's handkerchief on her lap. 'But nothing happened the last time I made a statement,' she protested. 'How do I know it will now?'

'Because you have my word,' Gerald said kindly. 'I've not long sent out some men to arrest him and bring him back in for questioning, so if you can hang on here I'm going to sort out an identity parade in the yard for you, and the young girl, to see if you can spot the man who accosted you both. If you choose the same man it will add a substantial amount of weight to this case.'

'But I know who he is!' Lottie snapped.

'Yes, I know you do,' Gerald said. 'But it would help us if we see you make a formal identification and if you both pick out the same man it will all strengthen the case.'

'I have some information that might help, too,' Tom chipped in. 'I'm a *good* friend of Lottie's and I witnessed an altercation in the street where he accosted Lottie a few days previously.'

'Even better.' Gerald looked like the cat that had got the cream. He glanced at Lottie. 'There's still something wrong, what is it?'

'I'm really concerned that he's been poisoning his wife from things he's told me. My aunt and I went to see Mrs Steed, but she'll have none of it.'

'Don't you worry, we'll see if we can find out more about that. I'm sorry you've been put through this, Lottie. And when the judge has thrown the book at him, he won't get his job back at Bryant and May, believe you me!'

For the first time in a long while, Lottie felt relief flood through her. Gerald kept them both there for another couple of hours while he took a statement from Tom and brought in the other girl, who Lottie knew in passing, though she was a little younger. The girl, Connie Murphy, Molly Murphy's eldest daughter, looked a lot paler than Lottie remembered, and she guessed it must have been down to the trauma Steed had put her through.

Lottie gave her a big hug. 'He did the same thing to me too, Connie. We shan't let him get away with this.'

Connie smiled, her feelings of relief palpable in the air.

Eventually, a Black Maria drew up outside the building, and Lottie heard Steed being bundled into the station and shouted at by a policeman. It was obvious he'd resisted arrest by his yells of protestation, but Lottie and Connie were safely on the other side of the wall, in Mr Simpkins' office and even if Steed's shouts upset them a little, he could no longer touch either of them ever again.

Outside in the yard, several men were lined up, and one at a time, Lottie, Connie and Tom had to pick out the offender. It was Lottie's turn last of all, and she deliberately stood in front of Oliver Steed and glared at him. His face was red and his eyes bulged with pure hatred towards her. 'That's the man!' she pointed. 'The man that tried to rape me!'

'You little whore!' he shouted.

Lottie shivered, but she stood her ground. 'That's the man who lied and said he knew my father. The man who promised to take care of me. The man who tried to seduce and then rape me, a young girl not much older than his very own daughters. And I can't prove it, but he's been poisoning his wife, I'm sure of it!'

Steed spat at her feet and Gerald Simpkins led Lottie away. 'You did very well, young lady. I want to get you away from here as he's not a very nice man at all. I don't want you to hear all the things he's been saying about you.'

Lottie froze. 'What things?'

'Never you mind.' The detective's face clouded over. 'When it comes to court you shall have your say.'

Lottie swallowed. Who knew what horrible things Steed had said about her?

Once back inside the office, Tom looked at her. 'What's wrong, Lottie? Did that man upset you?'

Lottie nodded. 'It's not just that, but Mr Simpkins said he's said some terrible things about me.'

'Aw, sit down.' Tom ushered her to a chair. 'That's normal practice, he's probably been to see a lawyer and they're trying to discredit your evidence. But they haven't banked on you and Connie both speaking up, and me, too.'

Tom's remark made Lottie feel a bit better. Gerald Simpkins entered the room. 'Tom is perfectly right,' he said. 'Don't worry, we have enough evidence to nail him. Now, how about a nice cup of tea?'

Connie, who was sitting huddled in the corner with a blanket around her shoulders, nodded gratefully.

As they waited for the tea to arrive, a young constable entered the office and spoke to Mr Simpkins. 'Sir, the search team discovered several interesting items at Steed's home which might tie in with the suspicions of poisoning,' he said. Trembling, he held out his hand which cupped a small silver lidded bowl.

'What's that?' the detective asked.

'It's a sugar bowl, sir. I think this is where he was hiding the arsenic in amongst the grains of sugar.'

Gerald Simpkins forehead furrowed into a frown. He approached the officer and lifted a silver spoon from the dish allowing the sugar grains to fall from the spoon into the dish. 'That's entirely plausible. Please mark it up as "possible arsenic" and for goodness sake, get it out of my office as we're about to have a cup of tea. I wouldn't want anyone here succumbing to accidental poisoning. We'll look into it. What made you think he might have been sprinkling it in the sugar, Henderson?'

P.C. Henderson's face flushed pink. 'I . . . er . . . found a key on his person when we went to arrest him. I asked him what it was for and he replied that it was for a medicine cabinet. When I unlocked the apothecary cabinet, there were several strange items in it. I've transported it whole and the items contained within to the station, sir. There were other things like a glass syringe, pieces of rope and a dagger. Several things in fact that made me think the young lady . . .' He glanced at Lottie, ' . . . the young lady's suspicions were correct about him poisoning his wife.'

The detective raised his eyebrows. 'Is his wife aware of any of this?'

The policeman shrugged his shoulders. 'She mentioned the young lady and her aunt had paid her a visit, but she hadn't believed them. She's just arrived at the station now, sir. I've put her to sit in the interview room until you have time to see her. She's in shock as you can well imagine.'

The detective nodded. 'Thank you, Henderson.'

P.C. Henderson nodded, seemingly pleased with himself that his decisions had passed muster with his superior and he left the room.

Lottie mulled things over as a lady dressed in black, sporting a long, white apron, appeared with a tray of tea. Poor Mrs Steed obviously had no clue to her husband's activities. Lottie cringed at the thought of it all. Still, at least now Aunt Dorothea would be pleased that the ball was rolling at long last – she couldn't wait to tell her later.

Chapter Eighteen

It was another couple of hours before they left the police station. Tom insisted on staying with Lottie, but he used the time wisely by writing the outline of his article for *The Star* newspaper. Out of five applicants, one would be chosen for tomorrow evening's edition. Whenever he had a question, he asked Lottie her thoughts on various issues to do with the strike.

Finally, Gerald Simpkins told them they were free to leave the station.

'So, what's the outcome then?' Tom asked finally, going into journalist mode.

Gerald glanced at Lottie as if seeking her permission whether to discuss such matters in front of her. She nodded her approval. 'Oliver Steed has just been informed he has committed the offences of attempted rape on one count and attempted murder on another. He will be up in front of the judge in the morning and charged with both offences,' he told the pair of them. His kind eyes twinkling as if pleased that justice would be sought at last. Connie was sleeping in the corner and murmured in her sleep. 'Don't worry, I'll tell her the same when she awakes properly,' he said. 'Looks like she hasn't slept in days and needs it. I might allow her to bed down here for the night if she has no place to go. Her home life is difficult. Her poor mother gets knocked around a fair bit from what she's told me.'

'Yes, Mr Murphy gave his wife a right shiner when she went on strike with us. He blamed her for not having enough food in the house,' Lottie replied, as she looked at the girl who had gone back into a deep sleep. Lottie remembered how Connie's poor hardworking mother was knocked around from pillar to post, while her brutish father cared more about drinking at the ale house rather than putting food on the table for his family. 'She's probably safer here until her mother goes back to work. Then Mr Murphy might not be so angry with her ma.'

The detective rubbed his chin, thoughtfully. 'Your Aunt Dorothea will be pleased to hear the news?'

'Yes, of course, and thank you, Detective,' Lottie said, smiling.

'Please pass on my regards to her.'

As they left the police station and hailed a hansom, Tom asked, 'What are you chuckling about, Lottie?'

'I'm just thinking Aunt Dorothea doesn't realise just what a desirable older woman she is!'

He furrowed his brow. 'I'm sorry. I'm not quite with you?'

'She has two gentlemen who are enamoured by her – the detective and the agent from the theatre!'

'Oh?' Tom said, helping her into the cab that had just pulled up at the kerb. 'Allow me to escort you home and then I'm off to see Floss to catch her before the curtain goes up tonight, if she can spare me the time! If I could I'd take you to see her performance, we'll have to do that one evening!'

Lottie settled herself into her seat and Tom followed suit. 'Yes, I'd love that, thank you.' She glanced across at him. 'I think you're burning to write that article, Tom!'

'Pardon the pun, but I'm all fired-up, m'lady!' He tapped the carriage roof to indicate they were ready to go. Meeting Tom again was bringing her good fortune and it was about time her luck changed for the better.

When Lottie arrived back at her aunt's house she burst into the drawing room. 'Great news, Auntie! Bryant and May have given in to the matchgirls' demands and not only that, Mr Steed has been picked out in an identity parade by three of us after being arrested today!' Dorothea's eyes were downcast and dull as she sat in the chair, her hands curled up into balls on the arm rests.

'What's the matter, Auntie, aren't you pleased for me?'

'It's not that, dear child, of course I am, but there are other pressing matters afoot. Please sit yourself down.' Aunt Dorothea stood and walked towards her. What was going on here? She felt her aunt's arms around her and inhaled that familiar lavender scent, as she led her to a chair.

'Auntie? What is it?'

Her aunt reseated herself and sitting forward in the armchair said, 'It's your mother, Lottie. Your sister, Bessie, called here earlier to let you know that your mother has had an accident.'

'No, no, not Ma?' She blinked as she digested the news, then bit her knuckle. Finally she asked, 'Is she all right?'

'I'm afraid she slipped on a tiled floor at the church hall while carrying a pan of soup. Fortunately, the soup wasn't too hot or else she would have scalded herself, but she slipped on something and fell backwards and hit her head. She's unconscious. Your sisters are taking care of her. Mrs Munroe from next door has been over to help and a Mr O'Hara has been lending a hand as well.'

Lottie nodded. 'I must go to her, Auntie. I haven't even had the chance to tell you what the bosses have agreed to and that we're to recommence work tomorrow. It should be good news for me, but now it's far more important I take care of Ma and the kids. They all need me.'

'Very well,' Aunt Dorothea said. 'But first, I'm feeding you up. You'll be of no use to any of them if you faint. How have you been gone so long, anyhow?'

'I'd meant to tell you it all when I came in but I've been taken aback by the news about Ma. They brought Mr Steed in for questioning a second time, and there was that identity parade, I picked him out alongside another young girl he'd accosted just afterwards. Also, my friend, Tom, made a statement that he'd seen him mistreat me recently on another occasion. He was also able to pick him out in the line-up. Mr Steed is up in front of the judge in the morning. They also found evidence at his home that he'd been poisoning his wife.'

'That poor woman . . .' Auntie's eyes glazed over.

'Oh, and Mr Simpkins was asking about you, Auntie . . .'

'Was he now?' Her face flushed pink like a young girl's. 'Never mind about him,' she said, skilfully changing the subject, 'I'll get Alice to bring you a plate of fish pie and a nice cup of tea, then I'll come over to your house to see what can be done.'

Lottie smiled. Although her aunt and mother had never been bosom buddies, it was nice to know she still cared.

It was late by the time they arrived in the deserted street and Lottie and her aunt arrived the back way. There was a lantern burning brightly in the scullery, Lottie noticed Shamus O'Hara standing there in the shadows of the flickering light.

'Lottie, I'm so glad you've shown up. Mrs Munroe is upstairs with your ma, I managed to bring her home from the church on the back of my horse and cart. I wish I had the money to pay for her to go to hospital, but I did manage to pay for a doctor to come here earlier.' His voice was full of concern.

Lottie removed her cape and bonnet and her aunt followed suit. 'Thank you, Mr O'Hara. How is she now and what did the doctor say?'

'She hasn't really regained proper consciousness I'm afraid, although she is murmuring a lot. I thought I heard her say your name . . . The doctor said he thinks that's a good sign and for us to keep talking to her. He said we should have some idea within the next day or so if this is temporary or not.'

She looked at Shamus's heavily hooded eyes and for the first time realised how desperately in love he was with her mother. She laid her arm on his forearm. 'Thank you for all you've done, Mr O'Hara. Are the children all right?' She felt it right to hold her composure; she wouldn't want the children to see her fall apart.

He nodded. 'Aye, the boys went to bed a couple of hours ago, but the girls are still chattering away in their bedroom, they're too upset to sleep no doubt. T'will be some time before we know if your ma is out of danger.' He wiped away a tear on the back of his hand.

'Well, I'm here now and we'll get Ma well again,' Lottie said, with a note of determination in her voice.

'Yes, we will do that,' Auntie agreed. 'Is there anything I can do?'

'Boil the kettle, we'll have a nice cup of tea,' Lottie said, trying to sound lighthearted, 'and please make a cup for Mrs Munroe and Mr O'Hara, they're probably in need of one. I'm going to take over and spend the night by Ma's bedside.'

Ma looked so pale by the candlelight as she lay in her bed. She could hear the soft sounds of her shallow breathing, evidence she was very much alive. Lottie looked at Mrs Munroe, who shook her head, tears in her eyes.

Lottie reached out and gently touched her mother's hand. 'Thank you for being here, Mrs Munroe. Has Ma showed any signs of regaining consciousness yet?'

Mrs Munroe slowly shook her head. 'I've been here since before the doctor arrived, Lottie, and she hasn't shown much sign of coming to apart from mumbling your name and one or two other words I couldn't understand.'

Lottie nodded. 'You go down stairs for a break, Mrs Munroe. My aunt, Dorothea, is brewing up tea. You can have it in the scullery with Mr O'Hara. Were the kids all right?'

Mrs Munroe stood to give Lottie her seat. 'Yes, I bathed the boys in the tin bath in the yard and put them to bed, then

Shamus read them a story till they fell asleep, but I think the girls are still awake. You go in to see them for a couple of minutes, while I hang on here.'

Lottie smiled and popped across the landing to Bessie and Daisy's room. When they saw her, they jumped out of bed and rushed to her side. 'Oh, Lottie, where have you been? We've missed you so!' Daisy said.

'And our poor ma just won't wake up after that bump on her head,' Bessie added.

'Now, now. I'm here to help, never fear.' Lottie soothed, as she hugged the pair of them. 'I was silly to stay away after that quarrel with Ma. I am going to stay by her bedside all night and shall be here when you get up in the morning.'

Seemingly happy with that proposal, the girls smiled. 'Now into bed, the pair of you,' Lottie scolded in a joking tone.

The girls snuggled down top-and-tail style into the single bed they shared and closed their eyes, appearing delighted their elder sister was back home where she belonged.

Lottie relieved Mrs Munroe of her duties, then sent her to have that cup of tea, while she took her mother's hand and spoke softly to her as she sat in the armchair beside her all night. Her mother's hand was slightly calloused and rough, a testament to how hard she worked for her family.

Lottie had drifted off to sleep and by the time she awoke, sunlight was streaming in through the bedroom window, and a light breeze billowed the curtains. She rubbed her stiff neck, then went to pour some water from the jug in the corner into its matching bowl so she could wash her face. She glanced at her mother whose eyes were open and looking at her, blinking.

'Lottie! Oh, my dear Lottie, I knew that you would come 'ome,' she said faintly.

Tears ran down Lottie's cheeks as she rushed to her mother's side and took her hand as she knelt by the bed. 'My prayers have been answered. Please, Ma, take your time, you've been unconscious for hours. I feared you might d—'

'Sssh, child. I'm still alive, you won't get rid of me that easily, gal. My throat feels parched, please may I have a glass o' water?'

Lottie assisted her mother to sit up and propped up her pillows behind her. 'You can have as much water as you like, Ma. I'll go and get you some, then I'll ask someone to sit with you while I fetch the doctor.'

It would cost money of course, and since the strike, there was little money around, but Lottie knew Aunt Dorothea would gladly offer to help. She found her aunt downstairs seated, with her head resting on the kitchen table, but there was no sign of either Shamus or Mrs Munroe.

Her aunt stirred and looked up as she entered the room. Then she stretched and yawned. Blinking she asked, 'Is everything all right, Lottie?'

'Yes, Auntie, Ma is awake. Can you please take her a glass

of water? I'm going to run to get the doctor to ensure she is going to be well again.'

Her aunt stood and nodded. 'I'll stay with her until you return and I'll see to the children too.'

'Where's Shamus and Mrs Munroe?'

'I sent Mrs Munroe home a couple of hours ago. I thought it pointless we all stay awake and she has that son of hers to take care of since he's been out of work. Shamus is in the yard chopping sticks.'

'I'll ask him to take me to get the doctor on his horse and cart.'

'Good idea,' Auntie said, as she got ready to go upstairs with the glass of water.

'Oh, sorry. I wasn't thinking . . .'

'What's the matter now, child?' Auntie's eyes rounded like two saucers.

'It's just I remembered how you and Ma don't see eye to eye.'

'Stuff and nonsense!' Dorothea said sharply. 'She needs my help. I'm sure after all she's been through she won't give one furry fig!'

Lottie almost collapsed with laughter at her aunt's haughty behaviour and funny quip, but she stifled her giggles, there would be time for laughter later when she knew all was well with Ma.

Doctor Maguire arrived later with his black leather Gladstone bag. He removed his hat as he entered Ma's bedroom.

By now, she was sitting up in bed in a clean night gown having had a little wash and her hair restyled into a bun by Aunt Dorothea. Lottie released a sigh of relief, realising it meant that both women must be getting on well with one another.

The doctor took his time examining Ma, then asked, 'Any headaches or feelings of nausea, Mrs Perkins?'

'No. I feel fine, Doctor, just a little shaken, that's all.'

'And what year does it happen to be?'

'It's 1888!' Ma answered with great aplomb. She took pleasure in answering all the doctor's questions, passing the examination with flying colours.

When the doctor had departed, her ma looked at Lottie. 'What happened to Shamus?'

'I think he's still downstairs, I'll bring him up a little later.'

Auntie's hands flew to her face. 'Oh goodness me, no.'

Lottie and Ma looked at her in a curious fashion. 'And what would be so wrong in Shamus coming upstairs to visit me in me own 'ome, Dorothea?' Ma asked.

For a moment, Lottie feared that Dorothea was looking down on the relationship, but instead, she smiled. 'I was just thinking it might be bad luck for him to see you up here before you both wed!'

'Wed!' Ma gasped. 'Where did you get that idea from?'

'Shamus told me himself, he said if you recover he's going to ask you again to marry him.'

Ma opened her mouth and closed it again.

'Well, he did ask you some time ago, Ma!' Lottie exclaimed.

'But I can't. I was widowed less than a year ago, it wouldn't be seemly.'

'Stuff and nonsense!' Dorothea said, sticking her chin in the air. 'Being lonely for the rest of your life isn't going to bring my brother back. Those children need a father and you need someone to care for you. Now we'll say no more about it, except for one thing . . . Do you have feelings for Shamus?'

Ma nodded slowly. 'Yes, I think I do.'

'Then when he asks you, we shall arrange a nice wedding and you can have the reception back at my house, understood?'

'Yes, Dorothea.' Ma beamed.

Life was too short, Lottie knew that herself. She was so pleased that Ma was feeling so much better that she'd almost forgotten something.

'Crikey, I need to get to the court. Mr Steed is in the dock this morning!'

'What's all this?' Ma asked, her face suddenly changing from a happy one to one of angst.

'Mr Steed was arrested by the police yesterday, Ma. He also accosted another young girl. The detective, Mr Simpkins, said they've pushed to get him into court quickly as he's a danger to young women and of course, there's now evidence he tried to kill his wife.'

For a second, Lottie thought Ma would faint from the shock of it all, but when she'd closed her mouth, she said, 'I am so sorry I doubted you, Lottie. You're a good girl. To think I allowed that man in this house and believed his word over yours.'

'He was very plausible and charming, Ma. Also, he was one of the bosses at the factory. I shouldn't have lied to you either, so that fall out was partly my fault.'

'Come over here,' her mother said. Lottie leant down and kissed her mother's cheek. It was so good to see Ma back in the land of the living once again.

Chapter Nineteen

Mrs Munroe came to keep an eye on Ma while Shamus took Lottie and her aunt to the court to watch what happened to Mr Steed. Auntie had sent her carriage back the previous evening and, as they were short on time, Lottie said she'd just have to 'rough it' on the horse and cart. Secretly, Lottie thought by the smile on her aunt's face, she found it quite an adventure to bob up and down on the cobbles in all her finery on Shamus's cart. She got some strange looks from folk on the way to the court; she was like the Queen of Sheba bouncing up and down on the cart along the streets.

When they arrived at the court, which was part of the police station, Shamus helped the two women down from the back of the cart on to the pavement outside.

He pushed back his flat cap on his head to look at Dorothea. 'Thank you, ma'am, for having a word with Freda for me.'

Auntie smiled. 'Stuff and nonsense. That woman would

say yes to you, anyhow. Anyway, I think if you choose your time wisely all shall go well.'

He nodded with a big smile on his face. Lottie had never seen him looking so happy. 'And I hope all goes well for you, Miss Lottie,' he added.

Lottie thanked him. They watched him take his seat atop his cart and ride off back to Lottie's house.

'I think he'll make your mother a fine husband,' Dorothea said.

For the time being, Lottie had more on her mind than her auntie's matchmaking, and she gulped as she looked up at the grey stone building before her. As they entered, Gerald Simpkins was already waiting for them.

'What kept you both?' he asked. He appeared a little anxious and edgy.

'We must apologise, Gerald,' Auntie said, 'Lottie's mother had an unfortunate accident and the poor girl has been up with her all night long until she regained consciousness this morning. Poor Lottie hasn't even had a bite to eat as yet.'

Gerald ushered the pair into his office and sent for a pot of tea and a plate of biscuits. Lottie could hardly eat a thing, but she knew she had to, to give her strength for what was to come. Connie was still at the station from last night, still in the same poor ragged clothing, a blanket wrapped around her petite frame, but at least her face looked like it had seen soap and water. She munched happily on a biscuit while Gerald told them what was about to happen.

'After reading out the two charges of attempted rape and the poisoning of his wife, the judge will ask Oliver Steed whether he pleads guilty or not guilty. He has employed a lawyer, so we're expecting him to plead not guilty. If he does that then there will be a trial where you ladies will be required to give evidence, I'm afraid.'

Lottie felt sick to the pit of her stomach. 'Is Mrs Steed here this morning?'

'Yes, for obvious reasons we are keeping her in another room,' Gerald explained. Lottie's stomach churned with the guilt at how she'd allowed herself to be manipulated by the man while his innocent wife was neglected at home. Of course, now she could well see in hindsight that it had all been a ruse. His wife didn't misunderstand him at all, in fact, she probably knew him all too well.

Aunt Dorothea reached out and touched Lottie's hand. 'Are you all right, child?'

Lottie nodded with tears in her eyes. 'I'm just thinking what an idiot I was to fall for that man's charms.'

'No, not an idiot, Lottie,' Auntie said wisely, 'just an impressionable young girl, like poor Connie there.'

Connie looked at them wide-eyed and carried on munching her biscuit.

Lottie supposed her aunt was right about that.

The time came for them to enter the court and, feeling a little revived from the tea and biscuits, Lottie took her place in the court alongside Auntie and Connie. The corridor was full to bursting with people waiting for their court cases to be called, some in ragged or garish clothing, as in the case of some of the prostitutes. There were a couple of policemen at hand to order them to behave while they waited.

Several people, she did not recognise, were already at the court. One was a bald-headed man who had several papers in front of him. 'That's Mr Montgomery-Smythe,' Gerald explained, 'He's Steed's lawyer.' Behind him was a young man who was scribbling something in a small notebook, which reminded her of Tom. He appeared to be some sort of reporter. The public gallery was decked out with all sorts of men and women who had come to see the court cases of the day as if they were public entertainment. Some had even brought food with them. It wouldn't have surprised Lottie if they started to throw rotten cabbages and squashed tomatoes around the place, like at the old music halls if the audience wasn't pleased with the act. A thrum of collective chatter bounced off the walls.

'Shame on them.' Auntie sniffed. 'You'd think they'd have something better to do than to glare at the misfortunes and misdeeds of others!'

Lottie had to agree with her. It was a form of entertainment for the rabble – she guessed there were few in the court who really needed to be there. Then she saw someone seated on the other side: Mrs Steed with her head lowered and clutching a lace handkerchief in her hand. Lottie swallowed hard. It was all about to come out in court.

There was a deathly silence as the judge took his seat at the wooden dock, presiding over them all, as heads turned to look his way. 'Cor! Is that the beak?' Connie blurted out, breaking the silence.

'Sssh, girl,' Dorothea chided.

Lottie smiled at the girl and nodded. She wanted Connie to feel as comfortable as possible: she was a little younger than herself and didn't seem to have much in the way of family support at all.

Steed was escorted into the dock by two police officers. He stood there with a sullen expression on his face, the rings beneath his eyes testament to the lack of sleep he'd got overnight. His clothing was dishevelled, probably from having spent the night in a police cell instead of his comfortable bed back home, Lottie thought. He had lost that privilege, at least for the time being.

'Oliver Steed,' the judge began in a sombre tone of voice, 'you have been brought in front of this court on two counts of attempted rape and one count of attempted murder. On July tenth you wilfully pursued a young lady at the Mile End area where you grabbed her, ripped her underclothing off her person and tried to engage her in the act of sexual intercourse. Then when the young lady tried to fight you off to keep her honour still intact, you were disturbed by two people close by. That very same evening, you then pursued an even younger girl in the same area, but she was fortunate that you were caught in the act and she managed to get away. As a result of these heinous acts, evidence was found in your home that you have been poisoning your wife for the past few weeks, in small amounts, granted, but with a view to making her ill so you could carry on with your unseemly pursuits. But that poisoning could have led to her death . . .'

There was a loud gasp in the court. Lottie turned to see Mrs Steed had fainted and one of the policemen who was in attendance was trying to rouse her.

Steed just stood there, staring ahead as if oblivious to it all.

'Has anyone got any smelling salts?' the judge asked.

A woman in the gallery called out and a small bottle was passed along and waved under Mrs Steed's nose. Slowly, she regained consciousness and sat up.

'Would you like to leave the court, Mrs Steed?' the judge asked.

'No, most certainly not,' Mrs Steed answered. 'I shall be all right.'

The judge cleared his throat and carried on. 'Now, where was I? The poisoning could have led to the demise of your wife, Mr Steed. And with regards to both girls, if you hadn't been disturbed I am convinced that one or both would have been raped. On the first account of attempted rape, how do you plead?'

'Not guilty, m'lud,' Steed said, his eyes icy-cold, not the same eyes when Lottie had first met him.

'And on the second count of attempted rape, how do you plead?'

'Not guilty, m'lud.'

'That's it,' Lottie whispered to her auntie, 'he's going to deny everything!' She felt so downcast.

'On the third count of attempted murder, how do you plead?'

There was a long pause, you could have heard a pin drop in the court house. Lottie held her breath.

'Guilty, m'lud!'

Lottie could hardly believe her ears. She looked at her aunt, who appeared just as shocked as she did. 'What does this mean?'

Aunt Dorothea shrugged.

'In view of the fact that attempted murder carries a life sentence and attempted rape does not, then I see no point in putting these ladies through a trial if the prisoner will not get to serve any greater sentence because of it.' The judge then turned to Steed. 'Oliver Steed, you are fortunate in that your wife did not die as a result of your actions. So, as a consequence, I am going to order that you remain in prison as you present a danger to society and that you remain there for all the days of your life.'

Lottie gasped. It was a result at least, even if he wasn't

being charged with attempted rape, he would get to serve the remainder of his life behind bars.

'Take him away,' the judge said, and then he banged his gavel ready for the next case.

'He's lucky the judge didn't order that he be hanged,' Dorothea snorted, as she stood to leave the court.

Lottie felt weak from exhaustion when she returned back home. Ma was sitting at the scullery table peeling spuds when she walked in.

'Ma, what on earth are you doing there?' Lottie was astonished.

Shamus was looking on and smiled and said, 'I did try to stop her, Lottie, but she said she needed something to keep her mind off proceedings and what you were going through in that court this morning.'

'So, what happened then?' Ma looked up at Lottie and Dorothea.

'He's being put away for attempted murder, but he denied the attempted rapes, unfortunately.' Dorothea sniffed.

'But it doesn't really matter as he's being put away for life, so it wouldn't make any difference anyhow,' Lottie added. 'It wouldn't have added to his sentence.'

Ma put down her knife and wiped her hands on her pinafore. 'Let's all have a cup of tea, shall we?' She made to rise, but

Dorothea laid a hand on her sister-in-law's shoulder. 'Stay put, Freda. I'll attend to it.'

'Very well, there's a slab of fruit cake in the cupboard, we can all have a slice of that. And Shamus, for goodness sake sit down, you're making the place look untidy.'

Dorothea chuckled. 'You sound like a married couple already.'

Ma smiled. 'He proposed this morning and I accepted.'

'Then we shall all make it a celebration, Ma,' Lottie said.

'Congratulations!' Dorothea said, sending a wink in Shamus's direction.

Shamus's face reddened, but Lottie could tell he was pleased as punch that her mother had finally accepted his proposal.

They were all enjoying a nice cup of tea as the ladies discussed the up-and-coming nuptials, where the couple could wed and where they might live as Shamus also owned a house, when there was a knock on the back door. Before Lottie had chance to answer, Tom burst in with a wide smile on his face.

'Guess what?' he yelled, so full of enthusiasm that he forgot his manners to acknowledge the party.

'I've absolutely no idea whatsoever,' Lottie said, feeling a little affronted at the intrusion.

He took a deep breath before saying, 'My article about the end of the matchgirls' strike has only been chosen by the editor for this evening's edition!'

Lottie ran towards him and hugged him. 'I'm so pleased

for you, Tom. I think this might well prove to be the scoop of the year!'

'Well done, Tom,' Ma said, proud as if it was one of her own sons who had won the honour. 'Sit down and have a cup of tea with us, we have several things to celebrate today!'

'We have indeed,' said Dorothea, as she looked at him over her gold-rimmed spectacles. 'Young man, you haven't even asked Lottie what happened in court today!' She gave him one of her stern looks that Lottie knew only too well.

'I'm so sorry, Lottie,' Tom said, removing his flat cap. 'I was just so excited, I wanted to tell you immediately.'

'That's all right, Tom,' Lottie said softly. 'Did you manage to interview Floss afterwards?'

'I did indeed, and as she was at the heart of it all to begin with, I think that might be why my article was chosen by the editor. Two of the others had tried to present the same sort of article but it was mine he chose!' Tom's eyes were shining brightly, like two polished diamonds. 'Now enough about me, what happened in court today?'

'Mr Steed is being put away for life for the attempted murder of his wife, but not for the attempted rapes, unfortunately.' She let out a long breath. 'I know it won't much matter as the sentences would have run alongside his attempted murder charge, but it would feel more like justice for me and Connie if he'd admitted it. I just want him to own up to what he did to us both, that's all.' She swallowed hard.

'Never mind, pet,' Ma said, 'drink your tea before it gets cold. God's not sleeping, let him mete out any vengeance. That man won't get any luck for it, you mark my words.'

A cold shiver ran down Lottie's spine even though it was a warm day, Ma's words chilled her to the core. *Vengeance is mine, sayeth the Lord.*

They all remained chatting until the boys came inside, they'd been out playing pitch and toss in the back alley.

'Any cake left for us, Ma?' Freddy shouted, as his twin followed close behind.

Ma stood and smiled as she ruffled their hair. 'Aye, maybe if you wash your face and 'ands, you pair. An' I've got some homemade lemonade for you. I need to speak with you both any'ow, and your sisters.'

Bessie and Daisy came into the house about ten minutes later and Ma gathered her clan together. Shamus discreetly stood by the door and Aunt Dorothea and Lottie remained quiet as Tom tactfully went and sat in the yard.

'You all know how Mr O'Hara, Shamus, has been calling on me these past few weeks?' Ma began.

They all nodded. Bessie and Daisy exchanged surprised glances with one another. 'Yes, Ma,' Daisy said.

'Well, we've taken a liking to one another,' Ma continued, 'and now your father is no longer around, it's nice for me to have some company. And Shamus's wife died some time ago, so he's been a bit lonely . . .' She let out a long breath as if to prepare them all for the news.

'Are you getting married, then?' Freddy chipped in.

Ma smiled, her young son had made it easier for her than she ever imagined. 'Yes, we are, Freddy. How do you all feel about that?'

Freddy jumped up and down excitedly. 'Wahey! I like it a lot – now I can get to ride on Shamus's horse and cart and help him every day. I like his horse, Dobbin!'

Shamus smiled.

Davy just sat there and muttered something under his breath, kicking his heels. He'd come around eventually, Lottie knew he would. Bessie and Daisy were very happy about it all. 'Ma, we can help make your wedding dress!' Bessie exclaimed. Daisy nodded excitably.

'Thank you, girls, though I won't want anything fancy at my age and definitely not in white!'

Ma looked at Dorothea. 'Thank you for being so understanding,' she said.

Dorothea smiled and nodded with tears in her eyes. 'I just want to see you happy, Freda. It's all I've ever wanted. Mama and Papa were foolish to cut off Albert from his family. He married for love and he had everything in you. And I was very foolish to argue with you. It was over something and nothing, I realise that now. Will you forgive me?'

'Of course,' Ma said, as she walked over to Dorothea to give her a big hug. 'And I hope you'll forgive me too for not making things up with you sooner. Pride is a silly thing, it pays a high price.'

Dorothea nodded with understanding in her eyes. 'Of course you're forgiven, Freda.'

Ma nodded. 'And thank you for taking such good care of me daughter,' she whispered.

'It was a pleasure, Freda. Lottie has become quite the young lady and I hope from now on you and all the children will visit whenever you're able.'

'I'd like that very much, thank you. And you, Dorothea, are welcome here in our humble home, any time at all.'

The women drew away and nodded. They were finally singing from the same hymn sheet and that gladdened Lottie's heart.

Later, when everything had settled down and Ma and Dorothea were putting the children to bed, Tom and Lottie went outside for a walk in the direction of the factory.

Standing on the corner of Fairfield Road was a young boy selling copies of *The Star* newspaper. 'Come and get your evening extra, all about the end of the matchgirl strike!' he shouted. 'Come and get it 'ere!'

Tom flipped a ha'penny in the boy's direction. 'Thanks, guv!' the boy replied. 'Scoop of the year that is!' He handed Tom the folded newspaper.

'Yes, I know,' Tom said. 'I know the person who wrote it!'

The boy looked at him as if he didn't quite believe him.

'It's true,' Lottie said, 'Tom, here, is the journalist who wrote that article. Take a look, it says, "Written by Tom Harking".'

The boy's eyes eagerly scanned the front page. 'Cor, love a duck, it does say that name an' all!'

'There you are, Tom,' she said, 'you've impressed someone there!'

Tom unfolded the newspaper and read the title, '"A Fierce Flame Burns Brightly: The Story of Annie Besant and the East End Matchgirls" by Tom Harking.'

'I'm so proud of you, Tom.' She leant in close to him as he put his arm around her waist.

'And I'm proud of you too, Lottie Perkins.' He said and hugged her close.

In the background, stood the factory with its chimney stack, towering high above them like some monumental tower from a far-off castle in a fairy tale. Tomorrow, the girls and women would walk through the factory gates once more, and the chimney would puff out clouds of sulphurous smoke, but now there would be changes afoot. It wouldn't be the same as before, now the workers would have rights, and their health and safety issues would be addressed. They had been listened to at long last.

Lottie found herself short of breath as Tom swept her up in his arms and kissed her deeply. The newspaper boy rolled his eyes, mumbled something and moved on to find another pitch to sell his stack of newspapers, clearly not impressed with such a sudden display of passion. But Lottie didn't care. Nothing could spoil such a perfect day.

Tomorrow, it would be old news – today's papers would be used for some other purpose. Today, though, it was the headline. Everything about this day was headline news to her. Lottie's heart beat a loud tattoo and her feelings for Tom burned like a fierce flame. As the sun set behind the factory, they kissed one another with a fiery passion called love.

Epilogue

December 24th, 1888

Shamus O'Hara and Freda Perkins had just wed at the registry office and Lottie had waved them off as they sat in Dorothea's carriage on their way back to her house. The rest of the family, including Tom, followed in a couple of hansom cabs. The light was fading fast as darkness approached.

'Ma looked the happiest I've seen her in a long while,' Lottie said.

'Yes,' Dorothea answered, 'and you two look quite happy yourselves.'

Lottie smiled. Ordinarily, she would have been embarrassed that attention was drawn to them as a couple, but now she was used to being with Tom and everyone knowing about it.

Before Lottie had a chance to say anything, Tom said, 'Oh, we are, ma'am, and I plan to marry this girl someday.'

Lottie's heart thudded a strong beat beneath the new dress Auntie had got especially made for her for the wedding.

Dorothea smiled, then looked at Tom sternly over the top of her glasses. 'How old are you now, young man?'

'Eighteen and a half.'

'Old enough I suppose.' She sniffed. 'And what are your prospects for the future?'

'Well, I'm doing well at *The Star*. The editor has said if I carry on like I'm going then one day he'll make me a senior reporter.'

Auntie nodded with a big smile on her face. 'I suppose you have plenty to write about with all that "Jack the Ripper" business still going on?' She sniffed loudly. 'A prolific killer who has yet to be caught? Most women in the area are afraid to go to sleep at night and I can't say I really blame them!'

'Yes, ma'am. We are kept on our toes, that's for sure. He's a slippery character. There are so many theories going around at the moment, there's even talk he might have fled to the continent or New York.'

'Let's pray that someday he will be safely locked up, but preferably swung by the neck from the nearest gallows.' Then she turned her attention to Lottie. 'And what about you, Lottie?'

All the talk of Jack the Ripper sent a shiver coursing down Lottie's spine. It wasn't a subject she cared to dwell on, and she and her work colleagues were taking extra care not to be out alone after dark – it just didn't bear thinking about. Swallowing, she said, 'Well, I don't think I'll be staying at the factory much longer. It was a job I needed at the time and even though conditions are vastly improved since the strike, I shall look elsewhere in the New Year.'

'Too right you will be leaving that place, I have plans for you, young lady,' Aunt Dorothea said.

'Pardon, Auntie?'

Aunt Dorothea tapped the side of her nose. 'All shall be revealed in good time, my girl!'

Lottie and Tom glanced at one another in amusement.

As the cab rattled across the streets of London, Lottie watched people dashing hither and thither, getting ready for their own little Christmases in their own little worlds and she counted herself as fortunate to have her family, and especially her boyfriend, Tom.

When they arrived at Auntie's house, the party was greeted by Alice and Cook, the house was wonderfully warm and a lovely spread of roast chicken, brined ham and vegetables beneath matching tureens was laid out on the table in the dining room. Freddy and Davy ran to gaze at it in awe and began picking away at a bread dinner roll between them.

'Mind your manners, boys!' Ma shouted after them.

'Leave them alone, Freda, let them enjoy themselves. I don't mind at all!' Dorothea shouted.

Ma's smile lit up her eyes. 'You know, I've had you wrong all these years, Dorothea, you're not stuffy nor stuck up at all!'

Dorothea chuckled and leaned over to kiss Freda on the cheek, then, glancing at Shamus, said, 'Now you look after this lady for me, Shamus, she's a very special person, indeed!' Shamus beamed and wiped a tear away with the back of his hand.

'Aren't you the soft one,' Freda joked.

'You're all I ever want and more, my love,' Shamus answered as he held his new bride close to him, taking her hand in his.

There was a loud rap at the door and Alice dashed off to answer it, while Cook started handing out glasses of sherry to everyone.

Alice returned and looked at Dorothea. 'There's a lady here to see you, ma'am,' she said, looking puzzled.

'Now, whoever could that be?' Dorothea said, with a twinkle in her eyes as everyone looked around at one another with blank expressions on their faces. 'Well, show her in Alice,' Dorothea declared.

All eyes were on the dining room doors as Alice returned with a familiar figure in close proximity behind her.

Lottie opened her mouth to say something, then closed it again. Tom though had a huge smile on his face as if he was in on some sort of secret.

'Hello, Mrs Besant,' Lottie said, as Annie smiled at her and nodded. Then Lottie turned towards her aunt and Tom. 'What's going on?' she blinked.

Auntie stepped forward to greet Mrs Besant, warmly

taking her hand and leading her into the room. Cook handed her a glass of sherry, which she gratefully accepted. Then Dorothea turned towards the room. 'Mrs Besant has kindly agreed to take Lottie on at *The Link* offices where she will become her assistant!' Dorothea proudly announced.

Ma clasped her hands together in delight and Lottie just stood there unable to take it all in.

Annie stepped forward so she was facing Lottie. 'As my assistant, you shall attend all my meetings and take notes for me, you shall have to learn shorthand of course. Tom knows all about that as a reporter, don't you, Tom?'

'Yes, ma'am, and thank you for all you've done for me, too,' he said.

Lottie looked at him blankly. 'Sorry, I'm not following you, Tom?' It was as if someone had written part of a story where she didn't quite understand the plot.

'Lottie, it was Mrs Besant who was my benefactor and mentor, she put a good word in for me at *The Star* which enabled me to be accepted for an interview. Remember it was you who told me she might help, so I went to see her.'

'Tom, you are too modest, if you hadn't been such a good reporter you wouldn't have got that job, and what a fine article you wrote about the strike, too!' Annie said with conviction. 'I only gave you a nominal sum to help you on your way and you made good use of it! You've already paid it all back!'

It was beginning to make sense now, how Tom had been

able to treat Lottie to coffee and cake at the coffee tavern that day.

'That's wonderful,' Lottie said when she found her voice.

'So how about it?' Annie asked. 'Would you like to come and work for me, Lottie?'

'Thank you for offering, Mrs Besant, but I wouldn't know where to begin . . .'

'Nonsense, child,' Dorothea said stiffly. 'Mrs Besant can see something in you, that's why she's asking you.'

'You mean it's nothing to do with you, Auntie?'

Dorothea shook her head. 'Of course Mrs Besant learnt of my involvement with you as I called to thank her for all she'd done for you girls after the strike. We got chatting and she said she was impressed with how you spoke out at meetings – it was all you; nothing to do with me whatsoever.'

There was a long silence.

'Well, Lottie, what do you say? All your aunt says is true, I am very impressed with you and what you don't know, you can learn.'

'Pa would be impressed, too,' Ma added.

'Yes, he would an' all,' Bessie chipped in, while Daisy nodded in agreement.

Lottie smiled through her tears, realising she was being offered the opportunity to work with someone she admired greatly. 'Yes, yes, please,' she answered.

'That's settled then,' Mrs Besant said, smiling. 'Come to see me next week and you can begin work in the New Year, you can say goodbye to that factory forever.'

Everyone cheered. They were about to raise a glass of sherry as a toast to the bride and groom and Lottie's good news, when the door knocker rapped again.

Alice tutted as she went to answer, shaking her head. She returned and looked at Dorothea wide-eyed. 'Ma'am, there are two gentlemen callers at the door, probably after money for charity or something.'

Dorothea quirked a silver eyebrow. 'I wasn't expecting anyone,' she muttered, then went to see who they were. She returned moments later, flanked by Wilfred and Gerald. 'How did you two turn up at the same time?' she asked.

'Well, I was invited by Lottie,' Wilf said, looking thoroughly amused.

'And I just popped over to see how you're all doing.' Gerald smiled.

Lottie whispered to Tom behind the palm of her hand. 'Neither man has a clue that the other has designs on Aunt Dorothea.'

He chuckled. 'Let's leave them all to it for a while, shall we?' he said.

They slipped away hand-in-hand through the front door, and stood on the doorstep kissing, as the first snowflakes fell from the sky swirling past their heads and falling to the ground at their feet.

'It's going to be a great Christmas this year, Lottie,' Tom said, breaking away as he looked up at the sky.

'I agree,' she said, cuddling into him and listening to his heartbeat. 'A very good Christmas, indeed.'

'Floss will be so pleased for you!' Tom said, removing something from his top pocket.

'What are those?' she blinked.

'Tickets to see Floss on stage at the Paragon Theatre on Boxing Night!' he exclaimed.

Lottie's smile went from ear to ear as, excitedly, she hugged Tom. 'I just can't wait! She's worked so hard. She deserves all her success!'

'Too right, she does. I'm going to write a piece about her performance afterwards.'

'Tom Harking, I thought you were taking me for a night out, not working at the same time!' Lottie pouted.

Tom sighed. 'I'm sorry, Lottie, I didn't mean to—'

Lottie began to giggle. 'I'm only teasing you. It will be fun and if anyone deserves a good write up, it's Floss and tomorr—'

She never got to finish what she was saying as Tom's lips were firmly planted on hers as the tickets fluttered to the ground at their feet. In the background, sounds of merriment echoed into the freezing night air.

Acknowledgements

The world is a better place thanks to people who wish to help others move up a rung on the ladder of life. One such person is the commissioning editor at Quercus Books, Emily Yau, who discovered *The Workhouse Waif* on Amazon Kindle and offered me the chance of a traditional publishing contract for not just that book but *The Matchgirl* and two future books in the series. Emily is a delight to work with and she has the ability to make my stories sparkle and shine. Thank you for giving me a chance to reach for the stars and be over the moon about it! It's the start of an amazing journey for me!

Will this little orphan girl find her happy ending?

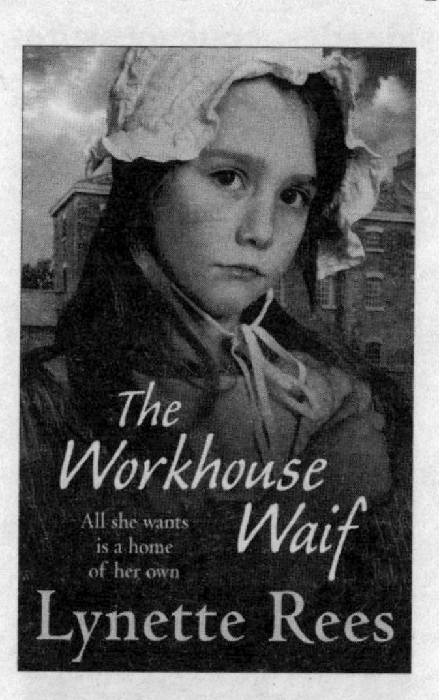

Separated from her family, Megan must learn how to stand on her own feet. Can she make a new life for herself?

For years Seren James has yearned for a child of her own . . .

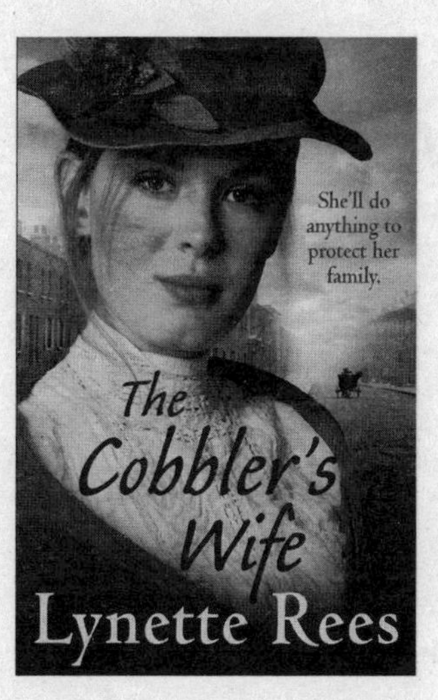

. . . but is she willing to pay the price for happiness?